The
Postcard

BOOKS BY CARLY SCHABOWSKI

The Ringmaster's Daughter

The Watchmaker of Dachau

The Rainbow

The Note

All the Courage We Have Found

The Secret She Kept

CARLY SCHABOWSKI

The
Postcard

bookouture

Published by Bookouture in 2023

An imprint of Storyfire Ltd.
Carmelite House
50 Victoria Embankment
London EC4Y 0DZ

www.bookouture.com

ISBN: 978-1-83790-603-1
eBook ISBN: 978-1-83790-602-4

This book is a work of fiction. Whilst some characters and circumstances
portrayed by the author are based on real people and historical fact, references
to real people, events, establishments, organizations or locales are intended
only to provide a sense of authenticity and are used fictitiously. All other
characters and all incidents and dialogue are drawn from the author's
imagination and are not to be construed as real.

For Janet.
My friend.

PROLOGUE

MIA

Wednesday, 14 July 2004

I stand on the pedestrian bridge that connects the Lusatian Neisse River and try and find the place that puts me exactly in the middle. When I do, I am satisfied – right now, I am exactly halfway between Germany and Poland; Görlitz, Germany, to my left and Zgorzelec, Poland, to my right.

The divide is not so big – a few metres in either direction but not many years ago, the distance seemed vast – Germans in the west, Poles to the east and a river separating the two countries.

A plane flies low above me in the warm summer air, whistling its way somewhere, leaving a trail of white in its wake, whilst below me, the river, algae green, makes its way sluggishly downstream. Amongst the reeds a family of swans feed, the cygnets fluffy grey, following the lead of their parents, their curved necks picking at the scummy surface of the water.

A family pass by me on the bridge, a couple with smiling faces and a young girl at their heels who is babbling about something. The child looks at me, her cherubic face smeared with strawberry ice cream, making her mouth redder than it should be. She grins and holds out the almost empty cone, and I laugh and shake my head.

The man picks up the girl and, with a slick movement, places her on his shoulders and soon they are gone – a happy family walking seamlessly from one country to another and I find I am envious of them.

I look back to the river where a small boat is chugging its way through the water, churning up the silt and mud that lies beneath. It is strange to think how just below the surface there can be so much hidden: dirt, mulch, and maybe more – perhaps trinkets that have been lost in the depths; a shoe, an item of clothing and, even, I suppose, secrets.

My backpack is full and I want to ease the straps from my sunburned shoulders, but I am afraid to not feel it against my skin, afraid that everything inside could disappear. Instead, I move the straps a little to relieve the pressure, then walk to my right. The heat of the midday sun is too much now, and I can feel droplets of sweat tracking their way down my legs and into the crease behind my knee. I need shade.

I reach the other side of the bridge and find myself in Poland. The ground feels no different here, the sun is still warm, the birds are still singing. I am not sure what I was expecting to happen, nor what I was expecting to be different. There are buildings here, painted in the lightest of pinks and baby blues, reconstructed after the war, and old churches, their spires grazing the skies, the cobbled streets shimmering in the heat.

Two nuns walk past me, deep in conversation, their gold crosses winking at me as the sunlight catches them, the only brightness visible amidst the black of their habits. Behind them, a coffee-coloured dog follows, his pink, damp tongue hanging out of his mouth as he pants in the heat. I bend down to pat him, and he accepts the gesture, raising his head up to meet my hand, his soft, endless brown eyes staring into mine.

The nuns stop and turn. One of them has a scar on her cheek, and she clicks her tongue to make the dog come to them. But he refuses and stays with me, his warm body leaning against my legs, his tail a frenzy of wagging from receiving so much attention.

The nun with the scar smiles at me, and I find myself wanting to ask her how she got her wound – who did this to her?

Finally, the dog is done with me, and trots off to his owners, the trio turning right into a church graveyard, shadows created by the whitewashed building offering them some respite from the heat.

I watch as they go inside, and have a strange urge to follow them into the cold silence that all churches seem to offer. But I know I have work to do – I must press on.

Ignoring the overflowing tables of tourists who sit like lethargic fattened flies under awnings and umbrellas whilst waiters rush about in white shirts that are stained darker under the armpits, I find my café – a café which I have decided I like because it is not like the rest. It has no board displaying daily specials, nor cutlery and polished wine glasses atop each table. It is simple, with one small plastic table and two chairs outside that sit under the shadows cast by an orange umbrella with a logo on it for some sort of drink I have never heard of, nor can I pronounce. I like it because it is sat in between a small, uncared-for church, weeds growing from every available crack in the mortar, and a school. As much as the church seems to be abandoned, every afternoon the bells chime out, echoing in the thick summer air. I have never seen anyone go in, nor anyone come out, and I have imagined that there is a ghost who rings those bells each day, bringing some joy, some music to those below.

I put my backpack on a chair and sit down on another. I drag the chair with my bag close to me and draw out its contents

– a box full of postcards, a writing pad, pen, letters and diaries and spread them out over the table as if I am commencing a day at work.

'*Proszę?*' a woman appears at my side. I have not met her before. Her face is red from the heat, and she is wearing a Guns N' Roses T-shirt.

'*Poproszę o wodę,*' I try in my best Polish accent, pleased by the way it sounds in my ears.

'English?' she asks almost immediately, and my pride is suitably doused.

'Yes. Water please,' I ask again and add a huge smile as an apology for her having to listen to me practise her language.

She nods and disappears inside where I can hear the whirr of a fan and the gentle thrum of AC/DC coming from the radio. Whilst she is gone, I spread out the postcards, trying to put them in order.

'You have many friends,' she remarks, as she places the glass of water down on the only space available. 'You write to all of them?' Before I can stop her, she picks one up, and then I see the frown.

She places it back down and gently shakes her head at me as if she cannot understand this strange woman, then takes her leave of me.

I pick up the postcard she has set down. The picture on the front is a sketch by Raphael. It depicts a man, holding an axe, blinded by the light of Christ's resurrection. At first glance, at least to me, it was of a man overworked and perhaps in the throes of death and I like to think that the sender thought the same – they misinterpreted it as it spoke to how they felt at the time. Although perhaps they knew the exact meaning of the painting and chose it because it symbolised hope. Either way, I like to think it meant something to them, as it has come to mean something to me.

It is, I suppose an innocuous enough picture – artwork

commonly found on postcards bought from a museum or art shop. But it is the reverse of the card that she noticed – a stamp bearing the face of Adolf Hitler, the writing underneath scrawled with pen and blurry with age.

I want to go inside and tell her it is not what she thinks. I am not a collector of Nazi paraphernalia. I am not some odd tourist who delights in buying trinkets left by the Reich. What I want to tell her is that this postcard means more to me than she can understand. That this postcard has brought me here, and kept me here for the past five years, just on the other side of the river, in Germany, where I once had a family. I want to tell her that it is complicated, unusual, and fragmented. I want to tell her the story as I saw it happen – how I imagined events unfolding.

But I can't tell her. Not just yet. Because first, I have to try and understand it myself and find the truth that is hidden in these postcards and letters, to find the past that has been hidden from me for so long, to hear the voices of the dead speak to me.

To finally put the ghosts to rest.

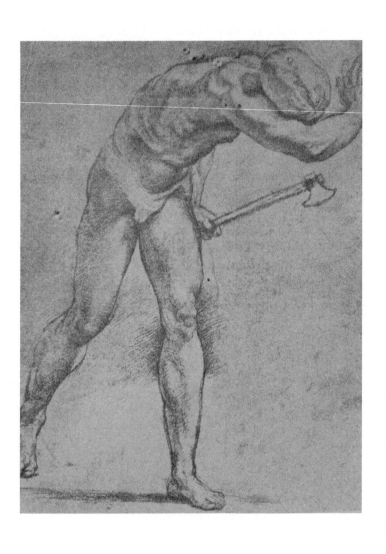

My dearest Tadeusz,

I hope this postcard finds its way into your hands.

I have been reading Mein Kampf. It is the only book that I can get my hands on.

However, pages 34, 60 and 72 are of interest to me as I think they will be for you.

We have a garden. We are allowed to plant and watch things grow. The potatoes will be ready in June.

Send books. Specifically, the Bible. I miss it. Psalms has always calmed my mind as I know it has yours.

Your cousin,

Szymon

ONE

MIA

Görlitz
Monday, 8 February 1999

Five years earlier, during the tail end of winter, I found myself outside a hospital in eastern Germany, a squeaking wheely case in one hand, the other free and scratching at the jeans-covered thigh of my left leg, at the eczema underneath.

It was a Monday. I remember that, as I felt it was appropriate weather for a Monday – drizzling rain and heavy low-slung clouds so that you couldn't be sure where the land ended and the sky began. As people bustled past me to go through the sliding doors, eager to get out of the rain, mumbling to themselves at the weather, I felt oddly comfortable standing outside, alone, wet and cold. Car tyres swished on the slick tarmac behind me, punctuated now and again by the lonely wail of a siren; then a moment of silence would come where only the pitter-patter of raindrops could be heard.

Beside me, a man sucked furiously on a cigarette next to a planter full of browning, dying shrubs, the soil covered in cigarette butts. He saw me looking at him, nodded at the cigarette, grinned and then shrugged as if to say, '*I know I shouldn't, but heh, what can you do?*'

The grey smoke that swirled in the air made me want to gag. I knew what the man would smell like, how he would be a mixture of aftershave and stale tobacco, a smell I had once liked, but now could not stand.

I didn't return his smile, and pulled my oversized black coat around me and looked at the doors that I knew I had to walk through, and yet, found that I couldn't.

Like most people, I hated hospitals. I hated the fusion of smells of bleach and overcooked vegetables and gravy that held a skin on top, now and again a hint of blood or bodily fluids adding itself to the mix. But my distaste for them started years ago, when a doctor with a shock of jet-black hair and large, blue-rimmed glasses came into the waiting room and broke the news to me and my grandmother that my parents had died in a car accident and there was nothing they could do to revive them.

I still don't recall the exact words that he used – perhaps he said dead or perhaps he said gone, but what I do remember is the smell that is universal in hospitals, the sound of the squeaking rubber soles of the staff on the linoleum floors and the doctor's blue-rimmed glasses.

But it was more than that – I knew that. My mind couldn't deal with this. I couldn't cope with what was held inside this building – not with everything else as well.

The automatic doors whirred open as a woman in a red coat approached them, letting out a stream of warm air, the bitter smell of medicine, of bleach and of something more sinister.

'*Ausweichen!*' the woman half yelled at me, as she tripped over my suitcase.

I knew what she had said – that I was in the way – but instead of replying in the little German I did know, I muttered in English, 'I'm waiting for someone...'

She narrowed her eyes at me, opened her mouth as if she

were about to say something more, then thought better of it and click-clacked on her pointy black heels into the reception area. I chewed at the inside of my bottom lip, the pain stopping the tears from coming. I felt foolish. Why was this stranger and her irritability with me making me upset – there was much more for me to be worried about.

'English?' the man with the cigarette walked past me to go back inside.

'Yes.'

'This is the entrance.' He nodded at the door. 'It's the right way.'

'Thank you. I'm just waiting...'

The confusion on his face said it all – why wasn't I waiting inside, in the warm and dry? He shrugged, then made his way inside, probably bemused by the stupid English woman.

I edged near the browning shrubs and checked the time – 1 p.m. She should be here by now. Shuffling side to side, with my arms wrapped around myself, I waited, the cold drizzle finding its way down the back of my neck. This was stupid – *I* was stupid. I needed to go inside.

As I turned to finally enter the building, she appeared as if by magic, my grandmother's best and oldest friend, Marlena.

She strode purposefully to me, waving a meaty arm in the air, shouting 'Mia! Mia!'

As she got closer, I could see the shock of dyed blonde hair that showed grey at the roots, and that she was wearing a purple kaftan with golden birds woven carefully throughout. Orange foundation was smeared thickly on her face, leaving her neck stark white in contrast, thick black eyeliner rimmed her lids with a dab of blue eyeshadow added to complete the look.

'*Darlink* girl,' she purred, taking me into an embrace that I was not expecting, my body crushed into her breasts, my face in her neck, nostrils clogged with Elizabeth Arden's Red Door perfume. 'You are cold and wet. Poor child. Poor girl.'

Noticing my reluctance, and possibly my rigid body that she held in her own two generous arms, she let me go and held out her hand.

'So like your grandmother,' she said. 'Like a stiff dead body. Go on. We shake. Like the English do.'

I took her bejewelled hand in mine, her arm pumping my own, making the thick gold bangles on her wrist jangle and clash together.

Despite the warm welcome, I did not know Marlena that well. Nearly every time I had visited Grandma, Marlena had been away on holiday – always travelling, always moving and collecting new fashions from the countries she visited. I had met her, briefly, just once over coffee and had immediately liked her. She was almost eighty years old, but you wouldn't have thought it to look at her, nor to listen to her. She had that way about her that drew you into her warmth and her lust for life, and I dearly wanted to be her when I grew up.

'You should be waiting in the inside,' she remonstrated. 'Is cold out here.'

'I know, but I just thought I'd wait for you here. I'm not really a huge fan of hospitals...'

'Oh, my *darlink*!' She raised her hand to her mouth as she gasped, her eyes growing large. 'Of course. Because before, your parents dead and inside hospital too, yes?'

I tried to answer her, but no words came out. My throat felt thick, and those damned tears from a minute ago were threatening to overflow again.

'Come, come on inside. We get you warm.' She ushered me in the direction of the doors.

'It was a good flight,' she said, as we made our way inside. I wasn't sure whether it was a question or not – her accent was thick and her intonation not quite right.

'It was fine,' I responded, following her down the slick corridors, the wheely case squeaking behind me.

'How is she?' I asked.

She looked at the case, battered from years of use, then at my hand that held it – the remnants of a bruise, yellowing now with age but still bright enough against my pale skin to attract attention. She raised a pencilled-on eyebrow at it. 'She is well. A sore head because that's what she fell on,' she elaborated. 'She fell on her head,' she corrected her English. 'Right on it. Blood everywhere.'

'Thank you for taking care of her,' I interrupted, my voice cracking slightly. I did not want to hear about the blood, not wanting to imagine my grandmother lying on the floor of her apartment, alone and in pain.

She shrugged her round shoulders. 'Friends are friends.'

I wasn't sure what that meant, but I nodded in agreement with her regardless.

'You are staying a long time,' she said in a way that was neither a question nor a statement.

'I'll be staying for a while,' I told her.

'Yes. I say this. You stay for a *long* time,' she huffed, as she shuffled along beside me.

'Well, I have to go back soon...'

'Why? You have no job. You have no husband. Nothing there for you' – she stopped and turned to me, placing a bangled hand on each of my shoulders – 'You stay here. Family is family. Friends are friends.' Then she kissed me on the cheek.

She was right, of course she was. I had no job, no husband nor boyfriend to speak of. But that didn't mean I didn't have a life to get back to. Yet I could already tell that arguing with Marlena would be pointless, so I let it go and continued our slow walk down those fluorescent-lit corridors.

I scratched at my leg again, wishing I could rip the jeans away from my skin and go hell-for-leather at the dry, itchy skin underneath.

'What is matter?' Marlena nodded at my leg.

'Eczema,' I told her. 'It gets worse when I'm... when I'm stressed.'

'Of course you is stressed!' She raised her hands up to the heavens. 'Your grandmother poorly, you with no job, no husband. It is very bad for you right now.'

I squirmed at her commentary on my life – yes, I had lost my job; yes, Will, my boyfriend, had dumped me; and yes, Grandmother, my only family was now in hospital, but I still did not want her pity.

'I'm fine!' I said a little too loudly, a little too brightly, which made a couple who were walking in the opposite direction eye me as they passed by.

'No. You are *no* fine. You are in *very* bad way.' Marlena was not to be deterred from her assessment of me. 'Here. Here is room,' she announced proudly as if showing me her own home. 'She is inside.'

Room 31 sat across from the nurses' station where the phone never ceased ringing and buzzers sounded every few seconds, sending nurses running to rooms.

'You go in.' Marlena opened the door for me. 'She's just sleeping,' she comforted.

My grandmother lay in the bed, her grey permed head sticking out from the sheets, a white bandage wrapped around it. Beside her a monitor beeped the rhythm of her heart, and two tubes from a drip ran under the covers, where I could imagine them attached to a bruised, blue veiny arm.

My breath caught in my throat as I looked at her. She seemed so small, so fragile and there was a part of me that couldn't believe it was her. Just months ago, I had seen her, strutting confidently about her apartment, cooking, cleaning, sitting across from me and berating me for my choice of attire, as according to her, a hoodie and jeans were boys' clothes.

I took tentative steps towards the bed. The baby-blue blanket that covered her was barely raised where her legs rested, and I was tempted to lift the cover away to see for myself just how wasted she had become. But I couldn't bear to, I didn't want to know.

What had happened? How could she, the strongest woman I knew, in such a short space of time, become *so – so delicate?*

Sitting beside her, I stroked her hair and then pulled my hand away. If she woke up and realised what I was doing, she would chide me for being sentimental and tell me to stop. But I wanted to touch her, so I placed my hand in hers.

'I get doctor,' Marlena said, then closed the door softly.

I doubted she would find a doctor, but I realised that if she did, whoever she found would be unable to say no to her and would be manhandled into the room whether they liked it or not.

'Grandma, can you hear me?' I spoke gently.

There was no response but a gentle snoring, as if she were simply taking a well-earned nap. I tried to imagine that was all it was, that we weren't in a hospital. Outside came the high-pitched squeal of a siren as an ambulance neared the hospital, making me remove my hand from my grandmother and wrap my arms around myself for comfort.

Whilst I watched her sleep, I felt the creep of guilt enter my brain once more. I should have been here – I should never have let her move here alone. What had I been thinking?

She and I had lived together after my parents died, in a small semi-detached house on a nondescript street in Cheltenham. It was the sort of street where everyone tended their tiny gardens at the front, commenting on each other's roses and how to get rid of aphids. It was the sort of street where everyone knew each other, would help each other, and yet, my grandmother was the only one who did not partake of its friendliness. Of course, she would talk to the neighbours, but briefly, almost begrudgingly and would wave away any offers of help – babysitting and the like – and return inside to mutter at how nosey the English were.

Everything about the street was banal. You could time the comings and goings of each neighbour, and indeed, Grandmother and I made a game of it, and would sit by the front window, guessing when Mr Clutterbuck was going to leave for work – delighting in the sound of his red Toyota engine roaring into life at exactly 8.10 a.m.

Mrs Clutterbuck would go to the shop each Saturday morning, precisely at nine. One morning, she left at 9.30, and the excitement it provided my grandmother and me showed how small our lives were together on that street.

When I had gone to Cambridge University, securing a place to read English, I had been glad to leave that street behind. Not my grandmother – just the street, with its red bricks and predictable routine. I had marvelled at the cobbled streets surrounding Cambridge University, the ancient buildings and bicycles everywhere: this was so very different from what I had grown up with – it was almost another world.

Yet, as much as I was glad to leave Cheltenham, it was home. It was a safety net; it was somewhere to return to, knowing that every Sunday Grandmother would make roast beef with all the trimmings, the windows steamed up from boiling pots, and we would sit and discuss the neighbours, what was happening on *Eastenders*, and share parts of ourselves with each other before snuggling down under my heavy duvet, the smell of childhood attached to the covers, the warmth of home that lets you drift into deep and undisturbed sleep.

It was a shock then, when I was in my third year, that Grandmother told me she wanted to return to Görlitz. For a brief holiday, she said, to see her old home from when she was a girl, and to visit friends that she had left living there. I had wanted to go with her, but she insisted I stay behind and concentrate on my studies. Two weeks later, she returned and told me she was moving back there permanently.

'I'm lonely, Mia,' she had admitted. 'I've never felt at home here. I want to go back to *my* home, to a place where I can speak my own language, where I can see friends from my youth. It feels like home there.'

'But what about *me*?' I had asked. She was leaving, which meant my home was disappearing too.

She laughed then. 'You're a grown woman now, Mia. You don't need me any more. Soon you'll be in London with your new fancy job, and you'll forget about me.'

I had hugged her to me then, feeling her stiffen at the gesture but doing it anyway even though I knew she hated it. 'I can't forget you. You're the only family I've got.'

'Ah now. Don't get all worked up.' She finally shrugged herself out of my arms. 'You'll come and see me, and I'll come and see you. It will be good for you too, to see where I am from, it's a part of you too, you know.'

Indeed, it was, and yet for my whole life she had never spoken of it, never spoken of the man she met, who became my grandfather, a man who died just three months after arriving in England, leaving a pregnant widow – a refugee – adrift in a foreign land.

I had asked her about her past, and about my grandfather, but she would never say anything other than it had been a diffi-cult time, and she no longer wanted to think about it. But despite her protestations, it had obviously niggled away at her all these years – she still thought of her past, her old home and now she was going back to reclaim it.

My grandmother had lived in Görlitz now for the past six years. I had visited when I could, but it wasn't enough, it had never been enough. And as much as she had provided a sort of home when I visited – still cooking a roast dinner – it wasn't the same and it had left me feeling adrift. Where was *my* home if she was here?

'Mia?' she suddenly croaked, dragging me away from my thoughts that rambled and knocked about in my brain, all clamouring for attention at once.

'I'm here,' I told her, feeling a catch in my throat. I would not cry. I could not cry. She would hate that.

'Water...' she mumbled, opening her eyes, which were red and dry.

I found a plastic cup on the table next to her bed with a yellow straw inside that was too long. She sucked on it a few times, but it seemed too much of a struggle and she soon gave up.

'You should go home,' she ordered, a glimmer of her old self returning. 'Why are you here?'

'Marlena called me. She told me you fell, and that she found you in the kitchen.'

'That *damned* floor. It slopes, you know. Slopes down to the sitting room. Hardly my fault at all.'

The way she spoke to me brooked no argument. If she said it was the floor, it was, and there was little point in me asking her if she needed help or whether she should really be living alone at nearly eighty years old, as she would tell me I was worrying for nothing and I wasn't her parent.

Indeed, I wasn't her parent, she was mine. In fact, I hated to admit it, but she was the only person I had left.

I didn't know I was crying until she raised her arm that the tubes were inserted into, wiping a tear from my cheek. 'I'm not going anywhere yet,' she said gently, with a small smile.

I nodded and wiped my nose on the back of my hand, then stood as she grimaced at what I had done and went in search of a tissue.

There were none to be had in the room, and I told her I

would be back in a moment. As I reached the door, she mumbled something.

'What did you say?' I asked.

'Szymon. When you're out there, see if you can find him and bring him to me.'

'Er, who's Szymon?'

She waved her hand in the air. 'Don't be stupid, Mia. *Szymon*. You know him. But then I suppose he wasn't always Szymon – he isn't really, but I still say he is. That's how I think of him – of them both,' she chattered away. 'One day you are one person, and *poof*, the next day someone else!'

I took a step nearer to her. 'I don't know anyone called Szymon.' I placed my hand on her arm. 'I don't know what you're talking about. Who's Szymon?' I prompted.

'How can you say you don't know him?' she asked with a note of incredulity in her voice.

'I don't,' I answered, not sure what else to say. 'Who is he?'

Suddenly, she looked confused – almost nervous. 'I don't know.' She looked at me, her eyes watery. 'Who is he, Mia?'

'Grandma, are you all right?' I stroked her arm. 'Who is Szymon?'

'I–I don't know.' Her bottom lip trembled.

I looked at the bandage on her head – how hard had she fallen? I needed to speak to a doctor; this wasn't right.

'It's okay. I'll go and fetch the nurse, or a doctor. There's nothing to worry about,' I gently explained. 'Just wait here and I'll be back.'

She nodded, and looked at her hands, turning them over to look at her palms then back again as if she had never seen them before.

'It's okay,' I repeated. 'I'll speak to the doctor.'

'And Szymon?' she asked quietly.

'Grandma, who is he?' I asked her again.

She looked at me. For a moment, she smiled innocently and then it was quickly replaced by a grimace of fear.

'What are you talking about?' she demanded. 'I don't know anyone called Szymon.' Her worry and confusion had suddenly been replaced by her usual stoical self.

'But you just said—'

'Said *what*?' she challenged. 'I say a lot of things. It doesn't matter.'

We stared at each other for a moment, then she turned away from me and lay back down, closing her eyes. 'Speak to the doctor if you want to,' she murmured. 'But I don't have a clue what you are talking about.'

Outside I could hear Marlena talking loudly to someone, a low grumble coming in response to her questioning.

'But you said you wanted me to find someone called Szymon. And that he wasn't always called that?' I continued, trying to ignore Marlena's raised voice.

She opened her eyes. 'I have no idea what you're talking about, Mia,' she hissed, then closed her eyes once more. 'Leave me now. I need to rest. I hit my head, don't you know.'

I was reluctant to leave her, but at the same time I needed to know how badly she was injured and why she couldn't understand what it was that she was talking about – or rather, who.

Opening the door, I found Marlena browbeating a tiny, young doctor who waved his hands in the air as he spoke, trying desperately to say something as Marlena talked over him.

'Here is *doctor*,' she announced proudly, turning from him and silencing him. 'He is like a boy, but he tells me he is a doctor. Not that I am very much believing him,' she harumphed and crossed her arms.

'I'm Mia,' I introduced myself and held out my hand. He looked at it for a second before taking it as if it were something to be mistrusted, and gave me a limp, slightly damp handshake.

'How is she?' I asked. 'And when can she come home? She

seems really confused and keeps asking for someone who doesn't exist – or at least she thinks he does, but then she couldn't remember who he was.'

He shook his head, then looked to Marlena who promptly looked at the floor.

'I am sorry,' he said, and his English was perfect. It was then I realised I hadn't even tried to speak the German that my grandmother had taught me when I was young, and I felt a little embarrassed that I had simply assumed he spoke English. 'But I'm afraid that your grandmother won't be going home.'

I was sure that he had misspoken and asked him again. Of course she would be going home – she had hit her head and was confused, but that didn't mean she wouldn't recover, surely?

'I'm sorry to say that her cancer is too far gone now. It has spread to a part of her brain,' he said. He opened his palms and shrugged. 'There is nothing more we can do. It is why she fell. She should not have been living on her own when she is so sick.'

'I think you're mistaking her for someone else,' I started. 'She doesn't have *cancer*!'

I felt like laughing at the suggestion. My grandmother was fine, she was the strongest person I knew. She was in robust health and would be around for years yet. She wasn't the type of person to get sick – I had never even seen her have a cold. It was absurd. She was the only family I had – she just *couldn't* be sick.

'I am sorry,' the young doctor said again. 'I thought you would know... She is dying. Maybe a month or two at most. I am sorry...' He placed his cold, damp hand on my shoulder. 'I thought her *family* would know.'

TWO

ILSE

Görlitz City Hospital
Monday, 8 February 1999

My hand is not working properly. It hasn't for a while, I suppose. But recently, and especially now, it seems foreign to me and will not obey my commands. My writing is almost illegible, and I suppose that is a good thing – who will be able to read my diaries now?

Mia and Marlena have just left the hospital. Mia was close to tears, crying about how I had not told her of the cancer, of the tentacles that had now spread out and reached my brain. I wanted to reach out and hold her to me, to let her cry on my shoulder and give her some comfort. Yet I did not, I stopped myself, just as I always do. Stoical, composed. That's what Marlena says about me – and worse. 'You're cold, Ilse,' she says all the time. 'Where did your warmth go – your love?'

I tell her all the time that I do love people, Mia in particular. But there is something in me besides this wretched disease, something that immobilises me, and I find myself retreating back inside, unable to show something – *anything*.

There is a part of me that wishes I had told Mia about the cancer. I wish I had allowed her to come here, care for me, sit with me in those long, lonely afternoons. We could have looked out onto the street and tried to guess which neighbours would leave home and when, just as we used to do when she was a child back in England. Not that I know my neighbours here, though. They are not the same as the Clutterbucks, who had a routine so solid that on the day that Mrs Clutterbuck died, I knew it before anyone else. Why, exactly? Because she had not put her bin out. Not at 6 p.m., not at 8 p.m., and that's when I knew something terrible had happened.

Wait.

My mind is whirring about, back to the past, back to the Clutterbucks. Why hadn't I told Mia about the cancer? It is hard to find the right thought, the right words now. My brain is just so muddled. Ah – no, there it is. I *couldn't* tell her, could I? There was something going on with her, something that she would not share with me.

When she last visited, I had almost told her, but she was so lost – her usual bright-coloured dresses abandoned in favour of jeans and baggy jumpers; her hair that was always so groomed, so sleek in its ponytails and other styles now lank and with split ends. Her hazel eyes were dimmed too – making them a dull brown; her usual wide smile now a pursed line. There was something wrong – something terribly wrong, but she would not tell me what it was. So how could I tell her about the cancer – how could I burden her with my troubles too?

I told Mia to go to my apartment. She was red-eyed, tired and needed rest. She wanted to stay with me, but I impressed upon her the need for my own nightgown, and a few toiletries. Now that she had a purpose, she finally left, her shoulders sagging a little, that wheely case of hers squeaking across the laminate floor, and the scene almost brought me to tears. But, still, I did not cry.

As soon as Marlena left me, I was able to think about what I had said to my granddaughter – *Szymon*.

I had said his name out loud without a second thought. How long has it been since I said his name, I wonder? My head is in pain all the time and my thoughts seem wrapped up in cotton wool, and as quickly as I think of something, it disappears, all wrapped up warm again and refusing to come out. The things I want to think about, the things I want to say will not come, and yet words, whole sentences even, slip out without my command, and then wedge themselves back into their nest. Oh, the irony!

I shouldn't have said his name, and as soon as the words were out of my mouth, I realised my mind was being careless, forgetting what to keep hidden. Mia had asked me about him, and I had brushed her off, telling her she had misheard me. But I know Mia and she won't let it go.

I hope that she does let it go. I hope that she doesn't ask more about him. I will have to speak to Marlena, that is, if I remember to, and tell her to keep her mouth closed. That, however, will be a challenge for Marlena as despite her good intentions, she cannot keep secrets for too long.

Does Mia think she can find him? I asked her to bring him here. Will that determined nature of hers raise its head? In a strange way, I hope it does, not for my sake, but for Mia's. Recently, she has lost a part of that resilience, that confidence that I was so proud to see in her, all because of that pathetic excuse for a man – Will, whom she was in a relationship with and who broke her heart. Can she find a way back to herself, I wonder, before what is growing in my brain drags me out of this world and into the next? But what of the next world, what do I believe? I am not sure any more.

I used to believe in God, in heaven, but after what I did, do I really belong there? It scares me to think of being judged, of being sent to hell.

But then, I suppose, that is what I deserve.

THREE

MIA

Görlitz
Monday, 8 February 1999

Two hours later, I opened the door to my grandmother's apartment block, with a weighted blanket of guilt on my shoulders. The doctor's words rang in my ears: *I thought family would know...*

He was right, of course. Family *would* know, *should* know. Yet I did not, and the deafening silence that occurred in that hospital hallway after he had spoken allowed Marlena and the doctor to see my incompetence and my utter shame at not having known.

But why had she not told me? There was a bubble of anger in my stomach that I could not ignore.

'She say she not want to burden you,' Marlena had told me, as we walked out of the hospital together. 'She say for me to say nothing. She will not even let me take care of her – she almost want to—' Suddenly, Marlena fell silent as she searched for the right word. 'She almost want to *suffer* alone.'

I hated leaving my grandmother in that room, with that

smell of disinfectant and overcooked hospital food, but she had insisted I get some rest and bring her some things the following day. I had kissed her gently on the head before I left, but she seemed not to notice, not to care that inside I was falling apart at the thought that soon, very soon, I would lose the only family I had left.

The light was already waning as I entered the foyer, the street lights aglow, the drizzle of rain making me wish for a warm bed and hot, sweet tea. I wrangled my case inside, letting the heavy wooden door slam behind me.

I loved this apartment block – made up of just three in a renovated house, with a grumpy man who lived on the ground floor and never spoke to me; a new tenant, a middle-aged woman, a cellist, in the middle apartment; and my grandmother on the top floor. The penthouse, she would call it, and giggle slightly, happy that she got the apartment with its large bay windows that looked out onto the meadows that ran down to the river; and just beyond it, you could see the town of Zgorzelec in Poland, tiny lights illuminating houses as chimneys spouted out grey warm smoke.

'*Nie trzaskaj drzwiami!*' a head with thin strands of white hair appeared through the lower apartment door. It was Mr Wójcik, an ill-tempered Pole, who seemed to hate everyone and everything.

'I'm sorry, I don't understand,' I said, first in English, then in a broken trail of German left behind in my memory from my younger years.

He shook his head at me. 'Door,' he pointed a bony finger at the offending item. 'No.'

'No door? Do you mean it was loud when it closed?' I looked to the door then back at him.

His face reddened. 'No English. No German,' he stated. '*No. Door.*'

He then slammed shut his own door, an irony if ever there

was one, and as I mounted the stairs, I muttered to myself, wondering how he could live in Germany and not speak German, and why was he so bloody angry all the time?

I finally reached the top floor, my breath coming in ragged gasps – I needed to do more exercise, that was clear. Fussing with the keys, I managed to find the right one and welcomed the sound of the *click* as it turned in the lock. I was home.

Yet it was not the home I had visited before. The apartment was in disarray. Clothes, books and shoes scattered about as if my grandmother had had a sudden urge to find something, and then left her belongings discarded to collect a thin layer of dust.

Normally, the plush green velvet chair by the door, positioned to allow her to sit whilst she put her shoes on, would be clear of any clutter. But now letters, newspapers and magazines were stacked on it haphazardly, spilling onto the hardwood floor that had lost its polished sheen.

As I walked further in, I noticed that the smell had changed too. Inside the open-plan living and dining room a stale air hung beneath the high vaulted ceilings. Gone was the light fragrance given off by the vases of lilies, roses or freesias that usually sat atop the piano in the corner, and on the round mahogany dining table, rarely used but always buffed with a special wax, so much so that the surface itself was as slippery as ice.

The table sat now with a sprinkle of white grime – dust motes that had settled when they had finished their swirling dance in the air. A handprint disturbed the otherwise dust-covered tabletop – small, almost like a child's, and I knew it was my grandmother's. Oddly, I placed my own large hand on top of the imprint and wondered why she had pressed just one palm into it. Was it to steady herself as the cancer made her dizzy and nauseous? Or was it to leave something behind to show that she had been here – that she was not gone yet.

Shaking my head at my silly poetic notions, I concentrated my gaze on the two sofas that sat facing each other in the middle of the room – one royal blue with yellow cushions, the other its twin in reverse: yellow with blue cushions.

I could see in my mind the day that she first bought them – maybe five years ago now – and how she had refused to sit on them for the first few days, not wanting to disturb their newness nor their perfectly arranged cushions.

It seemed she not only sat on them now, but she had been sleeping there too. Each sofa had upon it thick, tangled blankets, pillows from her bedroom, devoid of their pretty, white lace pillowcases, showing their slightly yellow-stained innards.

I needed to find her nightgown, a dressing gown and things she would need in hospital for the next day or two. And yet, looking at the scene in front of me, I suddenly felt the tiredness of the past twenty-four hours push down on me. I would have to clean this up, but I wasn't sure I had enough energy to do it.

Switching on every light in the apartment, I further investigated the life that my grandmother had been living with alone these past few months. Dishes were haphazardly stacked in the sink with dried-on food that would take a wire brush to remove; cups and mugs still half-full of coffee, tea and orange juice scattered themselves on every available surface, grey-green hairy mould growing on top of more than one. There was spoiled food in the fridge, whilst milk that was almost yogurt sat on the sideboard and a bin was overflowing, spilling its contents onto the wooden floorboards.

I ran the hot water tap and on finding no heat, went to switch on her boiler, suddenly noting the chill in the air too. When had she last turned the heating on? Had she sat here, cold, hungry and scared whilst I had been at home in London?

I wiped a tear away from my eye that was threatening to become an onslaught and busied myself washing dishes, tidying and emptying the bins.

Finally, having restored some order, I made myself a black, bitter coffee and stood at the bay window in the living room, looking out at the sliver glint of the river and the lights of Zgorzelec beyond it. It was then that my eyes looked left, even though I did not want them to. There, in the semi-darkness and lit by a single street light, I could make out the headstones, crumbling like rotten teeth. I hated that graveyard. There was something so strange about it, how it sat between two large houses, now converted into apartments and a hotel, and so close to the river, that unnerved me. It had been a family graveyard at one point – that I knew, as all these houses on the river had been exactly that – residential houses. And when Grandmother had moved here, she had insisted that she live in one of the big houses she had envied since her childhood, desperate to look out at the river each day.

Although the heating was on full blast, I felt a chill as I stood there and foolishly became afraid to turn around in case a ghost stood behind me.

'Don't be so pathetic, Mia,' I told myself, then turned and laughed at my stupidity. At that moment, a crash came from near the kitchen and my heart missed a beat, then settled into a sprightly rhythm.

I made myself approach the sound and saw that a silver photo frame had fallen off a side table and now lay face down on the floor. Picking it up, I saw it was me and my parents when I was around four or five. All of us alive – too alive, perhaps, especially them when I knew now what was to come for them just a couple of years later.

In this photo, we were frozen in time and place where nothing bad could happen. It felt odd to look at my parents – smiling at the camera, my mother showing neat white teeth, my father half blinking as the camera clicked, forever captured with one closed eye and a curious grin on his face. I was there too, in pigtails, chubby arms wrapped tightly around my mother's neck as I kissed her on the cheek. Looking at them was like looking at a family I didn't know.

They were my family, and yet they were not – they were gone.

I tried to imagine my father dressing that day, buttoning up his blue and white checked shirt in front of the mirror. Perhaps I had sat on the bed and watched him, and perhaps he had whistled a tune. Had he whistled? I had no idea, and much as I scrambled about in my mind, I could not remember what he sounded like, what he smelled like or what games we would have played. The same was true for my mother too – all my memories of them were hazy and perhaps made up by me, as every time I would look at a photo of them, I would create a false memory – trying to imagine them that day, what was said, what our life was like.

I always seemed happy in the photographs of us all – always smiling, always close to them – and there were times when I sorely wished they were still here to make me happy again. But there were other times when I didn't wish for them, didn't miss them – as how can you miss something that you don't even really remember?

All I had ever really known was my grandmother, who had taken their deaths with a stoical approach – life must go on, and it did. Together, we managed to find a way forward, and she did all that my parents would have done and more. Yet it was always hard for her to show affection, and I remembered one instance when I was eight or nine and had been laid up in bed with a chest infection. She had sat with me for hours, rubbing Vicks on my chest and bringing me endless mugs of steaming Lemsip, which I hated, so she would add two spoons of sugar to make sure I drank it.

As I drifted in and out with a high temperature, she placed her hand on my head and stroked my hair. It was the first time she had ever done so, and surprised, I flinched slightly under her touch. She quickly whipped her hand away and sat back in her chair.

I was annoyed at myself for moving away from her – I so desperately wanted her to do it again, but I knew she was not that kind of person. I had never seen her cry about my parents, nor had she ever spoken about her husband, my grandfather who died before I was born, making me wonder if he ever really existed.

I say that my grandmother never cried, but that was not entirely true. I did see her crying once. I was perhaps fourteen and was up late trying to finish some homework that I'd assured her I had already done. As I put my books in my schoolbag for the next day, I heard a moan, then a howl that at first made me look out through the window to see if it was a cat. But then I realised that it was coming from inside the house. Slowly I approached the noise and saw, through the half-open door of her room, my grandmother sat on the bed, hunched over, her shoulders heaving as she sobbed.

It had frightened me at the time to see her that way, and it had scared me so much that I did not know what to do. And so instead of comforting her, I returned to my own room and never spoke about it, never asked her anything. But in the years that followed, whenever I would think she was being overly harsh – telling me my skirt was too short, that I shouldn't get upset when a boyfriend dumped me, when I didn't get a first at university – I would remember that moment of her crying alone in her bedroom and try and understand that just because she didn't show it, that didn't mean that she wasn't in pain.

I set the photograph back on the side table and drew myself out of my memories, looking for what could have caused the frame to fall. I could not find anything but a small, latticed heating vent on the wall, from which I could hear faint music, mournful and bleak. It was the cellist below me – the vents were obviously connected. Normally, I would welcome the free concert, but after today, and especially now in this apartment where things weren't quite right, where the chill of the evening

still seeped in between the windowpanes, where the gravestones stood just outside, and where the ghosts of my parents
stared at me from a photograph, the music made me anxious
and oddly fearful.

To drown out my own thoughts and the emptiness of the
apartment, I switched on the radio and found a station playing
'Cruel Summer' by Ace of Base, and made myself dance a little,
trying to energise myself, singing along as I searched in Grandmother's room for her nightgown and toiletry bag.

I soon gathered a pile and searched for a bag to put the
items in. Finding none in the wardrobe, I searched underneath
her bed and found an old holdall, small enough for a few
belongings and big enough for me to get her dressing gown in.
As I pulled it out, I realised that it wasn't empty, something
heavy lay inside.

I unzipped it, revealing a battered cardboard box, a stamp
on the side stating that it had once contained tins of marrowfat
peas.

Inside was a bundle of letters and postcards, all addressed to
'Tadeusz' and all of them were signed with one name.

Szymon.

FOUR

ILSE

Görlitz City Hospital
Tuesday, 9 February 1999

Is it morning yet? I don't know. There is constant light here, constant noise too, and I want to go home and be in my own bed with the ghostly sounds of Leonie's cello floating up to me through the air vents.

Mia has not met Leonie yet – she moved in just a few months ago – and I wonder if I should have warned her that the music sometimes finds its way into my apartment, whispering in the still morning air. It might be unnerving for her to hear it, but then, perhaps like me, she will find it comforting.

A nurse has just been in and adjusted my pain medication as I told her it was making me too sleepy. 'You'll be in pain, though,' she warned me. I told her I didn't care. I don't mind pain at all – it reminds me that I am still alive.

However, I feel a burning now, a hot throb in my head, and I hope that it doesn't get any worse as I will have to down pen and paper and lie back and stare at the white ceiling, where a few spider webs have been missed by the cleaning staff.

I have thought of nothing and no one else since Mia left but *Szymon*. For years, I have had him locked away in a deep recess of my mind, along with other memories that I never wished to revisit. Of course, as it happens to all of us, during those strange witching hours between 3 a.m. and 4 a.m., when the world is trapped between the night and the break of morning, that's when your mind becomes flooded with worry and anxiety – when you sit bolt upright in bed and wonder if you can pay your bills, or if you left the back door open. My witching hour was always those locked-away memories and I longed to be plagued by a simple anxious thought instead.

I would sometimes wake suddenly, my mind flooded with memories of him and others. Sometimes, it would be a memory of my son, and I would wake, sure that he was there in the room and would go in search of him, turning on every light to make sure that I had not missed an inch.

No matter how often it happened, I could always control my thoughts during normal hours – I could place them, stack them away neatly and leave them alone. It took me years of practice to be able to do it. Years of an unwelcome memory visiting me before I was able to banish it again – but I did it.

Now though, it's as though the cancer has barrelled into that locked space, bashing open the door and letting all of the past come tumbling out. I cannot control them – I cannot put them back.

His name is ready on my lips, willing to be articulated once more. I did not let myself earlier, but now I do, and I say his name over and over again, making it feel normal to hear it.

But it will never be normal to hear his name, nor hear myself say it. It is laced with a sort of love. I say '*sort of*' because to me, love is not patient, nor is it kind, as it says in the Bible. Rather to me, this love was wrapped up with the silly romantic notions of a child, of excitement, then after that, with guilt. When I think of others in my life, the love I have for them is not romantic, nor easy. It is sometimes that of friendship when it should be something more, when it needs to be something more, and then the opposite can be true too – a love that's felt with a flutter in your stomach, but it is entirely misplaced.

How can all these things be true at once, I wonder. How can love be this complicated?

The pain in my skull is making itself known now with a hearty knock against my brain and I find myself clenching the pen tighter every few seconds, the ink smudging and making my already terrible handwriting even more childlike and illegible. But I will not give in to it, not just yet. I need to write this down. I need to remember Szymon as I once knew him – when everything was perfect.

I need to feel, to be back there in that moment in time, so that maybe, if I let myself remember him a little, then I will finally stop thinking of him and will not make the mistake of saying his name again. And then I won't have to revisit the spiky and unwelcome feelings that go with his name – the guilt, and sometimes, as much as I hate to admit it, a hint of utter regret.

But for now, I will remember only when I was a child, when I knew no better, when a boy called Szymon showed me how to fall in love.

FIVE
ILSE

Görlitz
October 1937

The Lusatian Neisse River was swollen from days of rain; it had crept up the banks, encroaching on the gardens of the large houses which sat alongside it as it rushed past, slurry brown and a dull slate grey. The trees bowed with the wind that bent them to its will, making them rid themselves of the last few leaves that hung on, leaving them with skeletal limbs.

I stood on the bridge with my friend Marlena, each of us dropping a stick into the tumultuous flow, then running to the other side to see them bobbing violently on the water, stolen away by the current.

'This used to be fun,' Marlena lamented, looking at me with her cat-green eyes. Her ruddy, chubby cheeks made her look much younger than her fifteen years.

I nodded in agreement – it had been fun when we were children, but now, strangely and without warning, all the games we had used to play had become tiresome and we had not yet found something to replace them.

We had tried spending time with my mother and her friends that afternoon as a dressmaker visited the house and brought with them the latest fashions. But soon, that too became a bore – the endless squeals of the women, the chatter and gossip, the talk of marriage and the insistence that Marlena needed to lose weight if she were ever to get a husband.

I had hated that comment. How dare they? These women, who filled their days and their minds with little other than fashion and gossip, had already decided our fate – we were to marry, and Marlena was too fat. I had wanted to say something in defence of my friend, but Marlena had handled it well herself, picking up a strawberry cake and stuffing it into her mouth, before grabbing my arm and leading me out of the room.

Now, standing on the bridge, the drizzle beginning to pick up its pace, I wanted to go home. It was cold outside, and we could sit in my bedroom until the women left. But then again, what would we do to entertain ourselves there, I wondered.

'Come on.' Marlena had started to run to the other bank, where the eastern suburb of Görlitz lay. 'Let's get *szarlotka* from Achramowicz's bakery.'

Although I was not hungry for the apple cake that Marlena loved so much, I hurried after my friend, always excited to reach the other side of the bank. Even though I knew that the ground I stood on was a part of my own German town, I was, *technically* at least, in another country. It gave me a thrill of adventure each time we ventured over the bridge. More shops had Polish names, more people spoke another, foreign, *exotic* language and I couldn't wait until the day I was old enough to travel the world.

Marlena had already slowed to a walk by the time I reached her, her cheeks pinker and eyes brighter. 'I have enough for two slices. Maybe three,' she said, as she examined the few coins that she had drawn out of her pocket along with an empty sweet wrapper and a piece of red string.

I took the string out of my friend's palm and played with it, winding it round and round my finger until it stopped the blood flow and made the tip white.

'Three!' Marlena exclaimed, delighted. 'I have enough for three pieces. One each and we take one home for later.' Then she noticed what I was doing and grabbed my hand. 'Stop, Ilse! You'll make it fall off!'

'Oh well,' I said, delighting in the fear on Marlena's face. 'If I lose a finger, maybe I won't have to go to school for a while, and I won't have to go to that stupid dinner party with Father and Mother.'

Marlena shook her head and narrowed her eyes but said nothing.

'What?' I demanded.

'Nothing. It's just... I don't know. You're *different* somehow lately. But I don't know how.'

I shrugged, ignoring her statement, then linked my arm through hers, both of us winding our way down the street, avoiding the puddles.

I let Marlena talk of the different cakes that we would see, a favourite topic of hers, whilst I thought of what she had just said, that I had changed.

Had I? I wondered. I tried to think back to a year before, and the year before that and picture myself in a moment in time. Yes, I supposed, I was different. Before, I was amiable with my parents, respectful and a dutiful daughter. I would dress how my mother wanted me to, I would read the books my father demanded that I read, I would play with dolls, brush my hair to a sheen, and do my schoolwork without being asked.

But things had shifted, and I was not sure when it had happened. Had it happened when the small buds on my chest had grown to make Mother exclaim that I would need support now? Or was it the day that the blood had appeared in my underwear, making me cry out for my mother, as I thought I was dying?

Either way, now at fifteen, I no longer wanted to do what my parents said. I did not want to wear pretty dresses, nor spend an hour styling my hair. I did not want dolls, toys, or even books, but as yet, I was still not sure what I wanted. This *unknowing* had caused a ball of anger, of frustration to grow in my stomach so that I was sure any day now, I would scream and yell, tear at my hair even, just to feel some relief.

We had not made it more than a few yards away from the swollen river when a high-pitched cry came from near the bank. We looked at each other, surprise and something else – something akin to worry – etched on both our faces.

'Someone's drowning!' Marlena yelled and pulled away from me, making her way back to the river, the thought of cakes gone for now.

I followed suit, soon racing in front of her, reaching the bank, then skidding down, the mud slippery and thick under my feet. Once or twice, I fell, my hands squelching in the moist dirt, but I did not care – I had heard a tale from a year ago of a woman and her child slipping into the river and being carried away, and the memory assaulted me now as I scrambled about.

What I was expecting to find was perhaps someone in trouble, perhaps a dog that had swum out and a distressed owner on the bank, calling its name. I found neither of those things. Instead, I was met with the faces of two older boys, almost identical in appearance, their faces in profile – both with sandy brown hair, blue eyes, and large grins that dimpled their cheeks. One was taller, broader and more muscular, the other thin, wiry even, and a few inches shorter than his companion. Both were shirtless, and both were whooping cries of joy, not of fear, as they stood, waist deep, hauling something oozing with silt and sludge from the water.

The rain was falling harder now and beat down on their

backs as they pulled at a length of rope, and I found myself mesmerised by the scene. I had never seen a man, nor a boy without a shirt, not even my father, and it stirred something in me that made me uncomfortable and yet exhilarated at the same time.

'What are you doing?' Marlena was beside me, the skirts of her dress hemmed with dirt.

The boys stopped, and on realising that they had an audience, turned to us. 'We found the treasure!' the shorter one exclaimed, first in Polish, and then seeing my confusion, repeated it in German. 'Come see!'

'You'll get swept away!' Marlena cried. 'Are you stupid?'

My feet began moving of their own accord, my body wanting to reach the boys.

'Ilse, don't!' Marlena warned. 'You could fall in!'

I ignored her and finally got to the edge and looked at the skinnier boy, noticing goosepimples on his skin. His eyes were a bright blue, spaced a little too close together, which normally I would have thought ugly, perhaps, but on him, it made him look intelligent. A long nose and a sharply angled face gave him the air of one of those Romans I had seen in a painting in an art gallery.

'Here.' He took my hand and I let him lead me calf-deep into the water as the taller boy continued to pull what was, to me at least, nothing more than a large tree stump coated in the thick river mud.

'We've been trying to get it for *weeks*,' he told me, not letting go of my hand. 'It fell in off a boat and we looked and looked but could never see it, but today, we could!'

He still hadn't introduced himself, nor the other boy, and whether it was his excitement at finding this hidden treasure that made him forget to do so, I was glad that he had. His hand in mine gave me a fizz of excitement, then he looked at me for just a second – perhaps a split second – where our eyes met each other's, and there was some invisible line that had suddenly tied us together.

'Ilse!' Marlena shouted a few feet behind me. 'Get out of the water! Don't go any further.'

'Your friend is probably right,' the boy said, suddenly losing the wide grin, his eyes creasing up with concern, finally realising that two young girls were here, and them with their shirts off, and my hand in his.

He walked back out of the river and helped me as my boots started to sink into the soft ooze, then he took his hand away and stepped back, and with an embarrassed smile, asked us who we were.

'Ilse,' I told him, trying to make him look back at me as his gaze had shifted to Marlena.

'And you are?' he asked her.

I looked to Marlena; her arms folded over her bosom like our teacher at school when she was cross. 'I'm not telling you.'

The older boy had now reached us and wiped his dirty hands on his damp trousers. His face was just like his companion's – long, angular but with a stronger, more adult jaw. They were so similar that, at first glance, you would think that if they were not twins, then at least brothers.

'What do we have here then?' He grinned at me, and the way he looked at me, head to toe, made me take a step back.

'This is Ilse, and the other one won't tell me her name.'

'Well. I'm Tadeusz, and this is my cousin, Szymon,' the older boy said, holding out his streaked hand ready for me to take it. But I did not.

Instead of being offended at my standoffishness, he simply laughed, then shook his head so that a damp swipe of hair fell over his forehead.

'Ilse. Let's go,' Marlena whined behind me.

'Don't you want to see our treasure?' Szymon asked, finally his eyes back on my face.

'I do,' I said, my voice coming out barely above a whisper.

'No. We. Don't.' Marlena grabbed my arm and dragged me away from the pair, who laughed at us as we slipped and slid making our way up the bank and to the road.

'Why did you do that?' I challenged. 'I wanted to stay.'

'Are you mad, Ilse? Look at us. Covered in mud. Those boys,' she pointed in the direction of the riverbank, 'have no *shirts* on!'

'So?'

'So? What if your parents saw us, or someone else?'

I shrugged. I didn't care if someone had seen us. I didn't care if someone would see me again with them. Because I was already certain that I *would* see them again. I had found the one thing that was missing from my life now.

Boys.

SIX
ILSE

Görlitz City Hospital
Tuesday, 9 February 1999

It was some months later before I saw the boys again, and we four became inseparable, forming a bond on hot summer days at the riverbank. For me, that summer is coated in the sugary sentimental glow of nostalgia where small boats parted the water, their wash slapping against the banks, whilst birds screeched in the sultry summer air, now and then diving down into the churned-up cloudy waters, skimming the surface for any food that had perhaps been dislodged by the boat's wake.

It was as though the world had shrunk, and all that was, and all that there ever seemed to be was four friends, youth still on their side, with hopes and dreams for their future and a childish, naive love that seemed so real and so eternal at the time.

I cannot pinpoint any exact memories of that time; it's as though I have locked them away for safekeeping, where nothing bad can happen and instead of being clear to me, they are simply a misty haze of warmth and joy. It is a memory I cherish, a memory I want to keep without the details, although I am sure that Marlena would remember it differently, as would Tadeusz and Szymon. Perhaps their memory of it would be clearer – more representative of the truth of our friendship, but to me, I shall keep it locked away, just for me, just a moment in time, frozen with endless joy and the possibilities that all the young feel.

I shall down pen now and lie here, looking at the silvery spider cracks in the white ceiling, and pretend I am back there, just for a while, to feel like I once did, to feel like the Ilse that I used to be.

SEVEN

MIA

Görlitz
Tuesday, 9 February 1999

I woke early to grey, muted light peering through a gap in the emerald velvet curtains. For a moment I forgot where I was, and what had happened and reached out in a dozy state to the other side of the bed. My fingers found only a cold sheet, and it was then that I realised I was alone.

Only a month ago, my boyfriend of two years, Will, had unceremoniously dumped me after confessing that he had found someone else and was in love. I still hadn't unpacked all the feelings that I had about it. I knew there was embarrassment, fear, anger, sadness, yet I couldn't let myself feel any of them and kept tucking them away when each one tried to grapple for my attention. It wasn't healthy, I knew that. I knew that I needed to cry, to wail, to call him and perhaps scream at him down the phone. But I couldn't. Even when he had sat me down to tell me that everything I had trusted and loved about us was now over, I had simply nodded, then stupidly had thanked him for telling me, letting him out of my one-bed flat with a wave of the hand and a promise to stay friends.

Now, remembering it all, I felt acute irritation that I had reacted in such a way. I wished I could go back in time and do it again, and this time do it properly and cause a scene, maybe even slap him. And yet, I knew really that just the sight of him would stop me from doing anything to him – he had a power over me, something that I could not break away from, and I also knew that deep down, if he asked me to come back to him, I would, even if I hated myself for it.

It seemed that the universe had felt that wasn't enough of a change for me and within a week, I lost my job at the advertising firm. And just two weeks later, here I was.

Utter exhaustion and failure suddenly barged its way into my mind. I was twenty-six. Alone, with no job and, soon it seemed, no family. There was a detachment from reality that had somehow invaded me these past few weeks. I had lost interest in everything – TV, reading, seeing friends – there was nothing there; no desire to behave like myself any more. On hearing that Grandma wouldn't be around for much longer, I had expected it to chisel through the thick protective layer that I had shrouded my feelings in. The fear of losing her, the worry and the pain simply wormed its way inside and found a home, making everything seem surreal and now, I was completely numb. In fact, everything seemed laughable, so unbelievable.

I didn't stay in bed long. I couldn't dwell on the thoughts and worries that fought each other for attention and got out of bed with some form of false vigour, like one of those people you see on adverts for morning cereal. They're always so happy, so energised and can't wait to greet the day. I *hated* those people.

Drawing back the curtains I wasn't surprised to find a light drizzle filling the scene outside. A few people walked about, huddled under red, blue and black umbrellas and I watched them for a while, wondering who they were, and where they were going. Perhaps I would be like them again – filled with purpose, with lives to live. I would be like that woman with the blue polka-dot umbrella, I decided. I would be her, hurrying to work on the damp pavements, my mind filled with thoughts about the day ahead. I would be eager, enthusiastic even to get to my job that I loved, and once there, I wouldn't even notice the time pass. At the end of the day, I would be filled with a satisfied tiredness, and make my way back out onto the streets, perhaps stopping off at a supermarket to buy myself a steak, perhaps even treat myself to a bottle of wine. Then I would find a new eagerness to get home, because in this future dream of mine, my house did not stand still and empty. Instead, there would be someone – anyone – there, with warm lights illuminating the windows, and I would know that when I opened the door, there would be someone there to greet me, to ask me about my day.

I felt a little comfort at the dream that I had concocted for myself and scoured the street to see where the future me with her polka-dot umbrella had gone. She had passed the tombstones and was nearing the river; then, just as in a dream, she had disappeared.

Before I turned away, I saw Mr Wójcik step neatly onto the pavement. He had no umbrella but wore a dark brown hat that matched his coat. He looked upwards and shook his head, no doubt at the cold rain that was falling. Then he caught my eye, and, for a moment, we found ourselves locked in some kind of stare-off. I would not look away first, I decided, and smiled at the old man, waving at him. He didn't return the greeting but continued for a few more seconds to glare at me, then, just as he had with the rain, he shook his head at me and turned left towards the centre of town.

I hurried around the apartment, collecting my grandmother's things, then my hand brushed against the postcards that sat neatly on her bed where I had left them the night before. I

picked up one and looked at the image on the front – an image I
had not seen before – a man, shielding his eyes, bent double, an
axe held in his hand. Turning it over I saw the names once
more, Tadeusz, the recipient, and Szymon, the sender. The
writing was scrambled, and I was sure it was not German –
Polish perhaps?

Tadeusz. Szymon. The names meant nothing to me, but I
knew one of these names meant something to Grandma. There
was a sudden chink in the armour I had built up over recent
events and I felt a flurry of something emerge. It wasn't excitement, but it was interest perhaps – interest in *something*. I
grabbed the first postcard, and as I held it in my hand, I felt a
comfort that had been lost to me lately. It was a lifeline I sorely
needed – something to think about, something to ponder whilst
the world around me fell away in huge chunks, leaving cracked,
scarred chasms. I tucked it decisively into my handbag and
decided that if she was awake, alert, then perhaps I would show
it to her and ask her once more about this man that she wanted
me to find. And by doing so, maybe I would find something of
myself too.

The hospital was a hive of activity when I arrived, as if
overnight everyone in Görlitz had suddenly become a patient.
Trolleys laden with prone bodies were rolled up and down
corridors by harassed-looking staff, whilst the screech of the
phones ringing competed with the buzzers from the patients'
rooms.

Before I reached my grandmother's room, Marlena accosted
me. Today, she had changed her appearance. Gone was the
kaftan, the heavy make-up, and in its place, she was wearing in a
white floor-length wrap dress, a large black shawl around her
shoulders, her hair pinned back in a tight bun, pink lipstick and
over-rouged cheeks. The bangles were still there, and I was sure

she had added a few since yesterday. Now, there was one with heavy red gemstones and another with azure blue. Her ears were adorned with weighty hooped earrings that pulled and stretched at her earlobes.

'She's sleeping,' she explained. 'I think you must leave her for now.'

Ignoring her, I stepped into the room, placed the bag on a chair and went to my grandmother, who lay so still that if it hadn't been for the machine bleeping her heart rate, I would've thought she had died.

I kissed her forehead, feeling her soft skin against my lips, noting that she had a scent of the hospital about her now, and decided that as soon as she woke, I would wash her and rub her favourite lily of the valley-scented cream into her pores to sweeten the smell. As I retreated, her eyes fluttered, and she mumbled something in her sleep.

'Grandma?' I whispered, placing my head next to hers to try and hear what she was saying.

'Szymon...' she muttered, followed by unintelligible words.

'I know,' I said, trying to pull the postcard out of my bag. 'I know he's real.' My bag seemed to have swallowed the postcard whole, and by the time my fingers finally found it, she had quickly settled again and her eyelids closed heavily.

'Grandma?' I tried to wake her, but she did not stir. I reached out and stroked her hair away from her face, feeling the silky strands so soft and thin between my fingers.

'Come. Leave her now,' Marlena whispered.

'I'll just stay a while longer,' I replied, still moving strand after strand off her face, smoothing it down on her head, telling my brain to remember this moment – to remember the exact feel of her hair, the way her eyelids fluttered as she slept.

'No, come, Mia. Let her rest,' Marlena was insistent. I knew she was right – she needed to sleep – so I reluctantly followed Marlena from the room.

Once in the corridor again, Marlena regained her bonhomie and suggested that we take a cup of coffee together in the canteen 'to talk, my *darlink*,' she said, wrapping an arm around my shoulders and drawing me close to the warmth of her body.

I managed to find a table in the cafeteria, which was teeming with visitors, all with the same look of worry and sadness on their faces. Marlena took her place in the queue, even though I had offered, and chatted with the staff and other customers, bringing a smile to their faces with whatever it was she was saying.

After ten minutes or so, she came to the table with a tray that was full with two cups of coffee, three different slices of cake, a packet of crisps, sandwiches and biscuits.

Seeing me eye the repast, she said, 'I eat when I am worrying. You eat too. You too thin, *darlink*. Men don't like thin women.'

Plonking her tray down and spilling coffee on top of the cake she had bought, she drew out a chair and heaved herself onto it.

'I look like a...' she paused, looking upwards as she tried to find the correct word. '*Ghost!*' she shouted, making the family behind her turn around in surprise. 'My face white when I wake up this morning. I try the make-up and my skin all dry, so I think to myself, fine, be a ghost then. But then, you know,' she leaned forward, wagging a finger at me, 'I still wear a little make-up. Can you see it?' She sat back and stared at me, waiting for my answer, but I wasn't sure what it was. Should I say I couldn't see the sticky pink lipstick? Or should I say I could?

Bored of waiting for my answer, Marlena picked up her coffee, slurped it back and let a trail of it land on her bosom.

She didn't seem to notice nor care. 'You sleep good? All alone in the bed? I cannot sleep alone. I have *meny* dogs. They sleep with me on the bed. All together like a pack. Your grandmother she hate it. She say it is not good for dogs to be on a bed, but I tell her all the time that it is nice, is warm. I think she like it now, but I don't know.' She shrugged.

I liked the way she said many – *meny* – it made me smile. *Meny* and *darlink*. It was lovely.

'Are you Polish, Marlena, or German?' I asked, never hearing my grandmother use that accent before.

'Both,' she muttered through a mouthful of cake. 'Father both Polish and German, Mother just German. But I like Polish more. I cannot say why. Maybe after war I am thinking more Polish these days, but I know some German there too. But what does it matter? I am me, you are you.'

I shrugged. Her reasoning was right.

'Tell me. Your boyfriend he is gone, yes? You are sad?'

I squirmed. I didn't want to talk about him, or anything else in my life. It was a shambles, and I couldn't deal with pity. The sleeves on my jumper had rolled up a little, and I quickly pulled them down, then wrapped my arms protectively around myself.

'You no have to say.' Marlena waved her bangled arm about. 'Men. They are problem. They bring *meny* problems.'

I nodded, desperately wanting her to talk about anything else but me. She seemed happy to oblige and moved the conversation on to her own romantic thoughts.

'Me, I no marry.' She laughed. 'Never. *Never.* Men are problems. Women are fine.'

Before I could probe more, she turned her attention to the couple at a nearby table who were talking in low, frantic whispers. 'See. They are angry with each other. You can see it the way they are talking. No good can come from men!' she declared.

I looked to the couple and wrapped my arms tighter around myself, my fingers seeking out a spot on my ribs that I could not help but pinch. The pain of my fingertips on my skin took my mind off the arguing couple, and I soon leaned in once more to the one-sided conversation with Marlena as she detailed the issues she had with men, with marriage and then, seemingly exhausted with her tirade, she stuffed another piece of cake in her mouth and nodded at it for me to do the same.

'I'm not hungry,' I told her. In fact, I hadn't been hungry since arriving here. There was a niggle of sickness in my stomach, and I was afraid that if food touched my lips, it would see me racing to the toilet.

'You so like your grandmother. She no eat either.'

'She hasn't been eating?'

'No. I try and try, but she say no food.'

'Did you know about the cancer?' I asked, and by simply saying the word 'cancer', I could feel a lump forming in my throat.

'I know. Yes. I try and look after her. Every day I am going to her and then she stop letting me in.'

'Why didn't she tell *me*?'

Marlena gently shook her head. 'She say she no want to bother you. She say that you have things on your mind – she was right, yes? You had problems?'

The eczema on my leg suddenly flared up and I reached down to scratch at it. 'She should have told me,' I said. 'How did you find out?'

'I went to see her, and she say she is tired. I knew that something can be wrong when she do this, so I go get my key and I let myself in and there she is, on the floor. Head and blood everywhere!'

The mention of blood and imagining my grandmother on the floor sent my stomach into a frenzy and I could taste bile in the back of my throat.

Marlena noticed my discomfort and reached out to take my hand, pulling my arm away from my leg and my frantic scratching. 'I am very sorry I no say to you what is happening. But she ask me to say nothing. She is secrets your grandmother. Always quiet and secrets inside.'

As soon as she mentioned Grandma's secretive nature, I remembered the postcard. Taking it from my bag, I slid it across the table to her.

'What is this?' she said, eyeing it with suspicion.

'I found it last night, under her bed. There's a box with others in it. If you look, it says it is from someone called Szymon. And she has mentioned him twice now, but I don't know who he is. Do you?'

Marlena raised one eyebrow. 'I don't know what it say.'

'I didn't ask you that. I want to know if you know Szymon. Or Tadeusz. That's who it is addressed to. Why does Grandma have them?'

She let out a huff and crossed her arms under her bosoms. 'I don't know no Szymon,' she mumbled.

'But why is she asking for him? She said something that didn't make much sense yesterday – that he wasn't really Szymon, but she still says he is – what does that mean?'

She shrugged. 'Is nice in here. Yes? Is nice and warm?' She tried to divert the conversation.

'I think you do know both of these names,' I tried. I could feel the tension coming from her and felt a flutter of excitement that she would be able to tell me who Szymon was and why Grandma had been asking for him.

'You do,' I insisted more firmly now. 'She keeps asking for Szymon. Tell me, who is he? Please, Marlena.'

'Why you want to know?' She slurped back more coffee, then placed it on the tray, positioning her arms heavily on the tabletop so that her bangles clanged. She raised her eyebrows at me in suspicion.

'My grandmother asked me to find Szymon. Yesterday and today. She's getting upset about him,' I offered.

'Is the cancer in her head...'

'No, it isn't,' I insisted. 'What are the chances that she asks for Szymon and then I find postcards and letters from a man with the same name. You know who he is, don't you?'

'I not know who he is *now*,' she emphasised. 'Only before—' Then she suddenly stopped herself, her eyes widening at letting out something that she was clearly trying not to say.

'So, who was he before?'

'I don't understand,' she tried. But her voice was smaller. She was wavering, I could tell and suddenly the fact that my sleeves had rolled up once more and the eczema on my leg were no longer bothering me.

'You do. Please, Marlena. It could be important. Maybe she wants to see him before she dies. Maybe I can do that for her.'

'You do so much for her. You no need to do this too.'

'She's done so much for me, Marlena. I haven't done anything for her. She raised me and took care of me the best way she could. Please. This is maybe something I can do for her,' I argued, not adding that it was something for me too – I knew I needed it, but I just wasn't completely sure why.

There was a minute of silence in which we both eyed each other. Then Marlena's face softened. 'You not going to give it away.' She leaned back in her chair and looked to the ceiling. 'You are going to keep going, keep saying same thing over and over, yes? Like my dog. My dog with his stick. Always over and over, chasing, bringing it back and will not give up.'

I wanted to say that in English the expression was 'like a dog with a bone', but I quite liked her comparison too.

'I'll be a dog with a stick,' I grinned at her, 'I won't let it go.'

Finally, she looked at me, and I could see that her lipstick had escaped the confines of her lip pencil and was approaching her nostrils.

'I tell you *some* things. Not all the things. Because not for me to say. But there is a little you can know because I think it is fine for you to know. But you no say anything to Ilse.'

'I won't,' I assured her.

Her hand grabbed mine and she squeezed it tight. 'You promise me. You say nothing to her for what I tell you. You say nothing. You understand, *darlink*. Please. Promise me.'

'I promise,' I said, squeezing her hand back to solidify my vow.

She nodded, then leaned back in her chair as far as she could, clasping her hands under her bosoms. 'My English not so good,' she said. 'So, if you not understand me, then you try and think what I mean, yes? You think in your head what I mean, what the story is, and you see it properly like this.'

'Yes,' I agreed. I would try and make sense of what she said.

'So,' she sighed, beginning her tale. 'Your grandmother, my friend, Ilse, she was here, living here before the war and there was a boy, a boy called Szymon...'

EIGHT

Görlitz
July 1937

The sixth of July was no ordinary day in the town of Görlitz. Although there were some residents who wished it were the case.

On what was considered by many to be the first true day of summer, a rag-tag bunch of players, gypsies and carnival folk descended on the town, making camp by the cool water's edge. Soon they would weave their way, playing music from decaying fiddles and tarnished brash cymbals down the rabbit-warrened streets, finally down Brüderstraße, passing old Mr Gliński's bookshop, eventually reaching the town square under the watchful eye of the Reichenbach Tower.

Ilse Klein's parents were in the group of people who wished each year that the players would not come, would not sully their town with their gold-capped teeth, unusual and too-bright clothing, nor their wares consisting of cheap woven bracelets and fake gold charms. But they had little choice in the matter, as Frau Meyer, who owned two large houses at the river's edge and a small, family graveyard that sat proudly between the two, enjoyed their company each year and always welcomed them back.

That day, Ilse sat in the garden. The weather was broiling hot; fat swollen flies had appeared as if from nowhere and smacked themselves against windowpanes, as if trying to escape the heat by finding some shelter and shadows in the house. She watched as the sheets that hung drying on the line flapped like ghosts in the warm breeze and deep down, seethed at her mother.

She had told Ilse that she could not accompany Marlena to the town square. It was not becoming of a young woman, she said. Nor was running about the town each and every spare moment she had. What would the neighbours think?

But Ilse had little concern for what the neighbours thought, and felt like howling in frustration at the harshness of her mother. She wondered; did her mother know why she had been careening around the streets so often? Did she know that she was still searching for the two boys from the riverbank, and one of them in particular?

No, she decided. She wouldn't know, couldn't know, and really even if she did, she would refuse to heed her words of warning.

She thought then of her father who had stood by her mother's side and said nothing, hands clasped behind his back, his feet rocking back and forth as her mother had spoken. He said nothing – nothing to help her, even though Ilse knew that her father liked the fair, he liked music, noise, and laughter.

He was a weak man, Ilse decided, although she had known this for years, both physically and emotionally. He had suffered throughout his life from breathing problems, and each year would have to go to a solarium in the countryside where he sought respite and cool, fresh air. He was thin – too thin, and pale even when the sun beamed down, whereas her mother was in robust health – curvy, bosoms straining at the front of her dress, thick fingers and ruddy cheeks that needed no rouge. Ilse had always thought them ill-matched. Her father a nervous, sickly man, who still delighted in conversation, art and music. Her mother, a tall, forbidding woman, who seemed to find irritation with other people's happiness. Yet Ilse knew that her mother had found something in her father that she liked – money. Money and power.

She fanned herself and looked at the garden – trimmed, manicured lawns edged by topiary bushes, and flowers, reds, yellows and purples, bobbing their heads in between all the green. She remembered only three days earlier, she and her father had sat outside together, talking and laughing, enjoying the time they had to themselves before her mother returned from shopping. In that moment, she had loved her father, and saw that underneath his quiet obedience he dearly loved her too. But she knew, as she always knew, that as soon as her mother returned, she would demand his attention. Marlena had once said that her mother was jealous of the love that her father tried to bestow on her, and Ilse could see that perhaps, as was so often the case, her friend was right.

She stood, brushing the back of her yellow sundress that she had picked out especially for the day. Earlier, she had brushed her chestnut hair to a sheen, admiring herself in the mirror for far too long, wondering if Szymon would notice her long eyelashes or her high cheekbones. She had sat, sucking in her cheeks, then letting the air out, an exercise she had seen her mother perform to make one's cheeks even sharper. Not that Ilse could tell if that had worked with her mother – her cheeks simply melted into the rest of her face, leaving it moon-like.

As she had readied herself, she couldn't help but still feel that strange agitation she had first felt at the river. Was this love, she wondered? She supposed it must be – the kind of love she had read about in books, where a prince sees his princess and their eyes lock and then that was it, they were *destined* to be together. Then her mind would flit to wondering how he felt – had he really noticed her, would he look at her with her little turned-up nose and think it was charming, or would he think she looked childish? All of a sudden, the excitement was replaced with fear, and she had tried to straighten out her nose with her fingertip, pushing it down, over and over again until the anticipation of seeing him returned and her confidence in their love was restored.

She had spent far too long in front of the mirror, but it was simply because she knew, she just *absolutely knew*, that today would be the day that she would finally find him – *Szymon*. And no one, especially her mother, was going to stop her.

'What do you want?' her mother asked, as she entered the house, sitting on a midnight-blue chaise longue, fanning herself weakly with a paper fan, her face red and puckered from the heat.

'Nothing,' Ilse replied as sweetly as she could. 'I think I'll have a lie-down. The heat is just too much, isn't it?'

She saw her mother raise an eyebrow and was preparing herself for some form of reprimand or questioning about what she was really up to, when her mother, seemingly overcome by another waft of thick air from the open windows, closed her eyes and waved the fan in the direction of the stairs. 'Lie down. Good girl.'

Ilse made to go up the stairs when her father appeared from the study. She gave him a quick glance, then turned away so that he would realise her annoyance.

'Ilse,' her father whispered after her. 'Come here.'

She turned and walked softly down the steps, her eyes flitting to the sitting room to see if her mother had heard.

'Here.' He grinned at her, opening his hand to reveal coins. 'Go on, go to the fair.'

'But Mother...'

He shook his head. 'Don't worry about her. Go and have some fun with Marlena.'

She kissed him on the cheek, delighted that he was enabling her escape, and delighting too that his grin spread as soon as she kissed him.

Exhilarated by her mission, she began to run down the pavements, bumping into families who scolded her for her unladylike behaviour. She laughed in response, then turned to one disgruntled couple, the husband's brow knotted like a rope, and blew them a kiss.

In the distance, she could hear the clamour of voices from the crowds that had descended on the town square and soon, the scent of frying fat, greasy sausages and sweet sugar for the pastries assaulted her nostrils. It made her run harder, faster, desperate to get to the life that was happening just around the corner from her drab and boring home.

As the pedestrians on the pavement thickened, she was forced to walk and, not for the first time in the past few months, she noticed the changes around her. She passed what had once been Jakob Abramowitz's men's clothing store, now owned by a German man, then a shoe store that was also now under someone else's ownership. Nazi flags flew from apartment windows, making a *flump, flump* as the breeze caught them.

She wasn't sure how she felt about the changes. How Abramowitz had had to leave – a man who had always been her father's tailor. She remembered going there once or twice when she was young to pick up a hat, or a tie with her father. Abramowitz had always been kind to her and let her try on hats and dance around in front of a long mirror, despite the looks from other customers. He had to leave because he was Jewish, and because a German deserved the business more than a Jew. That's what her father had said anyway. She wasn't sure that was true, and she couldn't see why it was fair to make the old man go, but what could she do? What could she say? Everyone seemed happy with the Führer and their new Germany, so if no one else seemed to care, it seemed pointless that she should worry about it too.

Soon she entered the square, and all thoughts of the changes around her were replaced by her mission at hand. She stopped to seek out her partner in crime, Marlena, who she knew would be here with her parents.

Tall apartment buildings edged the square and some families had found a spot on their balconies to enjoy the festivities from a height. Small children seemed to be everywhere; dashing over the cobbles, between and around people's legs, holding ice creams that melted down their arms. Just by looking at the children, Ilse could feel the stickiness of their hands on her own skin and absentmindedly wiped her palm on her dress.

A wooden cart sat in the middle, hiding the bubbling fountain behind it, yet Ilse could still smell the water – the freshness of it that comes on a hot day. Atop the cart a sad-looking jester juggled four yellow balls, his purple and blue-striped costume dulled and uncared for. No one seemed to be watching him, indeed no one seemed to be watching anything in particular. Instead, they ate and talked and drank whilst the blur of children ran around them, the screech of the violin and accordion whistling in the air. It was an odd scene and it made Ilse feel curiously uncomfortable. The people – so many of them packed tightly in – the sad jester still juggling as if for all eternity – had it always been this way?

Edging around the crowd, she tried to find her friend, and when she couldn't see her, she began to weave her way through them, feeling elbows catch at her ribs, a stray hand touching her back, a foot misplaced, crunching on top of her toes. The excitement was leaving her and becoming replaced with claustrophobia. The clamour of voices was too much, the cymbals crashing, the whine of the fiddle was discordant and making her feel anxious.

Just before she felt she was about to faint from it all, she found her. Marlena, dressed in a dark green shirt and skirt, a hand-me-down from her mother, which was ill-fitting and out of style, stood outside a bar where tables heaved with people, the white tablecloths already stained red from spilt wine.

'Ilse!' Marlena embraced her as soon as she reached her friend. 'You're all sweaty!'

'I ran here.' Ilse patted down her hair that was coming loose from its pinned moorings.

'They let you come. Did they come with you?' Marlena was on tiptoe trying to seek out Ilse's parents.

'No! They would never come here. But I had to come. I just had to, Marlena. I know he'll be here today; I can *just feel* it, you know?'

Marlena screwed up her face into a tight ball. One that she had adopted these past few months whenever Ilse had made mention of trying to find Szymon once more. She couldn't understand why her friend was so sour about it. Why couldn't she simply like the other boy, the older, taller one, and then they would be able to gossip about their new-found feelings.

'You'll get into trouble,' Marlena warned. 'They'll find out and then you won't even be able to spend time with me.'

'I'll always have time for you.' Ilse kissed her on the cheek. 'How could I not? You're my favourite person.'

'Am I?' Marlena was grinning now, her eyes bright. She took Ilse's hand in hers.

Ilse was about to reassure her once more when her eyes landed on something – no, not something, someone. *Szymon.* She had finally found him.

Her heart gave a little jump in her chest, and she dragged her friend away from her parents towards the face she had been thinking about for months. As she edged closer, she saw that he was talking to Tadeusz, the other boy, both of them wearing white shirts, showing their tanned arms from the summer's heat, their hair tousled and both seemed relaxed, leaning against the cool brick walls and shadows provided by the Holy Trinity Church.

Suddenly, Ilse stopped. 'What do I say to him, Marlena? Tell me, what can I say?'

Marlena was not paying attention. Instead, her focus was on her parents who were waving at her to return to them, then they smiled and pointed at the rickety old man who had appeared on a platform, playing an accordion as two women, wearing red, blue, and white dresses, spun around quickly in time to the tune.

'Marlena!' Ilse demanded her friend turn to look at her. 'Tell me. What do I say?'

'Just say hello.' Marlena shrugged. 'I don't know... Who cares? He won't mind what you say.'

Ilse was sure that he would care, and she was now only a few steps away from him. Then she was in front of him, and still, she didn't know what to say.

The pair had not noticed her and Marlena and were now chatting to two girls Ilse recognised from school. Their faces were not flushed like Ilse's, it was as though the heat of the day did not dare to touch their youthful, milky skin. They were laughing at something that Szymon had said, and he was joining in. Suddenly, this felt like a bad idea. She still had Marlena's hand in hers and pulled her friend away.

'Just say something if you want to,' Marlena said, but Ilse could see the relief in her face. 'You've been looking for him for ages. So just say *something*.'

'You saw who was there?' Ilse leaned against Marlena's arm, now despondent in her findings. 'Lena and Julia, they're the prettiest girls in school. He won't want to talk to me.'

Marlena stopped them both from walking away, turned, took Ilse's shoulders and made her stand in front of her like a soldier.

'You are the prettiest girl in school. We all know it, and Lena and Julia know it too. Go and say something to him. Do it *now*.'

'But I thought you didn't care. I thought you'd be glad if I didn't speak to him?' Ilse said, exasperated.

'I just want you to be happy. If he makes you happy, then fine, but just go and talk to him.'

Marlena's face, so earnest, so full of love, gave Ilse the confidence she needed. She stood straighter under the gaze of her 'marshal' Marlena, turned and walked back to Szymon.

She stood, awkwardly whilst the foursome chatted. Then she coughed, and raised her hand in a wave. No one noticed. No one saw her.

'Hello,' she finally said, her voice not really carrying over the noise.

Again, there was no response. 'Hello!' she tried again, louder now, and in an unfortunate lapse in time where the music stopped and it seemed to Ilse, at least, that the whole of the crowd went silent.

Szymon looked at her. His blue eyes trained on her. 'Well now. If it isn't the girl from the river. I've been looking for you.'

NINE

Görlitz
July 1937

The following days became a blur for Ilse.

A rosy haze had descended on everything around her – there in her bedroom, an old oak wardrobe had suddenly transformed itself into an almost regal piece of furniture, the curves of its legs, the leaf carvings were all so beautiful that Ilse found herself marvelling at it. All of her clothes were brighter, the material softer, and each morning she woke as tangled as her sheets with joyous nerves at what the day could bring.

Since finally finding Szymon at the fair, and he had uttered those words – that he had been looking for her – her world had changed. *Her,* Ilse Klein. They had spoken a few words that day, both a little shy as others listened in to their conversation. Then they had arranged to meet the following day at the river's edge, and Tadeusz and Marlena would accompany them.

But the meeting was as awkward as the first, and Ilse could not help but wonder where the confident Szymon she had met at the river's edge had disappeared to. It was as though he could

not find the right words to say to her, and as soon as he said
something, he would then retreat and quieten once more. But it
had not doused Ilse's conviction that Szymon was wonderful,
even though he spoke little – not like his cousin who never
stopped and would joke around with them all, telling them
stories he made up on the spot, wanting to be the centre of
attention. No, Szymon was quiet and reserved, and although
Marlena had queried whether Szymon was indeed right for Ilse,
she had doubled down on her belief that he was perfect.

'But you don't *know* him!' Marlena had lamented after their
third meeting. 'He barely talks and when he does, he says
almost nothing.'

'He's intelligent,' Ilse defended him. 'And intelligent people
don't talk much. They think instead.'

'Look.' Marlena had taken Ilse's hand and kissed her knuckles. 'I'm not saying I don't like him. I do. He's nice, I'm sure. It's
just that you are complete opposites. When you joke, he doesn't
laugh; when you get loud, he gets irritated and wrinkles up his
nose. I mean, wouldn't you think *Tadeusz* is better for you?'

Ilse took her hand away from her friend. 'You don't understand. It's love. I'm sure it is. And you can't help who you fall in
love with.'

'Love? *Really?*'

'It is, Marlena. Can't you just be happy for me? I love him
and I am sure that he loves me too.'

Marlena reluctantly said she was happy for her, though Ilse
could see that she was lying. But neither Marlena's worries nor
her parents, of whom she normally felt were hugely irritating,
could dampen her new-found bliss, and when her mother
scolded her for once again running off to Marlena's during the
day, she had not argued with her as she normally would have
done; instead, she simply laughed and kissed her mother's warm
cheek.

Stopping at the mirror that hung next to the coat stand in

the hallway, she stole a glimpse at her reflection and was happy
to find that her appearance was just as it should be – hair sleek
and tied into a loose knot at the nape of her neck; her eyes,
which usually seemed a boring shade of brown, looking almost
green as the sunlight caught them, her lashes thick. She even
batted her eyes a few times at herself, then laughed at her
silliness.

Slamming the door behind her, she walked quickly to the
river. The Lindenstraße was quiet, their neighbours at work or
shut away inside their homes, subdued by the midday sun. A
tinkle of piano keys accompanied her for a few steps, the music
trickling out from underneath a flapping net curtain. She found
herself stopping for a beat to listen. She did not know the tune,
but it matched how she felt – light and happy.

Smiling to herself she carried on, only stopping briefly to
pat Frau Koch's elderly miniature white poodle that sat stubbornly in the middle of the pavement, refusing to move no
matter how much the old woman tugged on her lead.

Turning left, she reached the riverbank, the water receding,
the banks showing parched brown mud and grey silt, where
small shells embedded themselves. She bent down and picked
one up, turning it over and over in her palm, delighting each
time that the mother-of-pearl interior glistened from inside. She
turned away from the river, to the thick conifers which obscured
the gardens of the houses, their scent of lemon and pine mixing
with the heat whilst sparrows chirruped as they fluttered almost
invisibly beneath the foliage.

A small gap led into their meeting place – the graveyard
belonging to Frau Meyer's house. When Szymon had first
suggested that this be where they should meet, she had shud-
dered at the thought of being so close to the dead. But, the idea
had soon grown on her. The graveyard not only provided shade
from the heat but was hidden from prying eyes.

Ilse edged around the gravestones, stopping at one that had

sunken at a right angle into the ground. Tangled ivy obscured the inscription and in places the stone was stained and darkened with age. She lifted a strand of ivy away and ran a finger over the engraved letters – something she had done a few times before, feeling as though by doing so, by tracing the person's name, she was remembering them somehow and that they, if they knew, would appreciate the gesture.

Otto. She traced the O, wondering, as she always did, who he was when he was alive. Had he come to the banks of the river in the scorching summer days; had he fallen in love with a girl, had he found friends to while away the time – talking about everything, but really saying little of any importance? She soon finished tracing his first name and moved onto his surname, beginning with the S, then the C, then H. But before she could complete his name, a voice sang out behind her.

'You're *obsessed*!' It was Marlena.

She turned to see her friend. 'I'm not.' Ilse let the ivy fall back into place, covering Otto's name. 'I just hope that when I die and when I'm buried, someone will remember me.'

'I'll remember you,' Marlena promised solemnly.

'I know you will, but maybe a stranger will stop by, too, and look at my name and wonder who I was.'

Marlena tilted her head to the side and looked at her for a moment too long.

'What?' Ilse demanded.

'Nothing. It's just – I don't know. You surprise me sometimes, I think.'

Before Ilse could question her further, footsteps alerted them both to the fact that the boys had arrived.

Szymon and Tadeusz appeared from in between the bushes, both of them wearing brown trousers and white shirts with their sleeves rolled up their forearms, again seeming so identical that, for a split second, Ilse looked to Tadeusz before Szymon.

Correcting herself, she turned her gaze back to Szymon, who, in turn, gave her a smile that was just for her.

'How are you?' he asked her with a formality that he seemed unable to shake, yet she liked it – it made their meetings all the more exciting. When would he brush his hand against hers, when would he comment on her hairstyle or dress – the anticipation of it was just as good as when it happened, and Ilse revelled in it.

'I am well.' She tried to sound coy, but her voice was loud and childish. She saw Tadeusz suppress a laugh, then he shifted his gaze from her and concentrated on Marlena who was picking at the bark of a tree, seemingly bored.

'And how are you, Miss Marlena?' Tadeusz asked, then gave a theatrical bow.

Marlena quickly cottoned on and curtseyed. 'Why Sir Tadeusz, I am well, if a little tired from this hot weather we have been having.'

'Why, Miss Marlena, it is summer, and we must endure it. Come, give me your hand and let us sit in the shade.' He proffered his hand to Marlena, and the two of them fell onto the cool ground, laughing.

'They're laughing at us,' Szymon said. Ilse watched as his nose, dotted with freckles, wrinkled with annoyance at the pair; then he looked to her and his face relaxed and a smile returned.

'Shall we?' He nodded to Tadeusz and Marlena who were now discussing a local farmer whom they both knew and how his cat had had kittens.

Ilse took Szymon's hand and let him lead her to the others, where they sat, their hands still entwined, and Ilse thought at that moment that life could not get much better.

'You see, I think I would ask for two kittens, that way they could both be friends,' Marlena was telling Tadeusz, who shook his head at the suggestion.

'One. One is enough. That way you can train it better,' Tadeusz countered.

'Train a cat?' Marlena laughed.

'I'd train it so it would sit on my shoulders, and we'd roam about together and everyone would point and say, "Oh look, there's that mad Tadeusz with his cat!"'

'What about you, Ilse? One or two?' Tadeusz turned his attention to her, not before his eyes flicked to her hand that was firmly held by Szymon.

'I don't care for cats,' she said, trying to sound authoritative, a little like her mother, she realised, so she stopped herself and said, 'I'd get a monkey!'

This sent Tadeusz and Marlena into a new discussion on other animals that could be pets.

'A monkey? That's stupid. Where would you get one from?' Szymon asked her.

'When I travel the world,' she replied.

'And when will that be?' He gave her a wry smile.

She wasn't sure what the smile meant so she carried on, telling him about the adventure she would have, the world she wanted to see, and as she got more enthused by her subject, her voice rose, she became louder, her hand let go of his as she waved hers about, gesticulating at the countries she would go to.

'Over there, India,' she said, pointing to the river. 'Then over there to China.' She jerked her arm round, pointing in the direction of her house.

Szymon gave a soft laugh and pulled her arm down gently. 'That's not where those countries are! Have you ever seen a map?'

'Ah, it doesn't matter,' Tadeusz said. 'We know what she means.'

'It does matter. I mean, how can you go off travelling and not know where things are!'

A small argument ensued between the cousins, and Ilse felt

her face redden. She was a little unsure as to what was happening. Was Szymon saying she was stupid? Why couldn't he just get excited and listen like Tadeusz and Marlena did?

She tried to push the niggling thoughts aside and was thankful that Marlena, seemingly now bored once more with the topic, suggested that they sit by the water and dip their feet in it to cool off.

Szymon stood and held out his hand for Ilse to take. This time she took it with a little less enthusiasm than she had before, and as the foursome walked to the water's edge, she heard Tadeusz whisper, close in her ear, 'Your adventures sound fun. Can I come?'

She whipped her head round to look at him, to see if his face gave something away that somehow explained the comment, but he had already leaped ahead to Marlena, pretending that he was going to push her into the water.

Yet, even though he had raced ahead, Ilse could still feel the delicate skin on the back of her neck prickling from where his breath had been just moments before.

TEN

Görlitz
August 1937

There were not many places to find shade that summer.

As July turned lazily into August, the sun banished all clouds from the sky, leaving a blank blue canvas. Birds sang only in the early morning, then as soon as the day had fully begun, they quietened, too lethargic to call to one another. So it was that Ilse found herself spending most of her days in the graveyard and on the riverbank with Marlena, Szymon and Tadeusz, all of them dipping their feet in the ever-shrinking waters and lying under trees whose leaves barely moved in the still, close air.

One Saturday afternoon, as Marlena and Ilse walked past Frau Meyer's large house and the small graveyard, picking their way down to the bank, Marlena stopped. 'It's too hot!' she whined. 'And we do the same thing every day. Why can't we go and do something else? Go somewhere else?'

'Because,' Ilse said sweetly, holding her friend's hand, gently cajoling her. 'We're in love and when you're in love, you have to see each other every day or else you go *mad!*' Ilse giggled, hoping that Marlena would join in. She did not.

'He hasn't said he loves you,' Marlena pointed out. 'And every time you see each other, you're both so quiet with each other – you talk more to Tadeusz than you do to Szymon.'

There was that niggle again, deep in Ilse's stomach, worming its way upwards, into her brain. Marlena was right – she still didn't know him that well, and she found it hard to talk with him. But she so desperately *wanted* to be in love – for this to be the real thing – that she continued to ignore the small voice telling her that whatever thoughts of love she had were perhaps misplaced.

Before Ilse could disagree with her friend, the boys appeared, both of them arguing over which one was a better swimmer.

'You think you are because you are older,' Szymon said.

'And *stronger*,' Tadeusz added, sitting down on the dusty ground, pulling at a dried stalk of grass that he clamped between his teeth. 'And more handsome.'

'I think Szymon is more handsome,' Ilse said, turning to her beau whose moody face was angled to the other side of the riverbank, where two swans sluggishly swam about in the shallows.

'Szymon. I said I think you are more handsome,' Ilse repeated.

But he still didn't answer.

'Just ignore him,' Tadeusz said, as he lay down, shielding his eyes with his hand as he looked over at Ilse and Marlena. 'He's been like this all morning. Moody and argumentative.'

'It's the heat,' Marlena suggested. 'It's making us all crazy.' She plopped down next to Tadeusz.

'I don't think so. He's always like this, aren't you, Szymon? Always disgruntled about *something*. Just yesterday he got angry with me because I was late.'

'You're always late...' Szymon grumbled.

Ilse went to him and, from behind him, she wrapped her arms around his waist, resting her head on his back. But he stood as awkwardly and stiffly as Marlena. What was wrong with everyone today? she wondered.

'I have an idea.' Tadeusz suddenly stood, and dusted the back of his trousers. 'Come on! I can't bear this heat. We all need to cool down and do something else with our time.'

They all followed Tadeusz who stalked away in front, like a general commanding his troops, leading the way into town, past Ilse's house, towards Brüderstraße.

It was as though all the inhabitants of Görlitz had either fled their homes to seek cooler climes on the coast, or were locked inside, fanning themselves on couches with windows open, curtains fluttering softly with whatever breeze managed to appear.

They soon reached their destination. Mr Gliński's bookshop, which was crammed in between a baker and a fishmonger.

Tadeusz opened the red door, pushing against a small brass bell that tinkled in welcome.

'This is my uncle's shop,' Tadeusz announced proudly, spreading his arms wide and almost touching the shelves that lined each side.

Ilse could see that the narrowness extended further into the gloom and immediately liked the place, dismissing Marlena's worries that it was scary or haunted.

Tadeusz and Szymon disappeared down the aisle to find Tadeusz's uncle, and Ilse unlinked herself from Marlena and began to examine the books.

Bound in red, blue and green leather, their pages thin and mottled in places with age, each one had been read already. She opened one, and found it was full of poetry. Not one to appreciate verse, she placed it back on the shelf and moved further into the shop to discover what else it held within. As she did so, there was the smell of warm dust, and a faint vanilla tang. She asked Marlena if she, too, could smell it, but received an answer from someone else.

'It's from the paper.' A face appeared in front of hers, a wrinkled map of lines and shockingly clear blue eyes that sat behind eyeglasses under a heap of white, wispy hair that shifted in multiple directions. 'It's the lining in the paper,' he continued with a smile. 'When it breaks down, it releases the scent of vanilla. Here, *smell*.' He took a book of the shelf and held it open.

Ilse did as she was told and inhaled the musk. She liked it and smiled.

'I'm Mr Gliński, my dear. And you are?' He grinned back.

'Ilse. And this is my friend Marlena.'

Mr Gliński, noticing that someone else was in his shop, moved to Marlena with a quick grace that belied his age. 'My dear. How lovely to have such a beautiful young lady in my establishment!'

Marlena blushed and Ilse was sure that no man had ever told her she was beautiful before. She decided there and then that she would tell her friend of this fact each day. She should not have to wait for an old man to say it to her.

'My nephew here tells me that the heat has sent you all a little mad!' Mr Gliński made his way behind the register and found a wooden stool that he perched on. '*The day is hot, the Capulets abroad, And, if we meet, we shall not scape a brawl; For now, these hot days, is the mad blood stirring.*'

'Who is it? Who wrote that?' he asked of them.

Ilse shook her head, as did Marlena.

'It was Shakespeare, my dears! Shakespeare. *Romeo and Juliet*. Now, now, I am so glad my nephew brought you here, for I have so much to teach you, that is clear.'

'Leave them alone, Uncle.' Tadeusz appeared with Szymon by his side, both of them holding tall glasses of *kompot*, a fruit juice that Ilse knew Marlena's mother would make. 'We've just come to get out of the heat.'

Szymon handed Ilse a glass, then kissed the top of her head, his mood suitably restored.

'You can always learn something. Especially you, Tadeusz. You lack focus. You have finished school, have you not? But still, you have no thought as to what you want to do with your life?'

Ilse looked to Tadeusz – had he finished school? Of course he had. He was older than the rest of them. Why hadn't he said anything to them?

'Your parents spoil you, my boy. They give you too much. When I was young, you had no choice but to work. But you are allowed to sit and waste days at a time until you know what to do. I shall suggest to your mother, my sister, that you come and work for me.'

'Ah now, Uncle. I don't think so. What use would I be here? And besides, you live here, all the way over the other side of the river. I would have to wake early, would I not, to get here on time? No, no, I think it much better you find someone on this side of the bridge,' he quipped.

His uncle smirked. 'Lazy boy,' he said, then stood and walked to a shelf, drawing out a lime book covered with dust, then began to flick through the pages.

Ilse drank some of the *kompot*, finding that it was made from strawberries, and saw Marlena nodding in delight at the taste.

'Here. Put those down and come and read this. We'll sit near my office. Tadeusz, get some chairs. This will interest all of you, I'm sure.' Mr Gliński had a twinkle in his eye, as though he held secrets and jokes and, at any moment, he might give his audience access to one or the other.

'Now,' he began, as they sat on old wooden chairs, Ilse and Szymon holding hands. 'This is an interesting story. It is by none other than Arthur Conan Doyle – have you heard of him?

No? Well. You are in for a surprise. This man has written the best detective you shall ever meet. A Mr Sherlock Holmes. And today we shall read the story which is called *The Valley of Fear*.'

Ilse saw Tadeusz open his mouth to protest, but his uncle raised a hand – there would be no argument. Szymon complained that books were boring, and Marlena said she did not like how dark the room was.

But Ilse could only feel the charm of the bookshop – it felt safe somehow, comforting even, as if, while they were inside, the world outside did not exist.

ELEVEN

Görlitz
September 1937

September arrived with a warm south-westerly wind brought from the Sahara, leaving a thin layer of red dust on car roofs, smears on windows, giving the sky a pinkish hue. It was a wind that sent dogs into a frenzy, making them bark at the ever-moving branches of trees and debris on pavements.

Ilse and Marlena walked to Mr Gliński's bookshop, Ilse delighting in the strange weather and the excited behaviours it had brought, not just to the animals but to the people as well. Marlena, usually so accommodating of whatever Ilse wanted to do, was moody and withdrawn, refusing to link arms with her and giving grunts of reply in lieu of words.

'Don't you just *love* it!' Ilse cried, twirling on the pavement, ignoring stares from passers-by.

'Just think, Marlena, where this sand has come from – all the way from *Africa*. Isn't that magnificent? Think of that story we read – *Arabian Nights* – and we now have a bit of it for ourselves...'

'You should stop,' Marlena finally spoke. 'People are looking at us.'

'Who cares!' Ilse grabbed her friend's arm, holding on to it with both hands. 'Anyway, guess who I saw the other day?'

Marlena shrugged.

'Come on, guess!'

'I don't know,' Marlena sighed. 'Hans?'

'Have I told you already?' Ilse asked, racking her brain, trying to remember if she had told her of her new-found love.

'You told me that he spoke to you and that he smiled at you, yes,' Marlena deadpanned.

'Well, did I tell you I saw him again yesterday outside the library and we spoke for almost an hour?'

Suddenly, Marlena stopped walking.

'What is it?'

'What is it?' Marlena half laughed. 'What about Szymon? For months you were obsessed with him, then you found him, and within weeks you have decided Hans is far better.'

'It's not that,' Ilse squirmed. 'I like Szymon, I do. But he's so serious all the time, and I think maybe I didn't love him like I thought I did. And he's just always looking at me like he loves me, but I don't know how to tell him that maybe we should just be friends. And, and I don't know...' Ilse trailed off, running out of justifications for how she had acted the past few weeks.

'You do know. Well, at least *I* do,' Marlena said crossly. 'You wanted him when you didn't know who he was. Then you wanted him more when he was moody and uninterested in you. And now that he loves you, you are bored like a small child with a toy. You just discard things, and people too. You're a selfish, spoiled *child*!'

Marlena's words stung, and Ilse could feel her face flame red with embarrassment and anger. 'At least I like boys!' Ilse spat. 'And at least they like *me*!' As soon as the words were out of her mouth, Ilse regretted them.

Marlena turned pale. Her mouth opened and closed as she stared at her friend, but no words came out.

'Marlena, I'm sorry! I'm *so* sorry!' Ilse went to her friend and tried to hold her in an embrace. But Marlena shrugged her off and began to walk away from her, heading for home.

Ilse chased after her, but Marlena was unforgiving. 'Just leave me alone, Ilse. Just go and be with Szymon. Then Hans when you're bored. And then find someone else.'

Ilse stood and watched as her friend disappeared out of sight. A gust of wind brought a warm dusty air that swirled around Ilse's legs and set the dogs off howling.

Marlena had never spoken to her so harshly before. Yes, she scolded her sometimes, but this was different – this was new.

Ilse turned and continued to walk to the bookshop once more, her mind turning over the words that Marlena had spoken. Was she bored? Was she selfish? Yes, she had thought of breaking it off with Szymon as soon as Hans, an older boy in her school, had shown interest in her, but that wasn't her fault! Every girl liked Hans, and every girl wanted him to talk to them and he had chosen her! Besides, Hans was easy to talk to – he joked around and made her laugh. Szymon was just so *serious* all the time.

Ever since that day back in August, she had allowed that niggling voice that had told her she didn't really love Szymon to become much louder. Each time he tried to hold her hand, or simply walk close to her, she would step away from him, annoyed at his persistence. The more she made it clear that she wasn't as interested in him any more, the worse it became. He had started to send her love letters, and even pressed a daisy for her. But rather than having the desired effect of making her like him again, it had made her feel all the more irritated by him.

Why couldn't they just be *friends*? she wondered. How could she tell him that it had been a flight of fancy – a first, brief love, and now they should both part.

Before she realised it, she was outside the bookshop. She stopped, wondering whether to turn around and go home, but Mr Gliński's head suddenly appeared at the window, a book bound in green leather in his hands as he positioned it in a haphazard display. On seeing Ilse, he grinned and beckoned for her to come inside.

'You are alone?' he asked as soon as she entered.

She nodded miserably.

'Why so sad?' He placed his hand on her shoulder and steered her to the rear of the bookshop, sitting her down on a worn leather chair.

'It's Marlena,' she sniffed, suddenly feeling sorry for herself. She tried to swallow back the tears that were threatening, but soon gave in to them.

'She says I'm childish and selfish.' She wept as Mr Gliński sat across from her, murmuring in sympathy. 'She says I discard people like a child with a toy when they get bored with it. But I don't! I just don't know how to say things sometimes, and sometimes it all comes out wrong!'

After a few minutes of defending herself against the accusations Marlena had thrown at her, the tears subsided, and she gratefully took a handkerchief from the old man and wiped her face.

'Now. Tell me properly, now you have shed tears and unburdened yourself. Why would she call you such things?' he asked kindly.

Ilse shrugged, then sniffed.

'Come now. There must be a reason.'

Ilse squirmed in her seat. Yes, there was a reason, but she wasn't sure whether she should be telling Mr Gliński, especially as he was Tadeusz's uncle and knew Szymon well.

'It will just be between you and me, I promise,' he said.

The way he spoke, so softly and calmly made Ilse relax. She could tell him. She could trust him.

'It's because I think I like someone else. I don't think I like Szymon like I used to. And Marlena got mad at me. But I don't know why because it's not like it matters much to her.'

'Ah, matters of the heart!' Mr Gliński stood and made his way to a shelf, drawing out a small book, then sat back down. 'Here is a book about just that. Love. And sometimes heartbreak. And sometimes love that does not last. Here take it.' He handed it to her.

She opened it and read the title page: *The Poetical Works of Lord Byron.*

'It may help you to realise that you are not alone. Men and women have come before you who have felt the unease, the excitement and the flutter of love that you feel. But what you have to remember is that even when you do not love someone like you used to, their love for you is still a precious thing. So, you must always take care with their heart and make sure you do as little damage as possible.'

'I'm not sure how to do that,' Ilse began. 'I mean, how can I tell Szymon without hurting him?'

Mr Gliński let out a soft laugh. 'That is a tricky thing, I grant you. But it can be done. All you must do is be honest and kind. Maybe if you do, your friend will see that you are neither selfish nor childish.'

'But why should she care?' Ilse demanded, suddenly indignant. 'It's not as if I have said that I'm no longer friends with her!'

Mr Gliński stood, patted Ilse's arm and said, 'You'll understand one day, when your friend is ready. But for now, be kind to her heart too, Ilse. Always be kind.'

Ilse remained at the bookshop for an hour or more, reading the poems of Byron, seeing all at once what love meant to him and realising that she had not felt this way about Szymon, but realising that he perhaps did about her. She had to be kind, she decided. Just like Mr Gliński said. If people felt the same way about her as these poems, then not only was she lucky, but she had the burden upon her to ensure that she did as little damage as possible to their hearts.

The change came quickly and without much warning.

The day after visiting Mr Gliński alone, and with a renewed sense of purpose, Ilse came down the stairs that morning and was met by three strange men, all carting wooden boxes into the house. Her mother stood in the living-room doorway.

'Be careful with the china in the dining room!' she warned them. 'It's worth more than all the money you will earn in your life!'

Ilse stood on the bottom stair, dumfounded.

'Ilse!' Her mother turned her attention to her. 'We're moving to Berlin! Isn't it *wonderful*? Can you imagine the life we will have there?'

'*Berlin*?' Ilse managed to say.

'Your father has been clever...' Her mother came closer. 'For once in his life, at least,' she huffed. 'He has agreed to take over a factory there, and there is the promise of more to come. Munitions, uniforms, all sorts of things!'

'But I don't want to go to Berlin,' Ilse muttered, almost to herself. 'What about my friends?'

She looked to her mother, wanting to hear some words of comfort, but was met with an icy stare. 'You'll make new friends. Better ones than that fat little girl over the river. Now go and pack. We leave in three days.'

'But I—' Ilse started, when her mother took her roughly by her arm, bruising the soft skin of her underarm. 'Go and pack, I said,' she hissed.

Ilse did as she was told, her mind whirring over the thought of leaving, of never seeing Marlena again, of never going to Mr Gliński's again nor going to the fair each summer.

With each step she took towards her bedroom, a thick lump developed in her throat and, finally, her tears began to fall.

TWELVE

MIA

Görlitz
Tuesday, 9 February 1999

Marlena licked the tip of her index finger and dabbed up the crumbs of cake that were left on the tray.

'So... she left?' I asked, staring at my grandmother's friend.

'She did. She cried and cried all the time before she left and so did I. Even Szymon was sad – sadder and more serious than he usually was. Only Tadeusz tried to still make us laugh – telling us jokes all the time to see if he could make Ilse smile, but he couldn't.' Marlena shrugged. 'No one could make her happy on those days before she left.'

'And she broke it off with Szymon?' I asked.

'She had no need to be doing that. She was leaving, so that was end of it, I think. He was a funny boy, Szymon – not funny like you laugh with him, but funny strange. I knew him still, after your grandmother left, and it is like he went back to the boy we had met at the river that day – confident. I think Ilse, she had an effect on him – made him serious and scared, I think – like he was not sure how to be himself with her.'

I swallowed deeply. I knew that feeling – a feeling of inadequacy, of low self-esteem because the person you are with is so much brighter, so much better than you so that instead of blooming in their presence, you end up shrinking away into nothing. Not that my grandmother did it intentionally to Szymon, not like so many people do.

'So, you see, Szymon was just a first love or a thing we all have when we are children. It means nothing. He means nothing,' Marlena finished.

I wasn't sure how I felt about the story that she'd just told me. It sat uneasily with me – my grandmother was a little spoiled, a flirt and perhaps a heartbreaker? It didn't correspond with the woman I knew. And what of Marlena? I knew she loved my grandmother, that much was clear, but had she been *in* love with her?

As if reading my mind, Marlena started speaking again. 'We were all different when we were younger – we fell in and out of love with everyone. All of us were different then. Me, I was a scared, fat child, but now I am happy, confident. I no care what peoples think of me, you see? I grew up, and so did Ilse.'

I let those words marinate for a moment before I realised something.

'When did she see him again?' I asked.

Marlena gave a heavy shrug of her shoulders. 'When she come back to Görlitz, maybe five years later? I am no sure she did see him. But when she came back, everything was different. Changed. Was a war and that was that. People gone. Szymon and Tadeusz gone. People always disappearing in those days. I no think she saw him.'

'But the *postcards*!' I exclaimed. 'The postcards are dated in 1942. That must have been when she came back. So she *must* have seen him – why else would she have postcards between him and his cousin?'

Marlena looked everywhere in the cafeteria but at me. I

watched her realise that she had made a mistake in telling me this tale. She had tried to fob me off with a childish love story, not realising that I knew the date on the postcard. I knew the look on her face, I knew what was happening – it was the same look that I'm sure I got as a teenager when I was trying to find a way out of Grandma's questioning about where I had been, what I had been doing, and why I smelled of cigarette smoke.

'Is wrong date,' she finally said with a sigh.

'Are you joking?'

She pushed herself away from the table and stood. 'I go see Ilse now. You wait here. Then you come in a little while. I want some time just me and her, you understand?' Her tone was firm, unyielding and it caught me off guard, so I quickly agreed.

As soon as she was gone, I wondered why these postcards were so anxiety-inducing for Marlena and what secrets they might hold. I chided myself for not bringing all of them with me – maybe I could have asked someone here to translate them; maybe if Marlena had seen all of them, she would cave. She had obviously thought that by giving me this tale of teenage love, it would satisfy me, yet she had forgotten that a postcard had started this. A postcard dated after my grandmother and Szymon had been apart. *So, what was she hiding?*

I felt a little guilt, or perhaps shame that I was thinking about this. At the end of the day, my grandmother lay dying just three floors above me, my life in London lay in tatters and it was not lost on me that I should be thinking about more important matters. And yet, this mystery, this story that had yet to be told, held not only a diversion from my current circumstances, but was offering me some insight into my grandmother, and there might not be any other time to discover what was so hidden from me.

Sitting in the cafeteria, as the hum of conversation dulled a possible silence, I thought of who my grandmother was – to me at least. *Stern* was one word. Another was *distant*. As I knew, she loved me deeply, but there always seemed something about her that was unable, or unwilling, to demonstrate it. Another word for her, a new word, was *secretive*. In just one day, I had found out that she had had a whole other life – a life where she was a confident, rebellious teenager, who wore her heart on her sleeve, who loved her friend with a deep affection that had lasted all these years. She had been a girl with hopes and dreams, with a love of learning, of books. But where had that girl gone?

She was none of these things to me. She had been a middle-aged woman nearing her elder years when I had come into her care. A woman who had been married to a man called Otto, yet never spoke of him. A woman who had worked as a district nurse after her husband had died when her son, my father, was two years old. A woman who didn't travel. Never read a book, and had a constant air of sadness about her. I had always thought that the sadness was due to her husband's, and then my parents', death. But now, I wonder if it had been ingrained much sooner than that – that maybe she had never really had a chance to be happy, nor find contentment.

Looking in my cup, I saw I had a mouthful of coffee left. I drank it back, feeling it cold and bitter on my tongue. I had given Marlena enough time. I was going upstairs, and I would confront her again. I had to know more – it was the only thing that was going to stop me from falling completely apart.

Upstairs, my shoes squeaked along the lime-coloured flooring, as I hurried to get to Room 31. As I entered, I saw that my grandmother was alone, and that Marlena had gone.

Feeling dejected, I shored myself up and went to my grandmother who slept still. Sitting by her bed, I reached out and took her hand, feeling the bones beneath the papery skin.

'Why don't you tell me? Why *didn't* you tell me?' I implored her sleeping form. 'Why couldn't we have talked? Why didn't you say more about Grandpa or about Dad when he was young? Why did you keep it all inside, all for you. Why didn't you see that maybe I needed it too?'

The questions came thick and fast, coupled with tears, recriminations, sobbing, and eventually, silence.

I sat, exhausted. Alone. And scared.

'*Sie nimmt viele Schmerzmittel. Kommen Sie stattdessen später am Abend wieder – sie werde wacher sein, weil sie sich weigere, sie nachts einzunehmen, schreibt sie. Dann besuche sie,*' a nurse said, as she walked in, a blood pressure cuff in her hand.

I tried to translate what she had said – that she was on painkillers and she would be more awake in the evening – she was... What did she say? She was *writing* in the evening?

I tried my best to reply and to confirm what she had said – that Grandma spent her evenings writing. But the nurse shook her head. She did not understand me and wasn't about to try.

I picked up my handbag and agreed that I would return later. I had never seen my grandmother write so much as a letter – what *was* she doing in the evenings?

Outside, the weather had not much improved. The drizzle soaked my coat and hair, trickling down the back of my neck as I walked with no particular destination in mind. If I had known where Marlena lived, I would surely have descended on her, insisting that she tell me whatever it was she was so determined to hide.

I didn't want to return to the apartment, so I found myself wandering into the centre of the town, following the street names that Marlena had told me about. The old town of Görlitz was beautiful, even on a dreary day like this. The buildings were painted in yellows, pinks and soft greens, with shops and restaurants on the ground floors, and apartments above. A church stood in front of me, the river beside it, a plaque stating it was the Church of St Peter and Paul, its gothic spires disappearing into the low sitting clouds. Suddenly, the bells chimed out the hour of twelve, and a flutter of birds that had been taking shelter in its rafters streamed out into the sky.

As I retraced the steps my grandmother had once taken, I tried to imagine her life – how she would have felt that summer, how the heat hammered down on her, making beads of sweat drip down her back. How all around her there were the beginnings of Nazi influence – flags flying, Jewish shops being given to others – and how she was clueless about what it would eventually lead to. She had simply been young, feeling a naive type of love and hope where anything was possible. In that summer, she had no idea what was about to happen – no thought that there would be a war, and that one day she would find herself in England, raising a son alone, and then a grand-daughter.

Shop windows were steamed up from the warm, damp bodies inside as I passed, and I stopped in a few to buy bread, ham and a bottle of wine for dinner later in the apartment, trying to inject some form of normality in my life.

I searched for the bookshop and walked past it twice before I saw the slice of a shop, just as Marlena had described, narrowly squeezed in between what was now a florist's and a butcher's. The name on the window was the same –*Gliński's Buchhandlung*

The door was still a scarlet red, the bell on the door still tinkled as I entered and inside, I felt as though I were stepping into the past.

Used books filled the shelves, with wall lights emitting a soft glow between the shelves. A slight woman wearing a long, heavy brown cardigan stood at the wooden counter, a vintage brass cash register in front of her as she rang up a sale for a customer. She gave me a quick glance, a nod and a smile which I returned and then began looking at the volumes. I had expected that the books would be in German, but the shelves were filled with classics translated into Polish, German, French and more. I wondered if they actually sold much here – was there a market for foreign translated classics?

Approaching the rear of the shop, where Marlena had told me they had sat and read stories with Mr Gliński himself, I saw Mr Wójcik from the apartment block, sat on a dark purple high-backed chair, his face half-obscured by a large volume he was holding.

I coughed once, then again, trying to get his attention, but he was so absorbed in what he was reading that he barely moved. Finding the courage to talk to the grumpy man, I said a simple, '*Hello.*'

He looked up then and narrowed his eyes behind his glasses.

'Mia,' I said, holding out my hand. 'From Ilse's apartment. Her granddaughter.'

He eyed my hand as if it were something to be afraid of, then shook his head. 'No English.'

I tried in German, but that made him shake his head more. 'No German.'

Defeated, I stopped trying. 'You know, you are one of the *rudest* people I have ever met,' I told him, knowing that he wouldn't understand. 'Ilse, my grandmother, your neighbour is in hospital, dying, and you haven't even said sorry, or asked about her. She was your neighbour. Do you not care at all?'

He cocked his head to the side as I spoke, something I did when I was trying to concentrate, and I suddenly lost my bravado – perhaps he did understand, and I had just repri-manded an old man that I didn't know!

Feeling a heat creep over my face, I shuffled out of the shop in embarrassment and found myself walking into the depths of the town, only stopping when I found a café where I could while away an hour or so.

It was only when I sat down and ordered a coffee that I realised I had in my hand a book from the shop that I had been looking at when I spoke to Mr Wójcik. *Shit.* I'd have to go back, and he would probably still be there.

I drank my coffee quickly, and raced back, hoping that the woman with the brown cardigan hadn't noticed what I had done.

As soon I entered, I breathed a sigh of relief; Mr Wójcik was gone. I placed the book back on the shelf and then browsed for a moment or two.

'Can I help you with something?' the woman with the brown cardigan was by my side.

Had she seen me? Did she think I was a thief?

'We have books in English.' She smiled and I relaxed.

'How did you know I was English?' I asked.

'I heard you.' She pointed to the now empty purple chair. 'Before, when you were talking to Tadeusz.'

Tadeusz.

As soon as she said his name, my breath caught in my throat.

'We have poetry and some of the classics in English – most are first and second editions so are a little pricey, but if you love books like I do, it won't matter!' she babbled.

'Wait, I'm sorry—' I held my hand up to stop her. 'Did you say that old man – Mr Wójcik – his name is... *Tadeusz?*'

'*Ja.* His Christian name. It is his bookshop. He is the owner. His uncle once owned this place, but he has no children, so I am not sure who will take this when he dies,' she said in a matter-of-fact tone.

'I'm sorry, but I have to go.' I almost rudely brushed past her and made my way out onto the dampened pavements and raced all the way to my grandmother's apartment.

Entering the foyer, I took a moment to catch my breath, then brushed my damp hair away from my face and knocked on Mr Wójcik's door. There was no answer, so I tried again, harder this time, hurting my knuckles.

'*Tadeusz!*' I tried, half yelling at the closed door, hoping that if he were inside and heard his first name, he would open it. But there was nothing.

Finally, I turned back out onto the street to go and see my grandmother once more. I was disappointed that he was not home, but he would be eventually, and I felt a shiver of excitement at finding out why, if he had once been my grandmother's friend, he did not speak to her now.

And, of course, where the elusive Szymon was.

By the time I reached the hospital, I was soaked through to the skin, and leaving a trail of puddles on the floor everywhere I walked. I apologised to a nurse who was eyeing the obvious hazard that I had left in my wake, and who immediately called for someone to come and mop it up. Before I even opened the door to my grandmother's room, a man had appeared in blue overalls, mop in hand. Ah, German efficiency was still alive and well.

Opening the door, I was met with an unexpected sight. My grandmother, seemingly asleep still, was not alone and it wasn't Marlena. Sat by her bed, holding a sheaf of papers in his slightly shaking hands was Tadeusz, reading to her in a calm, soft voice.

Hearing me enter, he looked up. His eyes were red from crying.

'Tadeusz?' I asked, and welcomed the look of surprise on his face as he heard his name.

He stood, looked at my grandmother, then stuffed the papers in his pocket, picked up his hat that he had laid on the end of her bed, and walked up to me.

'I want to talk to you,' I said, as he neared me.

He stopped and shook his head. 'No, Mia,' he said quietly, his English accent perfect. 'I will not talk to you. Please, if you will?' He gestured at the door.

I stood aside so he could pass, uneasy at the way he had spoken to me, and let him leave, then looked to my grandmother who was awake now and watching the scene, a smile on her face.

'Szymon,' she whispered from her bed. 'He came...'

THIRTEEN
ILSE

**Görlitz City Hospital
Tuesday, 9 February 1999
Afternoon**

My head is fuzzy. I can't explain it properly, but it's as though my thoughts, my past and my present, are all intermingled and I cannot pick out a proper thread. The pain is worse. Much worse, and now my eyesight is failing too. The lights which yesterday seemed so bright in here have dimmed, and the paper on which I write seems so far from me that it is making me feel nauseous as it dips and moves away from me.

Is this the end? Is this how it will go? Will I stop seeing? Will I stop being able to find a thought and verbalise it? I hope not... I hope I will die in my sleep, and if not, I hope that some medical person will do me a kindness and give me enough medication to take me softly away.

But again... Maybe I am meant to suffer. Maybe an easy death is not for me.

Marlena was here, briefly, telling me she had told some of my tale to Mia – about Szymon, and about that summer of ours.

I wanted to be angry with her, to yell at her, but I am too tired, too *old* to care any more.

Szymon was here too, earlier. I am *sure* of it – at least, I think I am. I hope it was not a dream, but maybe it was – it is so hard to say. I know that he told me a tale of his life – of loss, of horror and of bitterness, but I cannot imagine that this story could be true – I cannot imagine that he would come back to find me just to tell me that he suffered more than me, and not only that, has suffered since, *due to me*.

I wanted to say something to him as he talked, to tell him that I was sorry that I had made him feel this way and that I had felt guilt about it all my life. But the morphine was stopping me and all I could do was reach out to him, but he did not take my hand. Once more I have asked the nurse for less morphine this evening. I need a clearer head, I need to live these last few days before the cancer takes everything away from me and I am but a shell.

Can I remember what he said to me? No, not really... Not the details and this is making me irritated. I know he said he was angry. I know he said that he had hated me for a long time. And I know he said that he had been in pain. But what kind of pain? As soon as I think of what he said, it runs away from me and I cannot grasp it. If I had the energy, I would throw something across the room to vent my frustration, but alas, I can only just hold a pen that shakes across the page, let alone find the strength to lift something.

It makes me think back to when I was young. Of how I had endless energy and strength. Too much of it, I think now. If I was angry, I would yell and scream and perhaps break something of Mother's in secret – a china plate that she insisted was worth a lot of money, delighting as it shattered into tiny pieces on the floor. Or if I was sad, I would cry and howl like a demented animal and rub at my eyes with such force that I would pucker the skin pink.

I did a lot of this in my days in Berlin, I know that. God, did I hate it there. It was everything that Görlitz was not. It was neither pretty nor polite. There were people, cars, noise everywhere, and as much as Mother delighted in the life Berlin offered her, I detested it.

There were rallies constantly, and all of us were forced to go, saluting our Führer. That man. Hitler. I hated him then, and of course I still hate him now. Mother was taken by him, obsessed with him, Father less so, but glad of the opportunities he had with business – opening more and more factories across Germany, producing munitions for the war.

I, on the other hand, could see the cruelty of his regime. I knew that others did too, but I think we were all too scared, too ashamed, perhaps to speak out.

There were those who tried to oppose him and were arrested and killed. We all knew about them and maybe that fear was entrenched unwittingly under my skin, so I said nothing, I did nothing.

When I think of this now, I feel shame. Of course I do. I watched as Jews were rounded up and simply disappeared. I stood by, literally, on a pavement as a family right in front of me were loaded onto a bus, the mother crying, the father stone-faced. I waited until they were aboard, then continued my walk to the dressmaker's. I had pretended, as so many of us had, not to see it, to act as though it were normal for this to be taking place. But then, none of it was *normal*, none of it was right.

I was glad to leave Berlin behind. My father had expanded his factories in Görlitz and he was needed back to oversee them, especially since Görlitz was the most easterly town on the border with Poland and many workers had been brought in to help with the production of uniforms, guns, mechanical parts for tanks and other things.

I thought, naively, that by going back home, it would all be the same. That I would see Marlena again, would go to Mr

Gliński's bookshop. I thought I would perhaps see Tadeusz and Szymon, and that it would be as it always was – Poles and Germans together. Of course, it was stupid of me to think this way. Of course it was different, it was all so horribly changed.

When I think of those first few days back at home, it is like a dream to me now. I know I was there, I know I must have felt things, but it is as though I am outside myself, looking at a scene – like a film. I can see it, but I cannot *feel* the memory any more. Some memories are so real, so tangible I can relive them and remember every little detail. But this one, and some others are so distant to me that I wonder if it is the cancer, or perhaps it is simply age that does this.

But Szymon's visit today has made me think of it all again. How he said he was scared and in pain. I know that feeling. I saw it too. I will close my eyes for a moment and watch the memories play out on my eyelids, I the spectator this time, watching, observing.

And I hope that by doing this, I will understand how it was, not just for me, but for those I hurt.

FOURTEEN
ILSE

Görlitz
May 1942

Ilse stood in her bedroom with boxes yet to be unpacked stacked haphazardly around her. It had been five years, but nothing had changed; not that she was even sure what should have changed, but it all felt so familiar that she wondered if those years in Berlin had been a dream.

Her bed had been made up with a pale blue bed cover by a new maid – a girl who looked younger than Ilse and scurried about with eyes lowered at all times. Ilse had tried to introduce herself to the girl, but her mother had reprimanded her and told her that making friends with the staff was not the 'done' thing.

Her five years in Berlin had solidified Ilse's dislike for her mother. At times, she was sure she hated her, only in such a way that you can hate someone that you actually, strangely, love. All her mother cared about in Berlin was dressing nicely, showing off anything she bought, holding endless dinner parties for people Ilse neither knew nor cared about, and trying, yet failing, to make her only daughter into an image of herself.

Each time her mother had bought her a new dress, Ilse had refused to wear it, delighting in making her mother angry. Each dinner party Ilse refused to go to – even when her father, with his quiet, wheedling voice had begged her to and she had sat in her bedroom, alone, satisfied that she was not partaking of their new life.

She knew that she should have been happy at such a change in their circumstances – most girls at school envied the house they lived in on Wilhelmstraße, the money they had, the clothes she had. But Ilse found no joy in it.

Most of her friends had joined the Bund Deutscher Mädel, the youth league, pledging their loyalty to Hitler, and to the war when it started, yet Ilse had not, would not. The endless parades, the soldiers and the flags were a source of pride for so many, but for Ilse they made her nervous, fearful even, and she found it hard to put into words what she felt and why. So, she simply withdrew. She had no friends and instead wrote endless letters to Marlena, taking a snippet of joy each time she received a reply.

Now, though, she was home, and she felt a warm, relaxed glow on knowing that she would soon see her best friend, and that they could resume their friendship from where they had abruptly paused it five years ago.

The sound of the dinner bell chimed from downstairs and reluctantly, Ilse made her way to the dining room, hoping that her mother would not start with discussing social calls and dinners she wanted to plan to announce their return.

Her father sat at one end of the polished mahogany dining table, her mother at the other end, a vast stretch of wood between them. Ilse took her place on one side of the table, and spooned potatoes and carrots onto her plate, not waiting for the maid to do it for her.

'Ilse!' her mother reprimanded. 'You're acting like a peasant!'

Ilse grinned as she stuffed the potatoes into her mouth, making her cheeks bulge. Her father did not look up from his own dinner, a pile of letters by his elbow.

'Manfred! You could say something to her. To your daughter. Look at her – she eats like a wild animal. I've had enough of her. God knows I've tried with her, tried to find her a match – but who would have her? No one!' her mother screeched, finally getting her father's attention.

He looked to Ilse and gave her a smile, then it rapidly disappeared. 'You should listen to your mother, Ilse,' he tried. 'She knows the way of women.'

Ilse swallowed quickly. 'Some women,' she said. 'Not all. I am not like the women she knows about.'

Again, her father gave a small smile at her argumentative nature, then realising his wife was looking at him, turned his attention back to his plate.

'Is that it? That's all you will say to her? You let her get away with so much, Manfred. She could be married now and in high society in Berlin, but you said she could choose her own husband.'

'I thought you said no one would have her...' he started, trailing off on seeing the look on his wife's face.

Ilse's mother, sensing that she was losing the argument, silenced herself apart from the scrape and screech of her knife and fork on her plate, causing Ilse to grit her teeth with irritation.

'What is that? By your elbow, my dear?' Her mother changed tone upon noticing the envelopes by her father's side.

'These?' He raised his eyebrows as if he had forgotten they were there. 'Some of the workers did not have money for stamps, so I said I would post them for them.'

Ilse reached across and took one from the pile, noting the address somewhere in Kraków, Poland.

'Why would you do that?' her mother asked, her voice laced with exasperation.

'They have no money,' her father mumbled between mouthfuls of food.

'So on your first day, you help those *Poles*,' she spat the last word. 'They're criminals! And you, their overseer and you help them?'

'They're not criminals,' he replied calmly. 'They're prisoners of war. There's a difference, my dear.'

Buoyed by her father's sudden confidence, Ilse joined in. 'Why do they have to work for you, Father? Are they nice? Are they all Polish?'

'They are nice, yes,' her father answered. 'Very nice, in fact. They live over the river in a camp, but some of them are allowed to work. Some of them are Polish, some—'

'*Manfred*!' her mother yelled, then stood up with such force her chair toppled backwards to the floor. 'What on *earth* has got into you? Those men are criminals whether you like it or not! They are the enemy, and you want to post their letters for them and tell our daughter that they are...' she paused, then screwed up her face and said sourly, '*nice*.'

Her father stopped eating, and leaned back in his chair, a weariness taking over his whole body so that he suddenly seemed to Ilse much smaller than he had a moment ago.

'So, what would you have me do, my dear? Tell these men who are imprisoned that I won't send their letters and postcards to their families to let them know that they are safe?'

'Yes, exactly! Why do I have to be the voice of reason around here? Why is it always me?' She suddenly burst into hysterical tears and ran from the room, leaving Ilse and her father in silence with just the ticking of the grandfather clock for comfort.

Her father sighed, then scraped back his chair and picked

up the letters, taking them to the basket of old newspapers that sat by the cold fireplace.

'Father, no!' Ilse cried. 'You're not going to send them?'

A loud bang came from upstairs, and Ilse's father looked to the ceiling. 'It's easier this way,' he said sadly, then left Ilse alone and trudged up the stairs to placate her mother.

She acted quickly. The maid would light the fire either later this evening or tomorrow and she could not – would not – let those men's letters be burned. She retrieved the bundle from the basket, then lit a small fire in the grate so that if anyone asked where the letters were, they would assume that they had been destroyed.

Ilse ran upstairs and into her room, closing the door and locking it behind her. Sitting on her bed, she looked at each envelope, wondering who would be waiting to hear from a loved one, what their lives were like now, and of course, what the men had written.

Most were postcards, and thick black lines had erased some of the words, censoring what it was the men wanted to tell their families. She did not know much Polish, and could not read it well at all, but in most she could understand fragments:

Dear Mother and Father, how are you? Are you well?

Another read:

I want to let you know I am alive.

And another:

Will you please send food?

Soon, she became frustrated that she could not understand everything that was written and began to tidy them into a neat pile. It was then that she noticed a picture. It seemed an unusual choice for a postcard – one of a man shielding his eyes, an axe in one hand.

Then she turned it over, wondering where this would be sent to, and that was when she saw two names she knew, and an address.

The sender was Szymon, the recipient Tadeusz. And the address was Mr Gliński's bookshop.

FIFTEEN

ILSE

Görlitz
May 1942

Ilse did not sleep well that night. Her mind kept flitting to the postcard, the one with a picture of a man and an axe on the front. She had never seen the image before, but it evoked in her a feeling of pain, even of fear, and she couldn't decipher why.

She would try and sleep, but then her hand would reach out to the bedside table and her fingers would find the postcard once more. She would lie like that for some time, just touching the thin paper, wondering what had happened to put Szymon in the camp her father spoke of, and why Tadeusz was at the bookshop. It made her realise how much she didn't know, and perhaps how much she had ignored. Just because the war had not really touched her life, it didn't mean that those around her were not harmed.

By five in the morning, she gave up on sleep and sat at the window, waiting for the day to begin. Outside the street was already alive. Army trucks rumbled past in the direction of the river, their headlights too bright, their engines too loud. Ilse pressed her face against the window, trying to see the river in the distance, but she could not, and only saw her whitened breath on the glass. She tried to imagine the route they would take – over the bridge, past Achramowicz's bakery and into the streets, perhaps passing Tadeusz's or Szymon's homes.

Again, she wondered about her friends' lives: Who they had become in the past five years? And what had happened to them? She itched with the need for the sun to rise so that she could see Marlena, and ask her what had been happening while she had been in Berlin.

Her letters to her friend had never talked of the war, even though it raged around them. In their letters they spoke of fashion, music and each other's families and at the time, Ilse had been thankful for it, but now, she wished she had been brave enough to ask more – to ask what had happened to their friends and neighbours, to engage with politics more and understand what was really happening.

Moving away from the window, she grabbed the baby-blue bed cover and wrapped it around herself, and like a caterpillar in its cocoon, she flopped onto the bed and watched the clock tick away the minutes until she could begin her life again.

Later that morning, Marlena was at Ilse's before breakfast had been served. Ilse, whilst tired, was both delighted and relieved to see her friend, who had turned into a tall, beautiful woman, and radiated a new-found confidence that Ilse was desperate to find out where it had come from. Gone was the chubby girl and in its place was a curvaceous woman with large almond eyes, pouty lips that she had rouged and curling auburn hair that seemed to Ilse to come straight from a Rubens painting.

'I missed you so much!' Marlena squealed, as she took Ilse in her arms. 'Everything is so awful here now, we had to move into my grandparents' house as Mother thought we would be safer this side of the river. You know, you can't even cross the bridge any more – there are soldiers everywhere!'

Ilse held her friend tightly, not wanting the joy of seeing her to be replaced with the reality that was just outside her doorstep.

Marlena broke the embrace and held Ilse at arm's length. 'Look at you! You're so *beautiful*! Look at your hair, your clothes!'

Ilse shrugged despondently. 'Mother makes me wear them...'

'And where is she?' Marlena scoured the hallway, her eyes landing on the closed dining room doors. 'In there?' she nodded.

'She is,' Ilse sighed.

'Are things still so bad between you two?' Marlena asked.

Ilse nodded. She had been frank with Marlena in her letters, about how she and her mother could not find common ground, how mean and cruel she could be.

'Well, probably better that I don't see her. I mean, my father is half-Polish. She was never happy about it before, I doubt she's going to be happy about it now!' Marlena grinned.

Ilse smiled back, then clasped her friend to her once more. Thank God for Marlena! Thank God for her humour and brightness. Just seeing her made Ilse want to weep with happiness and relief.

Marlena laughed as Ilse held her. 'You've *changed*!'

Ilse let go. 'I have. Well, at least I think I have. I'm just so glad to see you.'

'And I'm so glad you're here. You cannot believe what it's like here now. Things are so different. People have just simply disappeared! Like one day there they are and the next they are gone. Do you remember Tadeusz? His parents are gone – taken away in the middle of the night. I couldn't believe it. But they had been hiding a Jewish family in their basement and someone betrayed them, so they were taken.'

'That's awful,' Ilse murmured. 'It's funny you mention him,' she added, keeping her voice low. 'Come with me, upstairs. Let me show you something...'

Marlena followed Ilse to her bedroom and plopped on her bed. 'What is it?'

Ilse handed her the postcard she had found and watched as Marlena read it. 'What does it say?' Ilse asked, then chewed at her nail with impatience.

'It says:

My dearest Tadeusz,

I hope this postcard finds its way into your hands.

I have been reading Mein Kampf. It is the only book that I can get my hands on.

However, pages 34, 60 and 72 are of interest to me as I think they will be for you.

We have a garden. We are allowed to plant and watch things grow. The potatoes will be ready in June.

Send books. Specifically the Bible. I miss it. Psalms has always calmed my mind as I know it has yours.

Your cousin,
    Szymon.

Marlena finished, and Ilse realised she had been holding her breath as her friend read.

'Where did you find this?' Marlena asked.

'My father said he would get stamps for some of the workers who said they had no money. He was going to send them, but then Mother had one of her outbursts, so he threw them in the paper pile for burning. And I took them.'

Marlena nodded, as if it all made sense to her.

'So Szymon... He works for my father now?' Ilse asked,

annoyed that the question sounded so stupid, yet she was still unsure why Szymon would be a prisoner of war, and why he would be working in her father's factory.

'I didn't know that he was. I knew that he and Tadeusz joined the army and then they disappeared. I didn't know Szymon was alive if I'm honest. It seems from this, that he's one of the prisoners, though. They're marched over the bridge each day into town then back again. There's a camp near where my aunt used to live. There are hundreds of them, apparently all kept enclosed behind barbed-wire fencing.'

'And Tadeusz?'

Marlena shrugged. 'He's at his uncle's shop.'

Ilse sat on the bed beside her friend. 'I want to give it to him,' she said.

'The postcard? Why? Just send it.'

'No. We were all friends once. I want to give it to him, to see how he is. It might be nice, you know, to go to the bookshop again, like we did that summer five years ago?'

'I don't know, Ilse...' Marlena warned. 'Things are not the same as they were. I told you Tadeusz's parents are gone. And Szymon is a prisoner of war. It could be... *dangerous*.'

'Dangerous how?' Ilse stood up, putting her hands on her hips. 'All we're doing is going to a bookshop.'

'Sure. Yes, but a *Polish* man's bookshop. And you are delivering something from a prisoner. There are eyes and ears everywhere, Ilse. It isn't safe. My uncle, he was arrested just because he refused to give evidence against his neighbour, who the police said worked for the underground army. He was beaten, Ilse. I mean, his legs were broken, so broken that he can't walk now without a cane. Who knows what people are seeing without us realising it.'

'But *you've* seen him, so why can't I?'

'Only a few times, Ilse. Just a few times and I promised I wouldn't tell anyone he was there.'

'But you just told me,' Ilse said with a determined grin.

'Well. Not really. I mean, the postcard—'

'Come on, Marlena,' Ilse interrupted her friend. 'I won't say you told me he's there. We'll just give him the postcard, say hello, and leave.'

Marlena began to chew on her bottom lip, tearing away a piece of dry skin, something which she had used to do as a child. Ilse could see that Marlena's confidence was not yet fully fledged.

'Come on, Marlena!' Ilse cajoled, placing her hands on her friend's shoulders and looking into her eyes. 'Let's have an adventure like we used to. It will be fine. There's no need to worry.'

Marlena shook her head, then laughed. 'I was wrong before when I said you had changed. You haven't changed a bit!'

'Is that a yes?'

'How could I ever refuse you, Ilse?' Marlena stood.

'You never could, and you never will!' Ilse wrapped her arms around her friend once more.

But this time she noticed that her friend did not hug her back.

SIXTEEN

ILSE

Görlitz City Hospital
Tuesday, 9 February 1999
Evening

'*Zeit für ihre medikamente,*' a nurse disrupted my thoughts and just like that, the montage of those first days disappears into the shadows.

I tell her I don't want any more medication, but she is insistent and takes a large syringe and injects it into the drip that is constantly attached to my arm. She's also told me I have to eat and has left a tray with a limp cheese sandwich and a strawberry yoghurt on my table. I know I won't eat it, but I told her I will.

She has hairy arms, the nurse. I notice this as she fusses about me, turning me and telling me I must move unless I want to get bed sores. I tell her it hardly matters – I'm dying and I can die with bed sores.

She ignores me and keeps pulling and pushing at me to make this broken body of mine move. She is wasting her time, and I want to tell her that she should go away and leave me alone, but I don't – I let her do her job until she is satisfied that she has done enough to keep me alive for one more day.

The medication is strong and is already starting to take effect. My mind is whirling and falling, as if I am on a roller-coaster and nothing seems to make much sense. I can still see that last scene in my head, though, almost like a painting. I am holding Marlena close to me. I am wearing a blue dress, light blue like cornflowers. My hair is shining and pinned back in a chignon whilst Marlena's hair is curly, voluminous, and escaping from the few pins she has used to try and secure it in place.

I am holding her, but her arms are by her side. If I could paint, I would render this scene, leaving in every deft brush-stroke to show how this moment, these few minutes of my life changed everything for so many people.

What would the painting show, exactly, to a viewer? Would they take away from it that my friend was giving in to me despite her own fears? Would it show my naivety, and I suppose my irritability with the life I had, and the desire for some excitement, ignoring the reality that was simply outside my bedroom window?

I would paint the window too, I have decided. It would depict those Nazi flags outside – the image saying much more about the dangers lurking than I ever could. And on the bed would be the letters and postcards from those men who worked for my father – or rather, were forced to work for him, whilst living in a prison, and never knowing if they would ever be set free.

Perhaps I would include a ghost in this painting too. Of Tadeusz's parents who perished in Auschwitz, and who were already dead at the moment I hugged Marlena to me on that day I first returned home, but we just didn't know it yet.

Maybe there would be other ghosts too – all of them stood silently in the background of a painting of two women, one holding the other tightly to her, the other resisting as the flags quivered outside, waiting for the embrace to end so that the spectres could follow them for the rest of their lives.

SEVENTEEN

MIA

Görlitz
Tuesday, 9 February 1999

After Tadeusz left the hospital room, my grandmother sat up in bed and demanded to know where I had been, ignoring my questions of what he had said and why she had thought he was Szymon. Was she getting the two of them confused perhaps, or was Marlena right, that nothing she said at the moment could be trusted? Was her mind becoming consumed by the cancer, and bit by bit she would disappear?

In the end, I ceased my questioning, and told her that I had walked the streets and done some shopping while I waited for her to wake up.

'What are you going to do, Mia?' she asked.

'Go back to your apartment, then eat, sleep and then come back here,' I told her simply.

'No, no.' She shook her head wearily, then reached out and took my hand in hers. 'I mean, when I am *gone*. What are you going to *do*? I need you to tell me.'

'I–I don't know,' I stammered. I wasn't prepared for this. 'I haven't thought about it.'

'You need to. You need to think now. Prepare yourself. I have arranged my funeral. Marlena has the details, so you don't need to worry about anything. I have money, too, that you will get as well as the apartment. You can sell it if you want to and then—'

'Stop!' I yelled. 'Stop it. I don't want to think about that. How can you talk about it as if it doesn't mean anything, like it's just, just...' I searched to find the right word: '*details*.'

She smiled kindly at me and gripped my hand tighter. 'I just need to know you will be OK. That's all. I just need to know, Mia. Think about what you will do and tell me tomorrow. I need to go in peace, knowing that you will be fine.'

It was then I realised my sleeve had rolled up by accident once more, revealing a darker bruise, blue and purple that had been so deep that in a month it had still not seen fit to wane into a greeny yellow.

'You won't go back to that man?' she quietly asked.

'No, of course I won't,' I said. Will wouldn't want me anyway – not that I would say that to her. I pulled my sleeve down to cover my arm.

'Good, good.' She nodded. 'Find someone who cherishes you. Promise me you will do that. Find a life for yourself that brings you joy every day. Don't just be like one of those people who work to live. Do a job you love. Find friends you love. Fill your life with love in everything you do.'

Suddenly, she gasped, then her head tilted back for a second. My heart stopped. I know it did. It stopped beating in my chest.

'Grandma.' I jumped up, looking into her eyes, then she took a rasping, rattling breath.

'I'm just tired, Mia...' she whispered.

I helped her get settled, then sat by her bed for an hour or more whilst she slept, watching her chest rise and fall, feeling my own breathing stop and start along with hers.

Eventually, I left – I had to. The nurse who introduced herself as Johanna made me. She had arms the size of my legs, and a voice that boomed. I wasn't about to argue with her.

As much as I did not want to leave my grandmother's side, I did want to see Tadeusz before it got too late. I just hoped he would open the door to me and decide that perhaps he would be willing to talk to me, after all.

I reached home just as the rain had started again. I was damp, cold, sad, hungry, tired – and more. I couldn't even find all the words to describe how I felt as I stood in that cold black-and-white-tiled foyer and knocked on Tadeusz's door, waiting, shifting from foot to foot and resisting the urge to cry.

Finally, due to my repeated knocking, Tadeusz opened the door, his eyes still red beneath his glasses.

'What you want?' he asked.

'I saw you at the hospital,' I told him in a voice that sounded more confident than I felt. 'I heard you reading something to my grandmother. So, why won't you talk to me?'

'Why do you need me to talk to you?' he countered.

'Because this is you.' I delved into my handbag and produced the postcard.

He took it from me and read it, his face betraying nothing. 'And?' he demanded, handing it back.

'You two don't speak to each other!' I half yelled. 'But you *know* each other. But then there you are in the hospital. Don't you think I deserve some explanation?'

Irritatingly, all he did was shrug.

'That's *it*? That's all I get?'

'Listen to me,' he said quietly now. 'I don't know you. You don't know me. You're trying to bring things up from the past –

with that, for one.' He pointed a bony finger at the postcard. 'The past is the past. Leave it buried. It has nothing to show you. Nothing to teach you. Yes, I knew your grandmother, a long time ago. She was a selfish woman and when she came back here, she was still selfish. She thought she could change what had happened to make herself feel better. But it's too late. Nothing can change.'

'But I don't understand...' I started.

He raised a hand to silence me. 'And you won't. Never. I went to see her because you told me she was dying. I went to see her to tell her some things I had not said for a long time. What I said is between me and her. Not you. Do you understand this?'

'Look,' I tried to inject some measure of calm into my tone. 'I don't mean to upset you. Really, I don't. It's just that she has been asking to see Szymon and then I found this postcard, then I find out you are his cousin. You can understand my curiosity, can't you? I mean, if I can find Szymon and maybe bring him to her, that will ease some of whatever it is that's bothering her.'

He smiled more kindly now. 'My dear, Szymon is dead. If you want to find him, go across the road to the cemetery. The one by the river. You'll find him there. She's known for a long time exactly where he is. So you won't be able to bring him to her.'

Shocked and saddened, I opened my mouth to say something but could not find the right words.

'Besides,' he said, as he gently closed the door. 'You know what that expression is in England – curiosity?'

I shook my head.

'It killed the cat.'

EIGHTEEN

TADEUSZ

Görlitz
Tuesday, 9 February 1999

Tadeusz closed the door on the girl and fiddled with the lock and the chain. Once finished, he placed his palms flat on the surface, then leaned his forehead against the door. He could hear her still outside, muttering to herself as she clomped up the stairs.

Why did she have to come here? Why did she have to find those postcards and dredge up the past?

He walked to his drinks trolley and poured himself a measure of whisky, then sat in his favourite armchair, pale green, the armrests worn through from years of use, horsehair poking through the thin material so that it scratched at his arms.

As soon as he sat, he felt tired. Not the usual tiredness that plagued anyone at his age, but a tiredness that seemed to fill his bones, taking away the marrow and replacing them with lead. His neck hurt, his back too and he could not sit comfortably.

'Damn it!' he shouted into the gloom. It was the girl. She had done this.

He shouldn't have gone to see Ilse, he should have left well enough alone, but after seeing Mia in the bookshop earlier that day, how angry she was, how she had said how ill Ilse was, he had felt as if it was time to at least put one ghost to rest. And so, he had gone to see her. Had talked to her as she half slept, and read words to her he had been waiting years to say.

Yet, instead of the calm and relief he thought that would bring, more ghosts appeared as if from nowhere – each of them whispering in his ear, each of them begging for him to remember them...

Annoyed that his evening was now ruined, he stood and found a record to listen to, hoping to focus his attention onto something else. He found an old Sinatra album and placed it carefully on the turntable, then slowly lowered the needle onto the spinning disc.

He sat back down and let old Frank croon about flying to the moon and New York, and tried to imagine himself in another life, where perhaps he had married, had children and was now sat with them, instead of alone in a dusty and echoing apartment.

'Damn it!' he shouted again at nothing, then drank back the whisky in one go and immediately poured himself another.

Those postcards were on his mind, taking him back to the war and to when Ilse had returned. He shook his head trying not to think about it, and found himself with a new memory, one which made him feel cold and sick with guilt.

He chewed his lip as he thought. Maybe, if he let himself go back there, then perhaps it would all go away. Perhaps the ghosts would be appeased for now, and he could go about his days again.

He closed his eyes and watched the colours dance and shift on his eyelids, and then he was there, in amongst the noise of battle, the smell of blood, the scent of musty earth and sweat scratching at his nostrils.

NINETEEN
TADEUSZ

Kierżno, 35 km from Zgorzelec
August 1939

The noise was too much for Tadeusz.

The constant wail and scream of the German Storches over-head, coupled with the rumble and boom of the tanks, then the *pip pip* of gunfire made his mind do strange things. He found that he could not concentrate when his comrades spoke to him, he could not follow a simple order, all he could think about was the noise. When it ceased for a moment or two, it gave him little respite as all he did was anxiously count, looking to the skies, down the rutted track on which they sat, and wait for it to start again. And when it did, he almost felt relieved, until, of course, it all became too much once more.

He sat in a trench with four other men, his cousin Szymon by his side, whose face was pale, streaked with mud, and eyes wide.

All around him, bodies were encased in the dirt, their blood mingling with the soil of their homeland, flies already drawn to them, landing on eyeballs. He wanted to swat the flies away, but it was a worthless task; as soon as he rid the bodies of a swarm, more would land with the same gruesome vigour as their counterparts.

The smell of death was new to Tadeusz, although the bodies had only been there for a few days at most. He always thought that it would smell rancid – almost an indescribable scent that would send any man retching. But the bodies around him still smelled sweet, the blood and the innards mingling with the dirt to create an air of something he remembered from visiting the butcher's. Not death – not *quite* – even though the bodies were far from alive.

'We can't win, can we?' Szymon whispered, taking Tadeusz's mind away from his musings on the dead. He looked at his cousin, whose eyes never left the horizon where tanks loomed in the distance.

'We can try,' Tadeusz said, but his words were hollow. He looked to his right where, just poking out of the mud, was the tip of a nose.

Szymon turned away and pulled out an aluminium water bottle, tipped it back and took a swig, then wiped the drips from his chin. He handed it to Tadeusz who drank too, the cool water soothing his parched throat.

'Not too much!' Szymon yanked the bottle back. 'We've only got a little left.'

Tadeusz nodded, then hunkered back down in the dirt, his rifle trained on the billows of smoke that seemed to be drawing closer.

'We have to move! Now!' Eryk, their lieutenant screamed at them.

Before Tadeusz could ask why, a huge boom came from the line of trees beside them, engulfing screams as debris came hurling at them. Tadeusz shielded his face with his arm, feeling dirt, stones, pieces of wood thwack against his body. Finally, the shower stopped, and Tadeusz was able to make out the shadows

of German soldiers moving closer to them. He turned to
Szymon, to tell him to run, but Szymon lay on his back, his face
a grimace of pain.

He scrambled to him and leaned over his cousin. 'Szymon!
Szymon!' he screamed at him, slapping his cheeks. 'Can you
hear me?'

His cousin nodded. 'My leg!'

Tadeusz looked down to where Szymon's leg lay at a strange
angle, his shin bent unnaturally to the right.

'I – we—' Tadeusz started, his eyes moving from the
shadows of men who were now becoming more human as they
moved out of the smoke, then back to Szymon's face that had
small bloody cuts on the skin. And then down to his leg.

'We have to move,' Tadeusz hurriedly said. 'Eryk – help us!'
he called out. Eryk did not respond, so Tadeusz went to him
and seized him by the shoulders to ask him to help him with
Szymon. It was then that Tadeusz realised Eryk's head was
leaning on his chest. He crawled round to look at him and
found Eryk's eyes glassy, staring at nothing, the lower half of his
body ripped apart by the explosion.

Tadeusz could feel heat and soot in his lungs. Each breath
hurt. His mouth was dry and yet he could feel tears dripping
down his face. 'I – we—' he gasped but had no idea what he
should say.

He crawled back to Szymon, ignoring a sudden pain in his
shoulder. The *pip pip* of gunfire was close, the shouts of 'Surrender! I surrender!' coming from his comrades and the harsh
growls of German in response, '*Sieg Heil!*'

'Szymon, Szymon,' Tadeusz placed his face close to his
cousin's. 'What do I do? Tell me what to do! I can't carry you
alone!'

'Stay with me,' Szymon moaned, his eyes opening and closing, the pain drawing him closer to unconsciousness.

Another round of gunfire and Tadeusz felt something jump

up and bite his calf. Again, ignoring it, he beseeched Szymon to tell him what to do.

'I will go and get help. I can. I can do it. I will try. Szymon, can you hear me? I will get help!'

Above them, planes screamed, and across the fields tanks boomed. More shouts came from the German soldiers, along with more cries for help from his comrades.

Tadeusz licked his dry lips and tasted the metallic tang of blood. Was it his? 'I can't stay here,' he said, his voice high and scared. 'I can't, Szymon!'

Tadeusz's mind felt like it was full of cotton wool. Nothing made sense. For a second, he placed his hands over his ears to try and drown out the noise, but he could still hear the sound of himself crying.

'Please, Szymon!'

'Don't leave me,' his cousin whispered again, then reached out for him. 'Please, Tadeusz. Take my hand. Don't leave me alone...'

Tadeusz took his own hands away from his ears and looked at Szymon's hand, black with mud, held mid-air, waiting for Tadeusz to take it and wait for a few more seconds together until their captors reached them.

'I'm – I'm so sorry,' Tadeusz cried, before he stood and ran. There was a pain in his leg and in his shoulder, but he did not care. There were shouts behind him for him to stop, to surrender, but Tadeusz did neither.

Carried by the cacophony all around him, he ran, dipping and diving, and did not stop until he could clearly hear his own breath coming in ragged gasps, the echo of war far behind him.

TWENTY

TADEUSZ

Görlitz
Wednesday, 10 February 1999

Tadeusz opened his eyes, allowing a few tears to escape. He wiped them away and stood to move the needle off the record which had started to jump and scratch at the vinyl.

He should never have let that happen to Szymon. He should *never* have left him. That one moment, those few seconds had changed everything and there was no going back to make it any different. He had left his cousin lying in pain amidst the filth of battle, enemy soldiers metres away from him, and saved himself.

The clock on the mantel chimed half past one – another day had begun. It was time for him to leave whatever thoughts and occurrences were beginning and go to bed.

He shuffled into his bedroom and changed into his pyjamas, lay down on the bed, closed his eyes and wished for death to visit him once more, and this time to take him away.

. . .

The following morning, he woke tangled up in his bedsheets, a layer of sweat on his skin. He couldn't remember the dreams that he'd had, yet he knew that they had troubled him.

'Damn it! Damn her!' he yelled at nothing. She had disturbed the carefully constructed life he had created for himself, drawing him into thoughts and memories that he did not care for.

He showered and dressed, then sat and drank one cup of coffee and ate one piece of dry toast as he did every morning. But this morning the toast clogged in his mouth, the coffee was burnt and bitter. He left his repast half-eaten and took his cane, hat and coat and made his way out onto the street.

Outside the rain had ceased and a cold, blue sky greeted him. Somewhere a bird trilled a spring song, and for a moment, his spirits were lifted. He would not let the girl get to him, he decided as he walked. He would do as he had always done, eat, work, sleep and eventually, the days would stack up and one day would be his last. And with that thought, Tadeusz was somewhat cheered.

As he turned onto Brüderstraße, he saw a figure outside the shop. He knew who it was and as he drew closer, the *tip tap* of his cane on the pavement made her turn around. Marlena.

'You,' she pointed a finger at him, 'I have to talk to you. Right now,' she hissed.

'And how lovely to see you too, Marlena. How long has it been? A while, no doubt,' he tried cheerily, but somehow his voice fell flat, and he felt a nervous flutter in his stomach.

He fussed in his pocket for his keys to the shop, then finding the right one, he unlocked the door, but did not hold it open for her.

But Marlena was not to be dissuaded, it seemed, and she burst in, almost knocking the tiny bell from its perch above the door.

'What do you think you are *doing*?' she cried, as he switched on lights and removed his hat and coat.

'I'm not entirely sure what you are getting at, my dear friend – what has it been, a year or more since you have come to see me? And this is the way you greet me?' He hoped his tone conveyed the sarcasm he so wished it to, but Marlena seemed not to care.

'I think the last time I came to see you, we argued, and you told me not to come back.'

'And yet, here you are!'

'You're such a moody, irritable old bastard, do you know that?' Marlena yelled at him, her nostrils flared like a bull that has just seen someone wearing red, and he had to stop himself from laughing at her.

'Such is the way with age. We all get a bit hot under the collar.'

'I'm only hot under the collar because you told me last year, and the times before when we would have coffee, that you wouldn't talk to Ilse and now I hear that you were there, in the hospital, saying something to her – what did you say, Tadeusz? Did you tell her, like you have been telling me all these years, how much you *hate* her – how you wished she would *never* have come back – how you preferred to think she was *dead*?'

As he heard the words repeated to him that he had so often said to Marlena, he felt a worm of shame turn in his stomach. Had he really wished her dead? He may have said it – he may have, but he was sure that he hadn't meant it...

'I didn't do anything wrong, Marlena.' He tried to sound confident, but his voice had suddenly grown smaller.

'What are you saying to her after all this time, Tadeusz? She has tried to talk to you, every day for six goddamn years and you have not muttered a word to her. And now, as she lies dying, *that's* when you choose to go and speak with her? Tell me! What did you say?'

Tadeusz sighed and sat on his chair behind the till. He looked at Marlena, his friend for most of his life. After the war had ended, they had seen each other about the town and now and again had had coffee. It was only when Ilse returned six years ago that Marlena had mithered him on an almost weekly basis to talk to Ilse, to let her explain – to forgive her. The bitterness he had stored away all these years came forth, and unfortunately his sort-of friend got the brunt of it and had been banished out of his life now for a year. Why did he do this to himself he wondered? Why did he force himself to be alone? Well, because he liked it, he supposed. Or did he?

He saw Marlena's mouth moving and realised she had been saying something, but that he had not listened. Now, she leaned into him, a gentle smile on her face, 'Why? Just tell me that.' Marlena asked softly, almost kindly now and it reminded him of when she was young.

He thought for a moment, trying to find the right words. When he had, he spoke slowly, trying to ensure that Marlena, and perhaps he himself understood why he had gone to the hospital and why he had suddenly found the need to speak to Ilse.

'Do you remember those days, Marlena? Do you remember coming here, to this shop, with Ilse that day with a postcard in your hands?'

'I do.'

'It changed things again for us all. I think about it every day when I come here. I cannot help but think about it. Every day I wonder if I had turned you both away, if my uncle hadn't been so trusting, then things would've been better for us all – don't you think so?'

Marlena placed her hands flat on the counter. He saw that she wore a bangle with tiny bells on it. She saw him take note of it and said, 'It's so people can hear me coming.'

He let out a chuckle, then shook his head.

'Look, it is the past,' she began. 'We can't change it now, Tadeusz. I don't even think about *what ifs* because it takes the joy out of life. But I see now that's what you have been doing all these years. Wondering *what if* – trying to find a better outcome for us all. But really you should have lived in the present.'

'It's too late.' He raised his arms and gestured at the books. 'This is all I have.'

Marlena slowly shook her head. 'No, it isn't. You have much more than that. And it's come to find you. I think it's about time that you, and Ilse, put all those old ghosts to rest and start to see what is right in front of you. It's not too late to be happy, Tadeusz.'

'I thought that was what I was doing when I went to see her,' he admitted.

'And has it helped? Do you feel better? Because you certainly don't sound like anything has changed for you.'

He didn't answer her, but he chewed on the inside of his lip as he thought.

The bell above the door tinkled and in walked his first customer – a tourist asking for a map.

He stood, smiled, then nodded at Marlena who took her leave, and left him to his day.

By the time he reached home, it was 4 p.m. The rain had started again and inside his apartment, the old plumbing clanged and clattered as it tried to heat up the radiators. He stood for a moment, his hands over a radiator, trying to warm himself. Then, he heard the front door bang as someone opened it and then the creak as it closed behind them.

Mia. He knew it was. He waited a second and recognised her footsteps on the stairs.

Marlena's words rang in his mind. He had tried all day to

ignore her voice, but he could not. He could be happy – could he?

He had thought that by seeing Ilse, and telling her what he had written down all those years before would relieve him of the burden he had been carrying – the unsaid words a heavy weight on his shoulders that had turned him from the light-hearted young man that he had once been into a suffering old fool. Because that was what he was, he decided, a fool. He had forgone happiness, forgone any light in his life and perhaps he had placed too much blame on Ilse for this. It wasn't entirely her fault – he knew that deep down. To be honest, it wasn't really anyone's fault but his own. He had swallowed bitterness and trauma every day, morning, noon and night, instead of dealing with it, instead of letting it all go.

He looked to his gnarled hands, their surface a polka-dot spread of age spots, the thick blue veins under his thinning skin pushing and throbbing against the prison that held them there.

He saw, then, that he had created a prison for himself too, and when he had seen Ilse earlier, old, frail and clinging on to a tiny bit of life, that perhaps she, too, had lived in a prison of her own making all these years. He knew that her son had died, he knew from Marlena that she had turned from a bright young thing into a recluse of sorts – never visiting Marlena, never allowing Marlena to come to here even. Always keeping everyone away.

He laughed – they were the same, him and Ilse. The only difference was that she had tried these past six years to make amends and he had resolutely refused her.

All he knew was that the feelings that were fighting for attention in his mind were throwing him off course and he could not let it continue. Maybe it was time to do something about them once and for all. Maybe it was time to go through what had happened, *properly* this time, and by doing so, under-stand where all this nastiness, this bile had come from and finally see if it had been right all these years to direct it just at Ilse, or whether he should have been directing it at himself.

With this decision made, he poured himself a half measure of whisky, drank it down, placed his hat back on his head and made his way to the door. He wasn't doing this for Mia, nor Ilse, nor Marlena, he decided as he turned the doorknob. He was doing this for himself – he was doing this so that he could understand what had gone wrong all those years ago.

He was nothing if not a learned man. And it was time he finally learned the truth about himself.

TWENTY-ONE

MIA

Görlitz
Wednesday, 10 February 1999

My day had not improved my mood. Grandma had been lucid and awake for an hour that morning, but then she had started to vomit constantly and had to be medicated, which had sent her into a deep sleep.

I had hoped to see Marlena at the hospital, and had called her that morning to tell her about Tadeusz and how he had been with me, and Marlena, in her way, had said she would deal with the problem. I had then waited around the hospital for her, called her a few times, but by 3 p.m., had given up and decided to come back to the apartment to rest.

But I knew I wouldn't sleep. I couldn't. There was so much going round and round in my head – the plea from Grandma to sort myself out; her secrets; the postcards; Marlena, Tadeusz. I wanted to cry but again, I couldn't. It was as if I was living, moving about and talking, but I wasn't really there, and all my emotions were so intermingled that I couldn't confidently pull out a thread of one and examine it properly.

I stood by the window and looked down at the graveyard where Tadeusz had said Szymon was buried. I had decided to go and find his grave, but the weather had turned again, and thick fat raindrops splotched down the windowpane, whilst depressed clouds sat heavy with the promise of more to come. A rumble of thunder alerted me to a storm that was growing, and I felt as though it matched my feelings – a storm was coming there too. Or maybe I was already in it.

Slowly, I rolled a sleeve up my arm, inspecting the bruises that dotted the skin. I traced each one with the tip of my finger, then pressed on them to feel the pain that they held. I wanted to feel the pain – I wanted to be able to understand what had happened and to sort this out in my mind too. There was so much I needed to think about, so much I needed to feel and let out of myself, but I was unsure where to start. Would pressing on these bruises do it? Would feeling the hurt of the past make me examine it more closely now?

A knock on the door brought me away from my thoughts and I went to it, expecting Marlena to be stood there, perhaps a bottle of something in her hand and a promise to tell me what had happened with Tadeusz that morning.

Instead, I was greeted with Tadeusz himself, his hat in his hand clenched between white knuckles. He shuffled from foot to foot, as if at any moment he would make a run for it. Then, he took a deep breath, exhaled, and stood very still.

'I have come to talk with you,' he said, not quite looking at me, but at something behind me.

I was so surprised I didn't know what to say for a moment.

'About what you said to Grandmother?' I managed. 'Or maybe explain why you have been so rude to me ever since I arrived?'

The irritation in my voice shocked us both for a second, and I saw his eyes widen. But I was on a roll now, the hurt and confusion over the past few days gushing forth.

'I've been polite to you, I've tried to talk to you, and you were so incredibly mean, as if you couldn't care less that a woman you know – no – a woman you've known since you were young is dying! And now you have decided to talk to me – *typical*!' I raised my arms in the air and gave a little laugh. 'Typical. It's typical of men to do this, isn't it – they decide when and how, but we get no voice – no one listens to us!'

'Mia.' He placed his hand gently on my arm, stopping me mid-rant. I could feel heat creep up my neck and face, not with embarrassment but with anger and something else that I wasn't sure had a name. 'Are you... all right?'

'I–I...' At that point, the fervour with which I had delivered my speech left me and I was unsure of myself – unsure of what was happening. 'I'm just... just – *tired*,' I finally said and saw him nod slightly, as if he understood with just those few words everything that I was feeling.

I opened the door further, gesturing for him to come inside. 'If you want to talk, we can talk. I'm sorry for the outburst.'

'No need to apologise.' He waved his hand. 'No need at all. It is I who must do that.'

'You'd better come in then.'

He looked to the hallway, dimmed lights illuminating the inside of the apartment behind me, and shook his head.

'No. Please. If you will. Come downstairs to my home. I do not feel quite right coming inside Ilse's home. It is still hers, and I am not sure she would want me here.'

'I don't think she would mind,' I said.

'No. Please. Come downstairs. And if you will, can you please bring the postcards you found? All of them?'

'You'll tell me what they say? What this is all about?' I asked.

'Yes, I will. It's time. You need to know, so that you can make a decision.'

'What decision?'

'You will see. Just bring them. I will tell you the best way I can.'

He turned and carefully walked down the stairs. Not wanting him to change his mind, I hurried into my grandmother's room and retrieved the postcards, then slammed the apartment door shut behind me and took the stairs two at a time.

His front door was open, and I walked inside to find an apartment with stuffed bookshelves on every wall, Persian rugs covering the floors and low lighting that barely gave much comfort in the gloom.

It was warm, though, and I was glad of that as the wind wheezed outside, smattering rain against the windows.

The old man sat at a desk, the shadows of the evening obscuring half of his face. I itched to switch on more lights, to bring some cheer into this dusty room, but I let him sit. He turned as I entered and nodded at a blue armchair that had a red woollen blanket draped on its armrest.

I sat, then, noticing his outstretched hand, I gave him the postcards that were in my own.

He quietly flicked through them, and in the gloom, I could barely make out his expression as he read them.

'First, I must apologise to you, for being so rude,' he said, still not looking at me, his eyes trained on the postcards. 'It was wrong of me. But you see, when I saw you and you asked about Ilse, about Szymon, it made it all come back a little too clearly for my liking.'

'I don't understand...'

'Neither do I.' He glanced at me and gave me a wry smile before turning his attention once more to the postcards. 'And that is why I am telling you this – this story – of me, of Ilse and Szymon so that perhaps I can understand what really happened and maybe why I have become this sour old man you see before you.'

Then he stopped, letting an air of silence fill the room as he thought. Then, almost to himself, he spoke again.

'He was not allowed to write letters,' he murmured. 'Some of them could. I think the English could. At one point, the Polish could too, but he had been told he could not – I don't know why. I think they simply made up rules to suit them and to make it hard for any prisoner they perhaps did not like. It would have been good to have letters; but, we made do,' he sighed.

He turned to me, his eyes wide as if for just a second, he had forgotten I was even there.

'Do you want a drink? I can get you one. It might make things a bit easier,' he asked, and once more, I was sure he was talking to himself more than he was directing it at me. He stood before I could answer and went to a drinks trolley. 'Gin? Whisky? Or vodka?'

I wasn't a spirit drinker, but I didn't want to offend him or stop him talking. 'Vodka,' I said. 'Please.'

He poured straight vodka into two thick cut-crystal glasses. I waited for him to add tonic, or water, or anything to mix it with, but he didn't and brought the glass to me.

I took it from him, and he clinked his glass to mine, looked me in the eye and said, 'Zdrowiei – cheers.' He sipped at the vodka, then smacked his lips in satisfaction. 'Polish vodka is the best. No need to add anything to it.'

I sipped at mine and found that it was smoother than I was expecting. It did not have that bite that I usually experienced with vodka, and instead I found the warmth of the alcohol comforting.

He sat down with a sigh, then turned his attention back to the postcards, shuffling them about. 'I need to put them in order. That way I can explain it properly.'

There were only maybe six of them, so it did not take long.
Then he turned to me and leaned back in his chair.

'You know Szymon was my cousin, yes?'

I nodded. I told him about what Marlena had said, and that
I knew little else.

'Ah, so. You don't know about Ilse coming back – about
when I saw her again?'

'No. She didn't say anything about that.'

'Ha!' he laughed.

'What's so funny?'

'Nothing.' He shook his head. 'It's just Marlena. She tells
me what to do when she won't do it herself. Typical...'

Not following him once again, I took another sip of the
vodka.

'Let me think for a moment – let me think.' He closed his
eyes, then opened them. 'I will tell you about me, about those
years. About what happened to Szymon. You won't find out
much from these postcards – there is not much hidden in there.
But I know what it was like for him, he told me afterwards. I
knew what his days were like, how he felt. So when I tell you,
you have to understand that I am mixing it all together – the
postcards, me, Ilse, my cousin – it is not all coming from this one
place – these postcards.'

'I understand,' I said.

'You must understand the *whole*, Mia, to really understand
what I am saying. I will tell you about the early days, about
what happened. But you must look at books, at history – then
you can see my story properly. You must try and see the whole
and not just what I am saying, to truly understand what it was
like for us all. I have books I can give you, texts that you can
read and bit by bit – maybe, just maybe you will understand.'

His voice was so eager, so demanding that I promised I
would. I promised that I would listen to his tale, as fragmented

as it was and that I would try and see it as he seemed to need me to.

'Good. And then at the end you can make your own judgement of it all. And then you can make your own decision of what to do.'

I wanted to ask him what this decision was, but I could see that he needed to tell me his story first and I had to be patient.

'So, I'll begin.' He closed his eyes and clasped his hands on his chest.

And then he told me his tale.

TWENTY-TWO

TADEUSZ

Görlitz
May 1942

Tadeusz sat in his uncle's apartment above the bookshop, trying to focus on the book in his lap. It was in Polish – one of only ten books that his uncle had managed to hide before having to only sell books in German and those approved by the Reich.

But he could not concentrate, he could not focus. His mind constantly went back to that day that he had left Szymon to his fate. And what fate that was, he did not know. It had been three years and he had not heard from his cousin – did not know whether he was alive or dead. His uncle had told him to pray for the best but to prepare for the worst. The only problem with that was that Tadeusz was not sure that he believed in God any more, and was sure that praying was not going to change anything.

He closed the book and looked outside the window that was smeared with grime. Through it, he could make out the shadows of cars and vans, people walking about, children even, holding hands with their parents, skipping and chattering.

Outside a whole world was alive, and here he was stuck inside, too scared to take one step into the fray.

His uncle had said that no one would be looking for him – that so much had happened that they would not be searching any more for one soldier who had escaped. But Tadeusz wasn't so certain. He had heard of random roundups, of Polish men and boys disappearing, taken into the German army against their will.

Every day the world was a strange place, for him, and for so many others. There were rules that changed on a whim, and he was scared to be a part of this world – scared that he would be stopped and asked for his *Kennkarte*, and that some soldier, guard, Gestapo would investigate him and find out who he was.

That day he had left Szymon, he had managed to find his way to a farmhouse where he had begged for help. The couple, whilst afraid, had taken him in, hiding him in their cellar, the wife treating the two neat bullet wounds on his leg and his shoulder.

'You are lucky,' she had told him as she cleaned them. 'Clear through. Your wounds will heal nicely.'

Tadeusz couldn't remember much of those first few days at the farm. He was in and out of consciousness, a delirium brought on by the pain and soon a small infection. It was only perhaps a week later that he was cognisant enough to understand the full repercussions of what he had done and that there was no going back.

Bidding his thanks and farewell to the couple at the farmhouse, and with clothes on his back that belonged to the farmer and were much too big for his frame, he made his way carefully home, walking for days at a time, hiding in wooded areas and relying on the kindness of strangers to give him food and water.

As he walked, all around him were the ruins of war. Huge craters caused by falling bombs littered fields, and those that had found a target had caused houses to crumble, broken pieces of furniture visible in the rubble, and in some cases an arm or leg that belonged to the house's past inhabitants, stark white in contrast with all the grey.

He would avert his eyes when he saw the bodies. He would pretend that they didn't exist, as he was so fearful that on arriving home, he would find his own parents crushed and battered underneath the wreckage of their house.

After more than a week, with red and oozing blisters on his feet, and wounds that still caused him pain from the constant movement, he reached Görlitz. But this was not the Görlitz he had left. The town was teeming with soldiers, flags flying from shops and houses and everyone, it seemed, walked differently, their heads down, their eyes concentrating on the ground.

As he stood and watched the day unfold all around him, he suddenly felt nauseous at the thought of going home – of seeing his parents who would ask where Szymon was. What would he say? Could he lie, and tell them that he had been taken? No, his mother would know – she would see immediately that he was trying to keep something from them and would soon wheedle it out of him.

He needed to see his uncle at the bookshop – that was who he would be able to tell the truth to – a man who would not judge him, but who would sit quietly whilst he explained that he had left his cousin behind and would offer words of comfort, of advice. Yes, his uncle was the only one who would understand and the only one who would know what to do.

As he drew close to the bridge that would take him to the other side of Görlitz, he saw soldiers and a few workmen erecting a checkpoint. They had not yet completed their work, the barriers still lay on the ground, the guards who were to stay stationed at each end sitting idly under a willow tree, smoking and talking.

The tiny hairs on the back of his neck stood up to attention on seeing the soldiers. He could not simply walk past them, could he?

He waited a few minutes in the doorway of an apartment block, trying to talk some sense into himself – it would be fine, they would not look at him, would not stop him. And yet, his feet would not move, cemented to the spot whilst his heart beat faster and sweat began to gather under his armpits.

Just then, he saw a family – the two children holding their mother's hands, the father striding a few steps in front, puffing on a cigarette. The children could not take their eyes from the soldiers and their shining guns, and the mother kept stopping to bend down, reassuring them that all was well.

He heard her speak – the family was German. Quickly, he left the sanctuary of the doorway and stepped neatly out in front of them, bidding the man with a cigarette a good day. The man narrowed his eyes at Tadeusz, as if trying to place how he knew him, but clearly not wanting to appear rude, he gave a smile and said hello.

That was all Tadeusz needed. He walked side by side with the man, the woman and children scurrying behind, their pace audibly picking up as they got onto the bridge.

'Can you tell me the way to the Trinity Church?' Tadeusz enquired as they walked, keeping the man in conversation with him. 'I've just come from Berlin to visit some family and I am afraid I have become quite lost!'

'Indeed, indeed.' The man removed his cigarette from his mouth and with a deft hand flicked it into the water below them. 'When you reach the other side, you go straight, then left and take the next right. You'll see it soon enough. If I were you, though, I'd keep to this side of the river now. Over there' – the man waved vaguely in the direction they had come from – 'it's not safe. More and more troops arriving each day. Stay on this side from now on. Too many Poles over there – always were. If you ask me, they should have got rid of them long ago. Stay here, on this side,' he said, as they reached the other bank. 'Our Führer will keep us safe here on German soil.'

There was a part of Tadeusz that wanted to tell the man that as far as he knew, where he had lived on the other side of the river was German, and that Poles and Germans had lived as neighbours. He wanted to tell the man that more troops arriving was not a good thing – not for Tadeusz and his family and friends – but he said nothing. Instead, he gritted his teeth and waved at the man as they made their way home.

As soon as he was out of sight of the river, and the bridge that held too many Germans, he half ran to his uncle's book-shop, almost weeping with relief as he opened the door, hearing the gentle tinkle of the bell to welcome him home.

His uncle looked up from a book he was reading at the cash register, the shop empty of customers. For a second, neither of them spoke. Then his uncle gave a wide grin, greeted him with his arms outstretched and took him into an embrace.

'My dear boy! My *dearest* of boys! How are you, my nephew?' His uncle wept into his shoulder as they held one another. He then kissed him on both cheeks, holding his face in his old hands.

'I am well,' Tadeusz replied, placing his own hands on his uncle's, seeing that the old man's eyes were still watery with tears. 'Or should I say, I am alive, at least.'

'You are! *You are!*' his uncle exclaimed, then took him into an embrace once more.

Tadeusz had spoken at length with his uncle about what had happened with Szymon, and how he had been afraid to return home.

'I think it wise that you do not go home for a while,' his uncle told him, handing him a hot mug of coffee and thick slices of bread and ham.

Tadeusz had torn into the meat, realising how desperately hungry he was.

'I'd say you could stay with me in my apartment, but I don't think that would be safe either,' his uncle mused. 'They could come looking for you – at your parents, at my house.'

'So where will I go?' Tadeusz mumbled through the mouthful of food that he was still chewing.

'You will stay upstairs!' his uncle cried, snapping his fingers as though the idea had suddenly come to him. 'Yes. You stay upstairs in the small rooms there. There is not much – just a bed and a desk – a space I know you know I use from time to time when I have perhaps worked late and drunk too much.' His uncle grinned. 'But there is the bookcase up there, the one that blocks the closet door. I think I could make that into somewhere you could hide if anyone comes to the shop. All I would need is some hinges and some clever ways of disguising the ruse. What do you think?'

What did he think? He was glad to have an ally in his uncle – a man who had told him what to do, a man who had literally calmed his fears within minutes, albeit not his guilt over Szymon.

'That will simply take time,' his uncle had reminded him over and over again on the days that followed. 'You did what you could. You had to get away. And one day, you will see that it was the only sane and rational thing to do at the time and I am sure that Szymon, wherever he is, forgives you.'

Tadeusz had listened to his uncle's reassurances, and on some level had agreed with them. He was just not certain that he could ever forgive himself.

Three years later and he was still in this room, still hiding, even though his uncle was sure no one would be looking for him any more.

But what was the point in leaving anyway? It was not as though he could go and see his parents or friends on the other side of the river; it was not as though they were still there, waiting for him. Because he had lost them too. He had lost Szymon and now he had lost his family – his mother and father had both been taken away for hiding a Jewish family in their cellar, just the year before. Despite his uncle's frantic searching, no one knew where they had gone, nor what was to become of them. Upon hearing the news of his parents, Tadeusz had not reacted, surprising his uncle who had expected either anger or grief. But he had said nothing, he had felt nothing. Instead, he had decided that it had not happened. He would look out of the window each day, his eyes automatically searching for the river, seeing church spires graze the sky on the other bank, and pretend that his parents were there, going about their days, waiting for him to come home. And one day, when the war was over, he would simply walk over the bridge and open the front door and they would be there.

This fanciful notion was the only thing that was keeping him from losing his mind in that tiny room. He could not bear to think that Szymon was dead, and he could not bear to think what frightening scenes his parents had witnessed, or were witnessing. No. It was better to pretend that they were alive and waiting and that Szymon was alive too – and that he had forgiven him.

The only person he saw besides his uncle was Marlena. She had seen him, briefly and by accident, as he had run up the steps to the small apartment one afternoon, after popping down to retrieve a book.

After his uncle had assured him that Marlena could be trusted, he had allowed her to visit him, the pair of them sitting upstairs, trying to talk of anything but the war, trying to talk about anything other than the people that had simply disappeared from their lives.

He had come to look forward to her visits, even wishing that they could have been more frequent. He felt almost special that she had chosen him, and only him to tell her deepest secret to. When she had told him, she had cried, perhaps expecting him to tell her to leave, to never come back – that she was not normal. But what Marlena didn't realise was that he had always known that she liked women, and not men. And, though he didn't dare say it, he and Szymon had always known that Marlena was deeply in love with Ilse. Had Ilse known, he pondered now? Had she known that her best friend was in love with her, just as Szymon had been?

At the thought of her, he suddenly became uncomfortable and irritable as he knew that he should be asking himself a question: had he, Tadeusz, been in love with her too?

Eventually, he turned from the window, his memories like the people outside, distorted and shadowy through the lens of grime on the pane of glass. He wanted to leave his memories there – outside the window, with all the complicated feelings that came from them.

He sat once more and fidgeted in his seat, hearing the gentle tinkle of the bell from the shop downstairs – an unusual sound these days as fewer and fewer customers found the need for books, even if they were those that had been approved by the government.

He heard a laugh – his uncle's – then the low grumble as he spoke. Then the click of the lock, the jangle of keys and then footsteps that clomped to the rear. But not just one set of footsteps: at least two – no, maybe three.

Tadeusz leaped out of his chair and checked the time – 2 p.m. Why had his uncle closed the shop? Who was downstairs? Would they come up?

Before he could even take a step to the false bookcase to hide himself in the safe alcove it provided, the lower door opened with a creak and his uncle's voice rose up to him.

'Tadeusz. Come downstairs. You have visitors.'

His uncle's voice was calm, happy even – there was no danger. It was then that Tadeusz saw in his mind's eye his missing cousin, Szymon. He had returned!

Racing down the stairs two at a time, he almost fell into the ground floor bookshop and looked about him, searching for Szymon's face, finding instead a woman whom he wasn't sure he knew.

'Tadeusz,' she said. She was tall and slim, with a wide smile that reached her brown eyes.

He shook his head.

'It's me,' she said. 'Ilse. Do I look so different?'

It was then that Tadeusz saw Marlena, whose smile at having Ilse back lit up her face and made her seem like the young girl he had met that summer all those years ago.

'You look pale,' Marlena said by way of greeting.

'I thought—' he started, then stopped himself.

'You thought what?' Ilse asked.

'Nothing. It doesn't matter.' Although disappointed that Szymon had not returned, he was caught in a strange trance. Just minutes ago, he had been thinking about Ilse – thinking of love and then, just like that, just like his memories, she had come in from the world outside as if she had been waiting there the whole time.

'I thought you would be *happy!*' His uncle slung an arm around his shoulder and pulled him close. 'I thought seeing your friends again would cheer you up.'

He looked to Marlena, and then back to Ilse, whose eyes were scouring the bookshelves. *Was he happy? Was he disappointed? What was he?*

Feeling that acute irritation bite at him once more, he told them both what he thought he should say, what was right and responsible for him to say: 'You shouldn't be here.'

'Why?' Ilse plopped down on the high-backed purple chair.

'Mr Gliński is glad to see us. Why aren't you? Marlena said she had visited you before, so why can she be here and me not?'

'It's not safe. Not for you and not for me,' Tadeusz told her, hoping that she would see that he was grown up now – not a boy who joked and larked about at the river. He was a man. And he wouldn't put anyone else in danger.

Ilse, seemingly uninterested or stubbornly not compre-hending what Tadeusz was trying to say, pulled something from her handbag. 'We only came to give you this,' she huffed at him. 'I hardly think the police are going to come and bash down the door because of it.'

He stared at her for a moment, seeing the young, impulsive girl he had once known. The same girl that had broken Szymon's heart after he had fallen in love with her, then disap-peared to Berlin.

He took the piece of card she still held outstretched, then briefly looked at it, ready to hand it back, until a name – *his* name – jumped out at him.

He read the postcard. Once, twice, three times, and could feel his heartbeat quicken. Szymon – *he was alive*! Relief flooded through him, and he could feel tears pricking at his eyes. All these years and he was *alive*.

'What is it?' His uncle leaned over his shoulder to read the postcard, then gasped. 'He's here?'

'You didn't know?' Marlena piped up.

'We had no idea, my dear,' his uncle began. 'We haven't heard from him at all. But now we know. We know, Tadeusz, that he is alive and close by. And see here – he remembered.' His uncle pointed at the request for a book and at the title that Szymon had said he was reading. 'I'll find a copy!'

'Wait, what's happening? What did he remember? What do you need to find?' Ilse was beside him now, her breath warm on his cheek. 'What does it mean?'

He turned to her. 'It means he remembered. A code. He can

write us and tell us more than what is written here. It means that I can help him.'

'Help him with what?' she asked.

Tadeusz felt so giddy, so suddenly light that he impulsively kissed Ilse on the cheek, then Marlena too.

'Thank you for bringing this – thank you!'

He could see the shock in the women's faces. Embarrassed, he coughed, took a step away from them and looked at the post-card again. Injecting some calm into his voice, trying to sound like the man he was now and not the boy that he used to be, he told them.

'I know how to help him escape.'

TWENTY-THREE

ILSE

Görlitz
May 1942

Escape.

Escape – the word sent a shiver of excitement down Ilse's spine. Tadeusz was going to help Szymon *escape*? Whether it was because she had spent years in Berlin, bored and restless, or whether it was that sense of impulsivity – of the feeling of excitement she got at just the whiff of an adventure – she could not sit still as Tadeusz explained.

Tadeusz sat opposite her, Marlena perched on the edge of the armchair and for a second, she felt happy – almost as if she had gone back in time to a moment in that summer when they would congregate here to listen to stories and discuss ideas. The outside world did not matter to Ilse in that moment. Nothing mattered as the excitement of some form of adventure was beginning to make itself known.

Mr Gliński hurried about, drawing books from shelves and condemning them to the dusty floor, swearing and lamenting that he may well have disposed of the book in question.

'I'll find it, I will!' he exclaimed, his long white hair as angry and frustrated as he, standing tall and wild.

'We played a game once,' Tadeusz began over the clamour of his uncle. 'After you left for Berlin. Szymon was...' He paused and looked directly at her as he said, 'not himself for a while once you left.'

Ilse squirmed in her seat and felt heat rush across her cheeks. She wasn't so stupid that she did not know what Tadeusz was implying, but she was damned if she was going to defend herself, or give him the satisfaction of a reaction. So, she smiled sweetly at him, as if the comment had not even registered with her.

She watched as he regarded her for a moment, then he turned to Marlena, drawing her into his explanation too.

'Anyway. To try and entertain him, my uncle gave him a book and said we could create our own ciphers so that we could leave small notes with more information hidden within.'

She remembered the book that had brought forth this idea – a Sherlock Holmes story called *The Valley of Fear* that had used a cipher, by utilising a book, in order to say more than what was originally written in the message.

'At the time it was simply a game,' Tadeusz continued. 'Something to while away the time and to get Szymon out of himself. We didn't realise until the war began how useful it could prove. When we were in the army, we taught others how to use the code too – again, just as a game – just something to do whenever we had a moment, and we didn't want our minds to wander too much. But then, one evening, three of our men had been captured and taken away. I said then to Szymon that if either of us were ever captured, if we were taken away but needed to get a note out to the other – if there was any reason we couldn't write what we wanted to – then we should use our game. Neither of us thought we would need to – neither of us thought that if we were captured, we would even survive...'

Tadeusz shook his head gently, then gave a weak smile. 'But we did. He did. He's *alive*.'

Ilse wanted to say that she was sorry for hurting Szymon. She wanted to say that she had grown up now and she wasn't the same young, foolish girl that she once was. But at the same time, there was a glimmer of excitement building and building inside of her. Ciphers, codes, Szymon in a camp and working in one of her father's factories. Her mind filled with the stories she had read over the years – the escapades of protagonists as they trekked the globe, or of fictional detectives as they solved a case. She could finally be like one of those characters – one of the heroes of the story.

'I'll help,' Ilse said, as much to herself as anyone else in the room. 'Let me help you.' She turned to Tadeusz. 'I can get the replies to him and get his replies to you.'

Tadeusz laughed. '*You?*'

'And what's wrong with me?' she demanded.

'It's not some *game*, Ilse. You look all excited like you used to. This is dangerous.' He shook his head at her, then repeated, 'It's not a game.'

Annoyed that he had seemingly read her mind, she drew herself up importantly. 'I'm quite aware it's not a game, Tadeusz. I think you'll find that I'm quite aware of what is happening around us.'

'Are you?' he interjected. 'Because if memory serves me right, you are German. And your family. And you are a fairly well-respected *German* family,' he emphasised.

'So, what are you saying? That I'm the enemy?' She stood, her hands automatically bunching themselves into fists.

'I'm just saying what's true. How can you, a German woman, with your family, have any idea what is happening, have any idea the suffering you are causing!' he yelled at her.

She took a step nearer to him, ready to tell him that she didn't agree with what was happening, that she had seen families taken. But as she rehearsed the words, they felt limp and useless.

It was Marlena who saved them from a fight.

'Stop! Both of you!' She stood between them. 'We were all friends, once. And I have still been your friend all these years. Just because you haven't seen Ilse, doesn't mean that she does not care. You know Ilse. You know who she is deep down. You can trust us.'

'Can I?' he asked. But his voice had changed, and Ilse knew that he was wavering.

'You can and you know it. Otherwise, why would you tell us about the code you used? Why would you even talk to us?' she countered.

Suddenly, Ilse saw his face as she had once known him – the old Tadeusz who always looked at her in such a way that she had often wondered if he had felt something more than friendship for her. She let the silent look last as long as she could between them, hoping that by doing so, he would see that she could be trusted, that she did care.

'Here! I found a copy! I just hope it is the same one. Same publication. But then, I can't see how it could be different,' Mr Gliński appeared from a cluster of books that were heaped on the floor. He smiled at her and then taking in the strange air in the room, raised his eyebrows in question.

'These two are deciding whether they are enemies or friends,' Marlena informed him with a sigh.

'Friends!' Mr Gliński cried. 'Oh, my dears. There is so much hate, so many enemies now. Neighbours have turned on neighbours, even families have been torn apart. Why do you think I stayed here? Why do you think I let those rogues come in here and take away my books, and replace them with what the Führer deemed appropriate?'

Ilse shrugged and was glad to see that both Marlena and Tadeusz were as contrite as she.

'Because… because…' Mr Gliński sighed. 'I wanted to stay. I wanted to try and bring joy, bring some harmony in learning, in books. I still sell books that are not permitted, but I do it anyway. That way, in some small way I am bringing people together. Even though I am persecuted. Even though I have to pay bribes to keep my shop from being taken from me. I will do it. And more. Ilse, you are German. Marlena, you are mostly. Me, I am Polish. Tadeusz too. But not so long ago, here, we were all as one. It didn't matter that Poles and Germans lived side by side. This was a town where we were all together – in it together. We cannot let that go just because of one mad man.'

'But Uncle,' Tadeusz said quietly, carefully. 'You know the danger in this. You know that Ilse could easily tell her father and mother. And if she did, we'd be arrested and possibly… worse. I mean, she wouldn't even have to intentionally do it – what if it slipped out – she and Marlena are putting themselves in danger.'

Mr Gliński approached them, then threw one arm over Ilse, and the other over Tadeusz. 'We won't let that happen, will we, Ilse?'

'No,' she said defiantly, not taking her eyes from Tadeusz. 'I won't say a thing. Neither will Marlena. You can trust us. I'm not like my parents and I barely speak to them anyway. Please, Tadeusz, you *know* me.'

'See! Remember your friendship. That lovely summer, when all four of you would fall in here laughing about something. How you would sit around and read books, discussing ideas. How you would all sit by the riverbank and talk. Remember those days, Tadeusz. Trust those days. Trust who you know Ilse was, and that she has not changed. I am sure not everyone has changed. Not everyone.'

Ilse could see that Tadeusz was not convinced, yet he did not argue with his uncle but gently shook his head in defeat like her father did when her mother got her way.

'Can we see what Szymon has written?' Marlena asked in a small voice, taking them all away from the argument at hand to the postcard and the code that was hidden in the book that Mr Gliński had found.

'Yes! Let's, my dears. Let's see how we can help him.'

Ilse sat back down as Mr Gliński flicked through the pages, muttering to himself and then consulting Tadeusz, who read out numbers, scrunching up his eyes as he tried to remember them.

After a few minutes, Mr Gliński raised his head and grinned. 'We have it! It's a small message. But it is here. It reads:

I am home. I work in a factory and am thin, but alive.

Tell Mother and Father that I am alive.

Guards are brutes.

There is no way out.

Mr Gliński stopped.

'Is that it?' Ilse cried in frustration.

'What were you expecting?' Tadeusz quipped. 'A long letter? A poem?'

'Don't be so childish,' Mr Gliński reprimanded. 'It is short because there isn't enough room to say much more,' he explained gently. 'But it is a start. It means we can send our own message back, and a copy of the Bible that he has requested. Then we can learn more from his reply.'

'But what would it matter, what he said?' Ilse asked, then felt a nudge in her ribs from Marlena. 'I mean. Why not just say it – why use a code? What's the point?' She felt the excitement drain away. What was she expecting from the code? What did she think he would say, she wondered?

'They censor everything,' Tadeusz told her. 'Even saying that the guards are brutes would have meant a thick black line throughout.'

'Do you think there is something we can do?' she asked. 'If we offer help and he can reply and tell us what we can do?'

'That's exactly what we shall do, my dear! *Exactly* that!'

Mr Gliński slowly stood and walked to his office, waving the book and the postcard in his hand. 'I shall get to work on it at once!'

'I'll get it to him.' Ilse eyed Tadeusz. 'I'll send it to him, with stamps so that he can reply. And anything else he needs. I'll do it.'

Tadeusz opened his mouth, but then Mr Gliński's voice called out: 'Thank you, my dear! Give me a few minutes and I will have you a reply.'

As they waited for Mr Gliński to write out the reply, Ilse asked Tadeusz about what had happened, to which he replied in gruff short sentences. She had then tried to make him laugh with a joke she had heard from a girl back in Berlin, but this had received no smile in return.

At times, though, he looked at her the way he used to, or smiled at something Marlena said with the same smile. It was as though he were the young Tadeusz and the older Tadeusz now all rolled into one – each competing with the other. Unfortunately, as the minutes ticked by, this new Tadeusz, a little sullen and serious, reminding her of Szymon, won and soon the three friends had little to talk about.

Ilse was relieved when Mr Gliński proffered the reply, sending them on their way.

'He's changed,' she said to Marlena, as the two of them walked back home.

'He's a little different – but we all are,' Marlena replied. 'After everything he's been through, how can he not be different?'

'He looks much the same, though,' Ilse added. 'The same... but different.'

She felt Marlena nudge her ribs. 'I seem to remember that you found him handsome once?' Marlena giggled and Ilse suddenly felt as though she were fifteen again.

'I thought Szymon was.'

'And what's the difference – they look almost identical. And I'm pretty sure that you once said that he was handsome – in fact, I'm *sure* of it.'

'Your memory is incorrect.' Ilse nudged her friends back. 'Maybe it's you that finds him attractive?'

Marlena laughed. 'Hardly, you know who I find attractive,' she began, then suddenly stopped.

Ilse looked to Marlena who had suddenly gone pale. 'Who?' Ilse asked.

'Nothing. No one. I misspoke,' she said, refusing to look at Ilse.

They walked on in an awkward silence for a few more steps, before thankfully, Marlena broke it. 'Are you sure we should do this, Ilse?' Marlena asked. 'It *is* dangerous. What if we are found out? What if your mother finds out?'

Ilse kicked at a random stone on the pavement and sent it skittering down the street. A man who was passing eyed her, confused that a grown woman was obviously acting like a child. Ilse laughed in response.

'I don't care that it's dangerous, Marlena.' She suddenly stopped walking, took hold of Marlena's arm and made her look at her. 'I don't want to be like the others. I don't want to do nothing, say nothing. I saw things in Berlin, and I didn't do anything. I stood there and did nothing. All of us are doing the same. I can't be like them, I can't. It's not just happening to people I have never met, it's happening to people I know – people I care about – that we know. I can do something, I know I can.'

Marlena cocked her head to the side as Ilse spoke, then

righting herself, said, 'There's a part of me that thinks you believe that, Ilse. But there is a part of me that thinks you like the idea of adventure, excitement even, despite the danger, despite how it could all turn out.'

Ilse wanted to argue with Marlena, but she knew it would be pointless. Her friend knew her still – after all these years apart, she still knew her inside and out.

'I promise I'll be careful. I promise I will be serious.' She kissed Marlena on her cheek.

Marlena let out a heavy sigh. 'I'm not sure you've ever been serious, Ilse. It's a blessing and a curse.'

Ilse knew that Marlena had been appeased and that she had won. As they walked, now arm in arm, Ilse felt a nudge of guilt, and perhaps worry, that she wasn't really taking this as seriously as she should, and that the promise of adventure was driving her far more than wanting to help Szymon. She tried to push the complicated thoughts to the back of her mind and engaged Marlena in conversations about the changes in the town, who owned what, and whether Marlena had any gossip. There was nothing to worry about. She was doing this for good, not for her own entertainment, she told herself, over and over again.

And by the time she reached home, she almost believed herself.

That evening Ilse sat in bed, the postcard that Mr Gliński wrote on the bedside table beside her, along with stamps and some blank postcards that Szymon could use to reply. Ilse had added some paper and envelopes, but Mr Gliński had said that letters may not get through as easily as a postcard that could be quickly read and censored, if needed.

She felt too much that evening. Angry at herself and frustrated that she was as uninformed as Tadeusz and even Marlena had suggested. And yet, excited that she had something to do – something that would give her some purpose in her life.

Lying down, she pulled the sheet up to her chin, then flopped her arms down straight on top and stared at the ceiling.

How many days in Berlin had she done this? How many days had she stayed in bed because she saw no point in getting out of it?

She didn't want to be like her mother. She didn't want to live the life of a wife and mother herself. She did not want to go to dances nor buy dresses. But, the thing was, she didn't know what she wanted. She never had, not really.

Her mind wandered over to the summer she had spent with Szymon. That summer she had decided her purpose was boys. And it had given her some excitement – that was true. But soon, that had waned and hadn't raised its head again when she moved to Berlin.

Now though, now, she had another purpose. She didn't need to be like anyone but herself. And herself was someone who, as naive as it sounded, didn't feel fear, didn't see danger; instead, she saw fun, excitement – *life*.

What's more, she decided as she turned onto her side, she was helping people. She was helping her friends. And she knew that if her mother found out what she was doing, she would be aghast at her behaviour, and that made Ilse happy too.

All in all, she couldn't see how what she was doing had any downside and she was sure that it would lead to bigger and greater things.

In fact, she remembered an afternoon with Tadeusz when he had told her this very thing: '*You are destined for great things, Ilse. Don't stop.*'

When had this been? Where were Szymon and Marlena? They hadn't all been together, and she wasn't sure why; but she had been at the river, this she knew.

Her mother had scolded her that morning at breakfast for not behaving properly.

'You're a young woman now,' her mother had said. 'You need to act like one. You come home each day after doing God knows what, covered in dust, your stockings ripped, mud on your dress! You're not a child any more!'

She had responded in her usual way, and irked her mother more by stuffing cheese and bread into her mouth so that her cheeks bulged and made her look like a hungry rabbit.

Delighting in the crease that developed in her mother's forehead from her antics, she had taken herself to the river to wait for the others. But why had Tadeusz only appeared? Surely the others came too, but her memory was slippery and she couldn't grasp at it properly.

But Tadeusz had appeared, she was sure of that, and they had sat side by side, dipping their feet in the water and watching a slow boat chug its way upstream.

'What will you do now you have finished at school?' she had asked him, her eyes on the boat, wondering who was aboard and where they were going.

'I don't know,' he had answered. 'Father wants me to go to university. Mother wants me to stay close by.'

'I'd go to university,' she had said wistfully. 'Or I'd go and be an explorer. Go to each and every country and find something new and never come back here.'

'An explorer?' he had laughed. 'You?'

'And why couldn't I be an explorer?' She had turned her gaze to him. 'Wait, don't say it. It's because I'm a girl, yes? Girls can't be explorers. We have to get married and have children.'

'I didn't say that. You can do whatever you like. I just meant that you didn't seem the adventurous type.' He had raised his palms in surrender.

'I am adventurous. It's just that there's not much adventure around here.'

'I like it, though. It's home, you know?'

She shook her head. It was her parents' home. Not hers. 'It's pointless, though.' She had looked back upstream to see how far the boat had chugged away from them. 'I'll have to get married and have babies and that will be that.'

'Says who?' he'd demanded.

'My parents. My mother would *die* if I did everything I wanted to do!' She'd laughed and was happy to hear Tadeusz join in.

'So, what is it that you want to do?' He seemed to have been closer to her and had nudged her gently on her arm with his own.

'That's the thing. I don't even know. I just feel...' she had paused. '*Frustrated.*'

'I understand that.'

'You do?' She had nudged him back with her arm.

'I do. But it's not because I don't know what I want. It's because I know what I do want. I just can't have it.'

'You should get whatever you want. Don't let anyone stop you. Tell me, what is it you want?'

'It's complicated,' he'd replied.

'Nothing is that complicated. You just have to sometimes be a bit selfish to be happy. That's what I think anyway. If I want to be happy some day, I'll have to do what I *want* and not care what anyone else thinks.'

'I think you're destined for great things, Ilse.'

'You do?' She had looked at him and saw that he was staring at her, a strange look on his face that she could not properly place.

'I do. Don't stop. Always be you.'

'I will, but only if you promise that you will get what you want too?'

He'd smiled sadly at her. 'I'll try.'

TWENTY-FOUR

ILSE

Görlitz City Hospital
Wednesday, 10 February 1999

'You're a force of nature,' the doctor said to me this afternoon.

He thinks I should be dead by now, but I'm not. And I'm lucid – well, most of the time anyway. I told him I was like that when I was younger – a force of nature – someone who thought she was destined for great things – and he laughed. But I told him it wasn't funny. There was nothing funny or brave about it. What I was, was a silly young woman, who knew very little, who was selfish and childish and thought danger was a form of excitement, a young woman who would risk not only her life, but those around her for some snippet of joy, or conversely, take joy in the fact that her behaviour would upset her mother.

God, how I hated that woman. I hated her so much that I did what I did because I was so desperate to be her complete opposite. I am sure of that now; if I saw one of those mind doctors – what are they called – I've lost the name of them – the ones that tell you why you do what you do – well, those doctors, they'd say that I had some form of complex. And I tell you now, they'd be right.

When I think of myself in those years, I cringe. I want to go back in time and rip that part of my life from my story. I was a narcissist. That's true too. I cared only for myself and what impact my choices would have on my life. Did I think enough in those days of how my decisions would impact Tadeusz and Szymon, Marlena even? No. I didn't. I wanted excitement and danger and adventure and life like you read about in books. But the thing is, I wasn't a fictional character, I wasn't a detective in Victorian England, finding out who had committed the latest murder. I was in a time and place, in a war that I had not understood the danger of. I was in a life where I had, like so many of us, shielded myself from the reality that stood outside our front doors, pretending that it was fine, it was normal even. And in that, I had romanticised it.

You see why I cringe now? Why I hate myself?

After the war ended, I went to the cinema in England. A neighbour took me, thinking at the time I was a refugee and not the well-connected German woman I was. The film showed reels, in black and white, of soldiers going to concentration camps and releasing the prisoners held within. The people were skeletons – skin stretched so tightly over their bones that I was shocked that they were still alive. They showed the piles and piles of bodies, all grotesquely woven together in a sort of death embrace. They showed smiling guards who offered cigarettes to the British troops, whilst behind them death littered the ground.

After watching the film, I remember going home and then running to the outside toilet to vomit. I threw up until my stomach was raw, and only bile and spit came out of my mouth. I had sat, my back against the brick wall and in that moment, I saw how stupid, how utterly childish I had been. This had been happening all around me. I had watched a family in Berlin loaded onto a bus, taken away, and now I knew what had become of them – or worse.

Years after the war ended, more and more information came out – the gas chambers, the shootings, the massacres. Every time I learned something new, I disappeared further inside myself – not wanting the old Ilse to ever come back. That Ilse knew *nothing*. That Ilse was *foolish*. There was no more adventure, no more joy for me.

That Ilse was dead.

TWENTY-FIVE

SZYMON

Stalag VIII-A, Görlitz-Moys
May 1942

Szymon was exhausted. His body ached constantly, and his skin was covered in a new rash that no matter how much he tried not to, he could not stop scratching.

'You got a new work detail today?' Stanislaw asked.

Szymon stopped looking at the bloody mess that his arm had turned into, and looked at his fellow campmate. 'Digging foundations for a new factory,' he deadpanned. 'Exciting.'

Stanislaw let out a bark. 'Better than me! I was stuck on the railway lines again. Do you know how heavy it is to carry those rails and then put them down, one after another after another?'

Szymon shook his head. No, he did not know how heavy they were, and he hoped not to find out. Despite all the manual labour over the past few years, he had gained no more strength; instead, he had grown weaker, his skin stretched over his painful muscles. He wished, and not for the first time, that one day his work detail might change and he would be allowed to go and work on one of the farms. Two Frenchmen, new arrivals had recently been given this honour, and when they returned to the camp each night, they bragged of the fresh milk, the eggs and the meat that the farm owners fed them.

Barrack 31 held thirty Poles. It was unheated, damp, and part of the roof was caving in, letting in a little slice of the night sky. Szymon had heard that some of the French barracks had heating: he was sure it was a lie, but as Stanislaw often reminded him, the Germans hated the Poles as much as the Jews, so he wouldn't be surprised if other nationalities got better rooms, food and work detail.

'Wait until they bring some British prisoners here,' Stanislaw would remind him. 'You'll see a difference. They'll have it so much better. I even hear that they're allowed food parcels – imagine that! That is, of course, if we survive long enough to see any more people arrive.'

Szymon was not sure where Stanislaw got his information from, but he was sure he was right. He had been in three POW camps before arriving here three months ago, glad, he said to come here and be closer to home.

Indeed, Szymon was close to home. Too close, tantalisingly so. He could almost taste his mother's cooking – the thick meaty stews that she made with fluffy dumplings, the freshly baked bread, the *placki ziemniaczane*, potato pancakes that she would serve with thick slices of roasted pork belly. He sometimes felt that it had been a cruel joke, being brought to a camp that was literally only a few miles away from everything he had ever known.

'You're thinking about food again, aren't you?' Stanislaw sat next to him and offered him a cigarette which he did not take.

He looked to his friend for a moment, watching as he lit the cigarette, his face folding with thick lines on skin that had been almost turned to leather from the amount of time he had spent working outdoors. He wondered what Stanislaw had once looked like before coming here – he was thirty-five, or so he said, but the creases in his face, and the sprouting of grey and white hairs in his black eyebrows and hair told a story of the hardship he had endured these past few years. Szymon knew that he, too, had changed. He had caught his reflection a few times and instead of seeing a young man, he saw a tired, thin, old face staring back at him. The first time he had seen his own face, it had scared him so much that he had simply avoided looking at his reflection again – ignoring it when a flash of an old man looked back at him.

Stanislaw's thick eyebrows hung heavily over his dark brown eyes as he dragged deeply on the cigarette, blowing out a plume of smoke so thick that for a second Szymon could not see in front of him.

'Here's how I see it,' Stanislaw waggled a finger as he spoke, making his point to an imaginary audience. 'I think that it's good you're near home. I mean, think about it. You know the area, you know where to hide when you escape.'

'If I escape,' Szymon interjected.

'*When* – *if* – either way. The point is, you need to stop turning it over in your head. Did you write to that cousin of yours again?'

Szymon nodded. He had written to Tadeusz at his parents' house, then his own parents, then to another cousin, but had received no reply.

Each day that passed with no word from his family had sent him into a spiral of worry. Were they all right? Why weren't they able to reply? Had they been killed by a stray bomb, and were lying underneath a flattened house, bricks and rubble covering their bodies? The questions and scenarios of what might have befallen them careered around in his mind constantly and could only be silenced when Stanislaw, upon noticing his reticence, would tell him a tale from when he was young and invite the other prisoners to do the same. Each of them taking turns to tell their stories, to laugh and sometimes cry, and for a few brief delicious minutes, Szymon's brain would be quiet.

His final attempt had been a postcard that he had bartered a meal for from a fellow prisoner who had a set of them, sent to Mr Gliński's bookshop, but Szymon was sure that he would've left – he would not have stayed and would have returned to Poland. He knew he would have. He was only allowed to send four postcards a month, or two letters, and had to space them out so that he would have a chance to reply if anyone did write him back. But, so far, he hadn't reached his quota – no one had spoken back to him.

'I had no stamp, and no money for one either,' Szymon told him, then reached out and took the cigarette from Stanislaw's hand and took a drag on it that made him cough.

'But you sent it, you said so?'

'The owner of the factory – Herr Klein, he sent it for me. At least he said he would.'

Stanislaw let out a bark. 'Ha! Probably said he would, then would throw them away.'

'He will send it. He's not like that. I knew him once – sort of.'

'You knew the owner? You should ask him if you can work inside one of the existing factories then instead of having to dig foundations for the new one! Maybe he'll have lunch with you, maybe he'll invite you for dinner!' Stanislaw joked with a grin.

'I did know him. But he didn't know me.' Szymon handed the cigarette back, then stretched out on his bed, his calf muscles sore and tight. He rubbed at his left leg and let out a groan.

'How can you know someone who doesn't really know you?' Stanislaw stood and went to the corner of the bunkhouse and bent down, carefully lifting a corner of a loose floorboard.

'He was the father of a girl I once liked. But then she left and went to Berlin. She always said her father was a nice enough man, her mother, not so much. He was nice to us. As nice as he could be under the circumstances. He told us to go and shelter when it rained and spoke to the guards who agreed with him. Then he offered us cigarettes.'

'Ah – feels guilty but not enough to help you get free!' Stanislaw remarked as he dug around under the floorboard. 'Does it to make himself feel better. It's not for your benefit – don't start thinking that they really care. They don't.'

'I don't really care why he did it. The fact is that Krzysztof asked for a stamp and then he offered to take any letters for us and said he would send them himself.'

The scratching and scraping from the corner was beginning to irritate him. 'Can you stop?'

Stanislaw turned, a grin on his face. 'It's good dirt. Soft. We can certainly try this for a tunnel.' Then he turned and went back about his scrabbling about like a rat.

Szymon turned onto his side. This was the life for all of them now – escape. It consumed the men and tales of those who had tunnelled out, or simply managed to outrun the guns were told each evening, each time the tales becoming wilder and more elaborate, to the whoops and cheers of the men.

At first, in the other camps, Szymon had joined in, buoyed by the idea that escape just lay below them: all they had to do was tunnel out – simple.

On a cold January morning, when two prisoners had not arrived for roll-call, the men had stood, a frisson of excitement running through each of them. Two people had escaped! It could be done – it was just a matter of time, and time was what they had a lot of.

The repercussions for the two men who had fled were immediate and severe. Three men, chosen at random from the line had to step forward. And with a swift *pop, pop, pop*, their bodies fell onto the snow-littered ground, their blood turning the pure white a deep shade of crimson.

Szymon had stood there with the other men, no one talking, no one moving, the sight before them so strange, so unexpected that he was sure it hadn't really happened. It was only when he and another prisoner were asked to move the bodies that it all became too real for Szymon. He was dragging a body that seconds ago had been alive, and excited at the prospect of escape, and was now dead, their eyes open but staring at nothing.

Because of that, the idea of escape became something that Szymon was too scared to yearn for – even for the other men. Whilst they devised plans and spent hours digging, using spoons and bowls as spades, he sat on his bunk, a shiver running down his spine as he remembered the dead men.

'What did you say to him anyway? I thought you hated him. He left you, right?' Stanislaw huffed as he worked.

'I don't *hate* him,' Szymon said, noting a slight pull, a heaviness in his chest as he spoke. 'It was the right thing to do. He got free – I hope. I mean, I don't even know if he did. Or even if he is alive. It was the right thing to do at the time.'

'I'm not sure whether it was or it wasn't. But if he is alive, he owes you. I mean, I don't think I would have left a man – not just a man but family – on the battlefield who was begging me to stay. But then, I suppose, who knows what you'll do in that situation.'

Szymon saw Stanislaw's large shoulders rise and fall in a prolonged shrug. 'Anyway. Did you ask him to send food? Always ask for people to send you food. Always,' he added.

'I asked for a book,' he said.

'A book? You must be mad!'

'The Bible.'

'Even madder! You can't eat that. Honestly Szymon,' Stanislaw said in an exasperated voice, turning to look at him.

'You've so much to learn. But don't worry. You've got me. I'll see you right.'

Szymon laughed, noting a catch in his throat as he did, and began to cough. A cough. A slight pain in his chest. This was new.

TWENTY-SIX

SZYMON

Stalag VIII-A, Görlitz-Moys
June 1942

The pain in Szymon's chest grew with exponential speed. Within a day of first feeling the tightness around his lungs, a cough, thick and hacking, came, coupled with a fever that made him delusional and cry out for his mother.

He did not remember being moved to the infirmary. He did not know how long he had even been there. His first memory came on a warm morning in June, when a Polish nun, her face crinkled with age, leaned over him and announced, 'God has saved you!'

Pushing himself up to sit, he found that his arms would not hold his weight and he quickly fell back against the thin mattress.

'You need food,' the nun said, nodding her head wisely and scuttled away, leaving him to take in his surroundings.

The infirmary was overcrowded – his neighbours so close to him that he could reach out and touch them. There was a smell too, a mix of sweat and bodily fluids that congregated thickly in his nostrils.

'Are you alive?' a voice came from the bed beside him.

'I think so,' he answered, then fell into a bout of coughing that scratched painfully at his lungs and throat.

'Tuberculosis,' his neighbour said, as his coughing faded. 'Most of them in here have it. That or dysentery. Me, I got lucky though, just a bad beating.'

Szymon turned his head to the side to see that his neighbour's face was a kaleidoscope of blues and purples, his right eye swollen shut and a large lump pushing against the skin of his forehead.

'What happened?' he croaked.

'Nothing has to happen,' he said. 'We're Polish, so I think that's the main reason.'

'Here.' The nun was back, a bowl in her hands.

Szymon slowly managed to sit up and let her spoon-feed him, tasting nothing but sugar.

'Sugar water to start,' she said firmly, ladling the spoon once more into the bowl. 'Then soon some soup, and maybe some bread. You have to start slowly and build it up.'

He managed to take three more spoonfuls before another coughing fit overcame him.

'You'd want to keep that up,' his neighbour said, as the nun gave up and retreated with the bowl, her eyes seeking out a new patient. 'They'll have you walking around tomorrow. And then you'll be back in the barracks. I'd keep up the coughing if I were you, that way you can stay here a bit longer.'

Szymon wasn't sure he wanted to stay in the infirmary. The groans of pain from his bed-mates, the sweet tangy scent of sickness and the coughing and hacking was too much for him. But he didn't want to go back to his barracks either.

As if reading his mind, his neighbour said, 'It's bad either way. At least here you won't have to work.'

Szymon agreed with him and introduced himself, learning that the other man was Pawel from Łódź, and had been held in Görlitz for over a year now.

'You should have been here last year,' Pawel told him. 'There was this Frenchman here – Messiaen I think his name was. Some famous composer from France. And wouldn't you know it, he composed this piece of music here. The guards brought him instruments and let him create music whilst the rest of us had to work.'

'Are you serious?'

'Absolutely,' Pawel replied. 'They treat them better, the French. But us. We're just animals. I heard him, you know. I heard the music. It was beautiful. When I leave here, and when the war is over, you mark my words that we'll hear that music and one day I can tell everyone that I was there the day he first played it. I was there when a famous composer found something beautiful in this place.'

'That's if we *ever* get out,' Szymon said with a sigh, turning away from him and closing his eyes, a sudden tiredness washing over him.

'We will. I will. You have to think positively, you know. You can't just give up.'

Szymon wanted to tell Pawel that he already had given up. That in a way, he wished he would simply die in his sleep, right here, so it would finally be over.

The next morning, he woke and managed to carefully manoeuvre himself to the edge of the bed. He looked to the window where a bumble bee was bashing itself against the glass, trying furiously to escape into the world beyond.

He placed his feet flat on the floor, the cold of the tiles shocking his warm skin, then eased himself to standing.

'Calm down,' he told the bee, whose fattened belly wiggled with fear as a human approached it. 'I'll set you free.'

It was only when he leaned over to the window that he realised it did not open, but the bee was insistent. How could he set it free, he wondered, noting the irony that the bee, like him, was a prisoner for no particular reason other than bad luck.

His legs felt weak beneath him, a tremble in his left thigh muscle reminding him that his leg from the break years before could not cope with his illness as well, but he was desperate to find a way to set this creature free.

Before he turned away from the window, he saw three men, all Poles walking on the grass beside the fence, the bottom of their trousers wet with the early morning dew, a soldier stood behind them with a rifle trained at their backs. One of them yawned at the early morning rise, another rubbed at his eyes. He knew the men – he had worked with them, slept in the same bunkhouse and shared stories with them late into the night. He pressed his palm flat on the glass, edging even closer to the scene of the men outside, oddly hoping that they would look at him, perhaps wave, and let him know that he wasn't completely alone.

Where were they going so early, he wondered? It was too early for work, so they must have some new work detail that had come through. He noted in the back of his mind to ask Stanislaw about it when he was freed from the hospital and see whether this new work detail may be something better than either one of them had at the moment.

The men suddenly froze, and a guard marched up to them, stopping just feet away from them. In a quick succession, there was a pop of gunfire, aimed at each man's head, and one by one they crumpled to the ground.

He had seen men killed before – seen how when they tried to escape, the guards were quick with their guns and mowed them down without a second thought. But this was different.

These men were not trying to escape, they had simply been walking.

The guards had walked away now, leaving the bodies on the grass, each one of them left for some other prisoner to deal with. He wanted to scream, to shout out that this wasn't right – they had been doing nothing – *nothing*!

It was then that he realised that all of the men killed that he had witnessed over the years had been doing nothing too – there was no need to shoot a man for trying to escape, a man trying to go home. How had he become so accustomed to it that he could not see that everything that was happening around him was wrong and that the guards' ultimate aim was to ensure that all the men died, one way or another.

A sudden hot pain rushed up his thumb. He looked down to see the bee, wiggling its bottom as it freed itself from the sting that it had left behind in his skin. Within a second, it had freed itself from its imprisonment, dropping onto the windowsill, dying from trying to save itself.

He scooped up the bee and sat on his bed, ignoring the throbbing pain in his thumb, and said a prayer as the bee finally became still.

If the bee could risk its life, then, Szymon resolved, so could he. Those men outside had decided his new fate – he would not resist Stanislaw's ideas for escape any more – it was time to act, and if not succeed, then to welcome death as he would an old friend, wrapping his arms around it until, either way, he was free.

That afternoon, Szymon drifted in and out of sleep, dreaming snippets of dreams where he was free and running through a field of buttercups, the brightness of their yellow outfits so real that when he opened his eyes, for a moment, all he saw was a haze of yellow. As his eyes adjusted and he realised he was back in the hospital, a doctor and a guard approached his bed.

The doctor was no ordinary doctor, not dressed in a medical coat, nor a suit or tie, but simple trousers and shirt that marked him out as a prisoner. The 'doctor' spoke rapidly and Szymon quickly realised that he was Russian, his face as drawn and as pale as the rest of them.

'He is good,' he managed in German and turned to the guard stood next to him. 'Tomorrow. He is good.'

The guard nodded and accompanied the doctor to Pawel's bed. Within a minute, he had made his diagnosis – 'he is good' and moved onto the next patient.

As soon as they were out of earshot, Pawel turned to Szymon. 'Shit. I was hoping for more time, you know? I don't even think he's a doctor. I think he said he was to get better work detail. You know the French get to go to an actual hospital? I heard that they did. The nun told me. She and a few others come here to help sometimes. Otherwise, it's down to us to help each other.'

'I don't know how I can be of any help,' Szymon said.

'You can – you just don't know it yet. Tell me, what barrack are you in?'

'Thirty-one,' he answered.

Pawel nodded. 'I'll come and see you there. Do you have any friends? Strong men?'

'One. Stanislaw. There are others, but I think they are as weak as me.'

'Good. One will do. I'll come and see you. You know, there were loads of us here before, and then they started taking more and more of us away. There's hardly any of us here any more. It won't be long until the rest of us are sent somewhere. We don't have much time left.'

'Time for what?'

'To escape. What else?' Pawel laughed.

Escape. That was exactly what Szymon had been thinking too. He smiled at Pawel, glad to have a new friend and a new ally. Together, they would come up with something; they had to be like the bumble bee – courageous even through the fear.

For once, feeling a nugget of hope, Szymon closed his eyes with a thin smile on his lips, and once more allowed himself to slip into a dream where he was free, where the yellow of a buttercupped field awaited him.

Returning to his barracks the following day, Szymon shuffled in, an arm wrapped around his waist as if trying to hold his ribs in place, which screamed with pain from the amount of coughing he had done.

'Welcome back!' Stanislaw roared at him as soon as he entered, a parcel in one hand, the other outstretched to take him into a quick, friendly embrace.

Szymon let his friend clasp him, savouring the warmth from his body, and allowed him to be led to his bed, where Stanislaw gently sat him down.

'Here. This came for you.' He handed him the parcel, loosely wrapped in brown paper. 'It was opened, of course. I don't know what they took from it.'

Szymon pulled the paper away to reveal the Bible, stamps, and a few postcards, one of which was written on.

He felt his heart leap with anticipation and turned it over to see words and names that made tears immediately come to his eyes.

My dearest Szymon.

Your words were well received. I too enjoy Psalms. As you will see, I have highlighted a few held within that I think will bring you much joy and calm.

At times, calm is what is needed. And reflection.

Indeed, I tend to read this on the days which I go to church.
I sit in a pew and look at the statue of Christ on the altar and
feel myself relax. It amazes me how it can make me feel.

Yours,

Tadeusz

'What does it say?' Stanislaw asked, interrupting his
thoughts that jumped about as he itched to find out what
message had been hidden within.

He read it aloud quickly, and ignored Stanislaw's laments
that the note made little sense and was amazed that they had
not sent food.

It was only when Szymon told him about the cipher that
Stanislaw quietened.

'So what does it *really* say?' he whispered, sitting down next
to him.

It took Szymon a few minutes, looking at the Psalms highlighted by Tadeusz to finally read the message that had been
hidden.

Message well received! We are happy to hear that you are
alive!

Tell us, what can we do to help? You are so close. Over the
river. We can help. Marlena and Ilse will also help. Tell us
more. As much as you can. Take heart. We are with you and
ready to do as you ask.

E. Gliński

As Szymon finished reading out the new message for Stanislaw, the door swung open, and a hobbling Pawel entered.

'I told you I'd come and see you!' Pawel shuffled up to them. 'What have we here?' He nodded at the open Bible and postcard. 'Are you praying for help? It won't come, you know. I've tried myself, but it won't come.'

Szymon looked up at Pawel. 'It has. It's arrived,' he said.

He waved the postcard at him and grinned.

TWENTY-SEVEN

TADEUSZ

Görlitz
June 1942

The days dragged more than they had before. It was as though God himself knew that Tadeusz was waiting for a reply from Szymon and was intent on keeping him forever in limbo. He paced the floor above the bookshop, disturbing the dust that floated up into the air, spiralling and dancing as sunlight met them.

Tadeusz thought of Ilse during those days. He imagined that she had betrayed them all and each time the bell tinkled its song downstairs, he expected that it was the police or worse, Gestapo here to arrest him. He smoked incessantly too. Dragging on each cigarette, making the tobacco crackle and hiss as it burned down to a nub near his fingers, then he would flick it into an ashtray and start all over again – smoke, walk, smoke, walk.

Would Ilse betray them, or was his uncle right – that they had been friends once and that Ilse was still that lively, bright girl he had once known?

Had she been kind in those days? What did he really know about her?

He thought back to the day that they first met, when he had been waist-deep in the cold waters of the river, dragging an old suitcase from the muddy depths, hoping to find treasure inside. What they had found was a collection of musty old clothes and shoes and he had been glad that Ilse and Marlena had not stayed around to see the pitiful find.

On the days that had followed, he had seen how Szymon had been taken with her. So much so that they had spent days walking aimlessly around the town, hoping to bump into her.

The problem was – and not that he had ever told Szymon this, although he often wondered whether he knew – that he had felt something for Ilse too. The way she had waded into the water, showing no fear, the way she had smiled, and the way she crinkled her eyes up as the rain spattered her face.

He couldn't tell Szymon. Of course he couldn't. Szymon had said that he had liked her, and so that had been that.

But when they had met her once more, in the summer next to the church, he had felt exhilarated at seeing her again. It was such a new feeling, and so overwhelming that on the days that Szymon could not see Ilse, he would cajole his cousin, making him abandon his chores and seek Ilse out, just so that he, Tadeusz, could be close to her.

In a strange sort of way, he had liked watching her from afar. He would sit as she chatted with Marlena, twisting blades of grass in her fingers, then snapping them free from the ground. How she would do the opposite of everything that anyone said – she was too loud – well, then she would be louder. She was too childish – she would stick out her tongue in reply.

He tried to make her laugh and was delighted when she did, much to the annoyance of Szymon who would then try to outdo him and make her laugh as well, but he never quite managed the same reaction that Tadeusz had got from her, and this had made him feel – well, glad.

But there had been one day – one afternoon in the bookshop when it had just been the two of them – a memory that gave him comfort and warmth when he thought of it, and one that he had nurtured and kept safe all this time. He was sure that there had been another day, another moment they had stolen together, but that was hazy and misshapen. It was this memory that was vivid and one which had meant something to him.

She had been in a mood. That much was clear. She sat in the purple chair at the rear of the bookshop alone, her arms folded like a small child who had been scolded.

'What's wrong with you?' he had asked.

'Nothing,' she'd replied, refusing to look at him, pouting and staring at the floor.

'I'll just sit here then.' He pulled a chair close to her. 'Where's Marlena?'

'Where's Szymon?' she countered.

'He's busy. His father wants him to help with the garden at home.'

'Lucky him,' she spat.

'Is that why you're upset? Because Szymon isn't here?'

'No.' She looked at him now, then kicked out her leg as if kicking an imaginary stone on the ground.

He couldn't help but laugh. Her whole demeanour reminded him of a small, cross child who was not getting her way.

'Don't *laugh* at me!' She sat straight and waved her arms about. 'Don't laugh at me like I'm stupid or silly. I'm not. And I'm not selfish either.'

'Who said you were selfish?' he'd asked.

'Marlena,' she muttered.

'Why did she say that?'

She shrugged.

'Come on. Tell me. Why did she say you were selfish?'

'It's nothing.' She sat straight and picked up a book that had been left half-open on the floor.

'Fine. Don't tell me then. What are you reading?'

She had sighed heavily and handed him the book. 'Poetry. Love poems.'

He felt his stomach drop. Love poems. Her and Szymon.

'They're stupid, though. I don't understand them properly.'

He flicked through the pages and began to read:

> *When we two parted*
> *In silence and tears,*
> *Half broken-hearted*
> *To sever for years.*

He read the entire poem, then looked to her to see her reaction. She simply stared at her feet, and he wondered if she had actually heard him.

Finally, she exhaled a heavy breath and turned to look at him. 'So that's what you'd feel like if you parted from your love? That's how it should feel?'

He nodded. 'Like if you and Szymon were parted. That's how it would feel,' he suggested.

'Yes. Yes, I suppose you're right,' she said, but her words did not hold a ring of truth.

'That's how you feel about him, don't you?' he probed, wanting her to say no, but at the same time to say yes.

She looked at him. Properly. Stared at him with those brown eyes of hers, that when the light caught them just right, turned green. 'I don't know,' she whispered. 'I don't think so.'

Before she could turn away from him, he seized the moment. 'Do you think you could feel it for someone else instead?'

She tilted her head to the side, then gave a wry smile. 'Maybe.'

He could not ask anything else as his uncle disturbed the moment and sent Tadeusz on some errand that took him away from her.

But he had held that 'maybe' in his mind for weeks, months and even years. Was that 'maybe' meant for him?

'Tadeusz!' his uncle shouted, breaking his reverie. 'Come down!'

He could hear the excitement in his uncle's voice – Szymon had replied. Taking the stairs two at a time, he clattered into the bookshop to see his uncle grinning from ear to ear.

'Here!' he proffered a postcard. 'He's written back.'

Tadeusz snatched it away and read the message, which was plain and uninteresting, but he knew that beneath the words there would be something more – something hidden just for him.

Szymon had given a few numbers, indicating page numbers and paragraphs and bit by bit, he and his uncle pieced together a brief message that had been hidden in Psalm 23.

We must escape. I am ill. TB. I cannot stay here. There are three of us. We are trying to tunnel out. Will need help on the outside. Please send food and money. Money is of the upmost importance.

Tadeusz read, then re-read the message, feeling a little let down that there wasn't more. Had he been hoping that Szymon would say he forgave him for leaving him? Was he hoping that a few words from him would take him out of this self-imposed prison he had created for himself above the bookshop?

'We'll do it. Send him money. We can try and send food,

but I doubt it will reach him.' His uncle had already taken the postcard back and was mumbling to himself, his eyes still on the card. 'We'll tell him that we are ready to help if he gets free.'

'We should tell him we will help him escape, Uncle. What use is sending money to him when he's a prisoner of war?'

His uncle looked up at him. 'Because, my boy, money buys you everything. Money could mean freedom. And that is how we are helping him. It is not as though we can go into the camp and get him free! My goodness! No. We wait for his instructions and be ready for when he needs us.'

Deflated, Tadeusz made his way back upstairs as his uncle wrote out the next message and searched for money that he had hidden in a few choice books.

Once in his small rooms once more, he stood in the middle of the floor, his hands in his pockets and started to wait.

As he did, he heard a buzzing. Looking about him, he saw that a bumble bee was wobbling its way about the room, bashing into the whitewashed walls, then inspecting the chair, before landing on his pillow.

He went to the window and opened it and sat in the chair, waiting for the bee to leave of its own accord. Soon, it sensed the fresh air and flew away from him into the afternoon. He went to the window and closed it, envious of the creature's freedom, and wondered, as he so often did, how this had all come to pass. How he and his cousin, once young, happy boys were now both locked away from the world, fear enveloping their days.

TWENTY-EIGHT

SZYMON

Stalag VIII-A, Görlitz-Moys
June 1942

Herr Groening was a young guard – younger than most – tall and thin with red-blond hair that would peek from under his cap with its unruly curls. He had a way about him that had intrigued Szymon, who had watched him closely for the past four days as he waited around the barracks with nothing to do until he was well enough to go back to work. He had been surprised to get a week of convalescence after his time in the infirmary, but then, seeing as he could barely walk without stopping to bend double in a coughing fit, he would be useless digging foundations.

Groening walked as if strolling around a new city, his eyes flitting to the trees, admiring the sparrows that sat on branches and sang, stopping to look at a wildflower that had bloomed, or simply standing, enjoying the warmth of the sun on his face.

He was new, and Szymon wondered how long it would be until he became like the other guards who seemed to delight in finding constant fault with the Poles, making them work late into the night, digging pits which they would then tell them to fill in. They loved these games – loved to see how tired, how frustrated they could make them. He wished in those moments that he hadn't been born a Pole. If he had been French, he would be in the other barracks, separated by a wire fence. They were allowed Red Cross Parcels, a chapel and even a movie night.

Although he was not permitted to talk to any guard unless answering a direct question, Stanislaw and Pawel had given him this task to talk to the youngster, to try and see if he was amenable to bribes.

So far, Szymon had not found the courage to speak to him, but today, he decided, would be the day. The sun was shining, the birds trilling, and only Groening was walking the perimeter, watching out for the handful of Poles, including him, who were not at work.

As Groening sauntered past, Szymon stood from his perch on the step of the barracks.

'Herr Groening,' he said. He waited a beat until Groening stopped and turned to look for the voice.

He raised his hand in salutation and continued. 'I am so sorry to talk to you like this, I know it is not permitted. However, I could not help but admire the shine on your boots as you passed. I was in the army too, once, and I don't think I ever got a shine like that on mine.'

Groening opened his mouth, then closed it and cocked his head to the side as if considering what he should do. Szymon held his breath, waiting, hoping until Groening put him at ease.

'I like to try, you know,' he replied. 'It's the little things that count. That's what I think anyway. Just because we're here, doesn't mean we shouldn't keep up with our training.'

Szymon nodded and smiled, realising Groening's naivety. He was a boy playing dress-up. Straight out of basic training and sent here with no real awareness of the war or what it meant to be a soldier.

'You should be commended. The others probably look to you as an example, of that I am sure.'

This produced a shy smile from Groening, who stepped forward, closer to Szymon, removing his cap from his head, letting the wild curls of his hair escape their confines for a minute.

He ran a hand through his hair. 'I don't know whether I am an example,' he said. 'They tease me about my hair and have said that it should be shaved off. But it grows so quickly, and I try and use cream to make it stick down, but it always tries to make an escape! I think they are right and that I am due another haircut.'

'You should try what I used to use,' Szymon said. 'My father made it himself – a mixture of beeswax, a little lard, and if you can, some scent of some kind. My mother would sometimes add lavender to it.'

'I'll try it – I will.' Groening grinned. 'Thank you.'

Szymon nodded. 'My pleasure.'

Groening turned to leave and then seemed to think better of it. 'It's a lovely day, isn't it?' he asked.

Szymon could see through the boy – young, away from home and lonely. He could play this game.

'It is. You are very lucky to be in this part of the country. The city is beautiful – have you looked around it yet?'

'I went to one bar.' He kicked at a stone, then seeing that it had scuffed up his shiny boots, bent down and wiped it clean. Standing straight once more, he continued. 'It was fine. But there wasn't really anyone to talk to. And I'm not one to begin the conversation, so I had one drink and left. But I will investigate it a little more.'

Before Szymon could ask another question, another guard

walked around the corner and Groening immediately slapped the cap back on his head and turned and walked away.

Szymon retreated inside the barracks and lay down on his bed. Even the brief conversation had taken its toll and his breathing was ragged, his lungs crackling. But, he decided, it had been a good day. Groening could easily be bribed; all he had to do was to get Groening to see him as a person – no, a friend, a confidante, so when the time was right, he could ask him for a favour.

He reached behind him and pulled out from underneath his pillow the postcard that Tadeusz and his uncle had sent. He had been so happy to finally hear from him that his excitement had clouded his mind, and in that moment, he had decided that escape was possible – Tadeusz could help, his family were there, just within reach and he was finally going to take the risk. That morning in the hospital when he had seen those men shot had solidified this for him. Shot simply for being alive.

He wished though that the message had come directly from Tadeusz. He wanted to hear his words – and perhaps something about what had happened that day. Did he blame his cousin for running away and saving himself? He searched inside himself and could not find blame there. Nevertheless, there was something that bothered him – the fact that it hadn't been mentioned, no apology offered. Not that he *needed* an apology – but still.

His mind turned over a leaf, much like a page in a book, and he started to think about the fact that Ilse had been mentioned in the note – Ilse who had broken his heart as a young boy, disappeared to Berlin, but was now, seemingly, back in Görlitz and helping.

The irony was not lost on him that her father was the owner of the factory that they were building, and his daughter was aiding a Polish prisoner. But then, knowing Ilse as he had that glorious summer, he expected nothing less from her.

Szymon allowed himself a moment to think of Ilse – the girl he had fallen hopelessly in love with and ended up making a fool of himself over. He cringed at the memory of how he had acted. Before her, before that day on the riverbank he had always thought himself a confident boy – joking around with his cousin, never really concerning himself with the way he looked or what people thought of him.

But then, she had changed all that. '*I've been looking for you*,' that's what he had told her that hot day at the fair. And he had. He had thought of nothing else but her since that rainy day and had made enquiries to friends and family, describing her in a muddled and useless way, simply forgetting the colour of her eyes or hair – such was the way when you liked someone, they became a blur, an ethereal being: you knew you were attracted to them, but no matter how much you dug about in your brain, you could not picture them in their entirety.

He knew that Tadeusz had liked the look of her too, as he didn't tease him as he normally would have and seemed just as eager to walk round the town, crossing the river almost on a daily basis with the hope of catching a glimpse of her.

Then, just like that, on the day of the fair she appeared.

She was more than he remembered her to be – more beautiful – her brown eyes seemed green when the light touched them, her cheekbones high, her small pouty lips never still, always chattering or smiling.

That night, he had looked in the mirror at home at himself. His nose was too big, his eyes too close together. He did not have the muscle on his body that Tadeusz sported, nor the square jaw, and for the first time in his life he thought himself ugly and unworthy of a girl like Ilse.

She would like Tadeusz better, he knew. He was louder, funnier and she would soon realise that she had chosen the wrong cousin and turn her attention to Tadeusz.

But Szymon knew he was more intelligent than Tadeusz,

and that he could play to his strengths. He would allow Tadeusz to lark about like he always did, and he would show Ilse how thoughtful and intelligent he was in comparison.

In the days that followed, a silent competition began between the pair, even though neither one acknowledged it – it was there, unspoken and constant.

When Ilse spoke, when she laughed, he wanted to join in – he had wanted to say something pithy in return, making her look to him and feel as though she were the lucky one to be with him. But there seemed to be a disconnect between his brain and his mouth and the words would get caught within an insecurity of his and refuse to come out of his mouth.

The more he could not say, nor could not be who he wanted to be in front of her, the more he could sense her pulling away. First, she would drop his hand instead of holding it with such force that it was sometimes painful. Then she would talk more to Marlena, or Tadeusz, and soon she would make excuses not to see him, but he would find her later at the bookshop with Marlena. The more she pulled away, the worse he became. His seriousness took on an edge that he did not like, and he found himself constantly arguing with his parents, with Tadeusz and even with Ilse. But he couldn't help it. He was so in love with her, felt so much for her, that he had morphed into someone entirely different, riddled with self-doubt and loathing.

When she had left for Berlin, those first few weeks he had simply locked himself away from everyone – refusing to see Tadeusz, refusing to even go to school and lamenting to his mother that he was sure he was dying. At the time, he had thought he was dying of heartbreak. He would place his hand over his chest at night to feel the drum of it, sure in the knowledge that at any moment it would simply stop.

But it didn't. Of course, it didn't. And bit by bit, day by day, the pain of losing her became easier to bear, and he soon found that he came back to life a little.

How strange, he thought now, lying on a small bed, a prisoner of war, that his love for Ilse had changed him into someone he did not recognise, that her leaving had allowed him to be free from the complicated feelings of youth. And now, she had come back – would he see her again and become a lovestruck fool? Would he escape here only to be ensnared in his love for her once more? Would he, simply, never be free?

'How did it go?' Stanislaw asked, his voice too loud in the quiet of the room, bouncing off walls and hitting Szymon's ear in such a way that he found it irritating.

'It went well,' he answered, his own voice low and calm, hoping that Stanislaw would follow suit.

'It better had. The hole we tried last night is no good. We need a new plan.'

Szymon painfully pushed himself up to sitting. 'What do you mean, no good?'

Stanislaw lit a cigarette and blew out a plume of smoke. 'Too much clay – too thick. It would take us years.'

'We can try somewhere else?' Szymon suggested.

'There isn't anywhere else.' Stanislaw sat heavily on his bed. 'Too many eyes. That was the only barrack close enough to the fence and far away enough from the guards and gates. That was our chance.'

'What now, then?'

Stanislaw's large shoulders gave a heavy shrug. 'I suppose we have to be patient. Something will come up, you know, it always does.'

'You don't sound like you believe it,' Szymon said, noting the tiredness in his friend's voice.

'I do,' Stanislaw rallied, plastering a grin on his face, a smile that did not quite reach his eyes. 'Something will come up. It has to.' He dragged heavily on his cigarette, flicking the ash, watching as it landed in a pile on the floor. 'It has to,' he repeated. 'It just *does*.'

TWENTY-NINE

MIA

Görlitz
Thursday, 11 February 1999

Tadeusz stopped. 'It's getting late,' he said.

I looked at the clock – 1 a.m. It was late, but I did not want him to stop – what happened to Szymon, how did he get free? Did he? I opened my mouth to ask, but Tadeusz shook his head.

'I'm tired.' He made to stand, but his legs didn't hold him and he plopped back down.

I stood to help him, but he waved a hand at me.

'No. No. I'm fine. I don't need any help. It's just that if I sit too long, they seem to stop working. They just fall asleep!'

He attempted a little chuckle, and I humoured him and laughed back.

After another attempt, he managed to stand upright, and stood wobbly like a newborn foal for a moment before he found his momentum and shuffled to the front door.

'Please. We will continue. I promise we will. I am just tired.'

As much as I did not want him to stop, it was not as though I could pressure an old man, late at night, to keep talking to me.

Reaching the door, I felt his hand on my shoulder. 'Mia,' he said.

I turned.

'Sleep well, OK. And come back tomorrow.'

He gave me a watery grin and before I could bid him a good night too, he began to close the door slowly. My time with him was over.

Upstairs, I sat in my grandmother's apartment, nothing interrupting the still, late-night air other than the ghostly wails of Leonie's cello, sneaking its way through the heating vents. I tried to make sense of everything Tadeusz had said, and his story about what it had been like for Szymon in the camp, what it had been like for him and my grandmother in those days.

Taking my notebook, I began to write, trying to see the picture that Tadeusz had been trying to paint for me with haphazard brush strokes. It was as though I were writing about someone I did not know. My grandmother, who was my flesh and blood, yet the girl that Marlena and Tadeusz had once known was nowhere to be found in the woman that lay dying in a hospital bed. She was not to be found in the woman that had raised me either – always telling me never to take risks, telling me to think things through. Where had that girl gone, who laughed so much she cried? Where had the girl from the river disappeared to – the one who fell in and out of love with such force it knocked all those around her down with it. Where was the woman who sensed adventure and excitement in every-thing, who quite naively did not see the danger she put herself in?

It was odd to think that, during the war, when so many terrible things were happening, that a young woman, *my grand-mother*, was quite oblivious to it – that as much as she loved or cared about others, her own sense of needing adventure took precedence over all of her decisions.

I wished that I could ask her if the picture that Tadeusz had painted of her was correct. Surely, she was not as naive and impetuous as he had made her out to be, and her own narrative of those events would be different – perhaps more thoughtful.

As my pen scratched against the paper, I realised that I was going to have to try and merge two different versions of the same person together – stitching up the seams with a neat hand so that she could become whole again.

Soon, I didn't notice the cello music any more. I didn't feel an early morning chill creep into the apartment. Their stories took all my focus, and it was not until 5 a.m., when my hand began to cramp, that I put away the notebooks and made my way to bed.

I had perhaps slept for a few hours when a ferocious banging on the door woke me. I staggered to the door, bleary-eyed and confused, and was met with Marlena who took me into a strong hug that squeezed the breath out of me.

'*Darlink* girl,' she murmured into my ear. It had happened, hadn't it, I thought. Grandmother had died.

I released myself from her grasp. 'Is she... has she...?' I said, not quite managing to get the final words out.

'Who? No! *Darlink*. Ilse is *fine*. I see her already this morning even though doctors and nurses say no visiting time. But I don't much care!' She flounced into the apartment, leaving a trail of thick perfume in her wake.

I shook my head and closed the door behind her. Following her into the apartment, I found her in the kitchen making coffee as if she lived here.

Today, she had adorned herself in orange. Head to toe. Bright orange baggy trousers and a blouse that gaped, showing her large bosom. Her earrings today were red gemstone hummingbirds that clashed loudly with her clothes, and she had completed her look with an equally crimson lipstick, that once more had escaped the confines of her lips and smudged itself underneath her nose.

She saw me looking at her. 'I feel I need *colour* today!' she declared. 'You need colour in your life – did you know that? Like a rainbow. Someone once said that to me when I was a girl – a gypsy man. He said always have colour in your life.'

I yawned, covered my mouth, then sat down at the kitchen table.

'Why so tired?' she asked, banging mugs on the countertop and pouring boiling water over coffee granules.

'I spoke with Tadeusz,' I said simply.

She stopped for a split second, then turned and smiled. 'You find out some things?' She handed me the steaming mug and sat down opposite me.

'Why do I get the feeling that you already knew I would have talked to him?' I asked.

She shrugged, then took a noisy sip of her coffee, leaving a red smear on the rim. 'I no know what you talking about.'

'I've also noticed your English gets worse when I ask you things that you don't want to answer...'

'It comes, it goes.' She waved her hand. 'Some days I have the words, sometimes not. Tell me. What he tell you?'

I relayed as much as I could, Marlena nodding along. 'Yes. Is right. Is correct,' she interjected now and then, putting her seal of approval on Tadeusz's memories.

'What was it like for you, Marlena? When Grandma came back – you must have been happy to see her?' I prodded, not sure of whether to tell her what Tadeusz had said to me, that she had been in love with my grandmother for years. Was she still?

'Of course happy! She is my favourite person. Always my favourite person. Even when she in England, we write and write.'

'But you never came to see her? Didn't you miss her?'

'Of course I want to go and see her. But things different here – Russians come and then you know – Berlin Wall – you remember this?'

I nodded. I did.

'We not have much. Not enough for ticket to England. And besides, she no want me to come.'

'Why?'

'Because she different then. She have baby and then life it gets busy and soon, before you can blink – it is gone!'

'But still—' I started.

'No.' She waved her hand again, stopping me. 'She no want me to come because son alive, everything okay and she maybe come. And then, he died. And she say to me, no come. I have to look after granddaughter and things not so good here. I think though,' Marlena leaned her cheek on her hand, and tapped an impatient finger against her skin, 'I think she not want me to see her because I remind her too much of before. Of everything that happened.'

'What did happen, though? I mean, Tadeusz told me that Szymon was going to escape. Did he? He must have, surely?'

'You like the dog with the stick again,' she moaned. 'Why we not talk about the weather? Yes? English people like to talk about the weather.'

'What happened next, Marlena? How did Szymon get free – do you know?'

'I know,' she sighed. 'Of course I know. But only some things. Not all.'

'And will you tell me? I'll be like a dog with a stick if you don't!' I joked.

She waited a beat, took another slurp of coffee, then stretched her arm out, her hand searching mine. 'I tell you what. I make you a deal, yes? I tell you a story, but then, you must tell me a story too. About the boy – Will—'

'Wait!' I interrupted. 'How do you know about Will?'

'Your grandmother. She tell me. So then you must tell me about you. Your heartbreak. Your life. Because, my darlink, right now you are like a ghost. All pale, sad, alone, scared and you need to be alive again. I promise your grandmother that I will help you be alive again. So it is a deal, yes?'

I saw her look at my bare arms. I had forgotten to put a cardigan on and sat there wearing the oversized black T-shirt I had slept in, that showed the bruises in all their glory.

'I see you, *darlink,*' she said quietly. 'I see you are in pain, and you are scared. Not just for your grandmother but for what he did to you. I promise your grandmother yesterday that I will help you, and I think that I can only help you if you tell me the truths – all of them – so you don't have to be afraid any more.'

I thought back to the previous day when Grandma had asked me what I was going to do when she died, how she had asked me if I would go back to Will and I had promised her that I wouldn't.

I hated the thought that she was worried about me, lying there, knowing that these were her last days and all she was doing was thinking of me and wanting me to be OK.

'I don't think I can talk about it,' I said quietly. 'I've been trying to ignore it, trying to think about other things.'

'You can't ignore it forever, Mia. You have to face it.'

'I... I just don't know if I can.'

Marlena took my hand in hers. 'Listen to me. I know what it is like to try and forget things – Tadeusz, he know too, and your grandmother – now look at us all! All old and arguing and shouting with each other. It is not good. I promise your grandmother that I would talk to you, I promise her that I would help. Is the only thing I can do for her – is the only thing you can do for her.'

A rogue tear escaped my eye and trailed its way down my cheek. Finally, I felt something – the worry, the tiredness, the fear, the thought of my grandmother dying, it was all there, right at the surface.

Looking at Marlena's kind face, I decided she was right. I needed to reassure Grandma before she died that I was fine, Marlena needed to do it for her too, and I suppose, I needed to reassure myself that I was okay, and that I could survive this.

'You have a deal,' I told her.

'Ah, good! *Darlink* girl, you will be glad you did. My story first, then you. Yes?'

I nodded, I needed just a little more time before the ghosts of my recent past were let loose in this house, hoping that as Marlena talked of Szymon and his escape, I, too, would find some courage to be able to begin my own.

'OK. Where are we? You say money is sent to Szymon. This is true. But it is Ilse and I who give it to him because you cannot send money in an envelope. So, me and Ilse we go to factory and we search for Szymon...'

THIRTY

GÖRLITZ

June 1942

Ilse patted the pocket in her thin coat for the third time in less than a minute. The money was still there. She walked close to Marlena, their shoulders touching, both seemingly scared of what they were about to do.

'Do you think he will believe you?' Marlena asked.

'He has to – I mean he *will*.'

'But you've never visited him before at the factory, won't he think it's strange that you're there?'

Marlena's questions were annoying her. She had thought it through. She simply had to make her father think that she was interested in working with him – that she had decided to follow in his footsteps. Her mother had lamented for months that no man would want to marry her, so she would play up to this, and tell her father that in the meantime, she wanted to make both her father and mother proud. She would ask for a tour of the factory and find a way to get to the workers outside who were erecting a new building and simply give Szymon the envelope full of money that Mr Gliński had given her that morning.

'It has to be today,' Mr Gliński had warned. 'The postcard he sent said that they needed money, then he sent another saying they had found a guard to bribe. This might mean that he has a chance to escape, but we must act quickly.'

Ilse had looked at Tadeusz who had barely uttered a word to her so far. Instead, he stood with his arms folded, chewing at his lower lip. Was he afraid – was he afraid for her?

'I can do it,' Ilse had told them both confidently. 'You can trust me. I can do it.'

She had taken the money and left with Marlena, telling them both that she would be back that afternoon to let them know that it had been accomplished.

But now, as she stood outside her father's factory, the whir and grind of the machines within leaking out into the day, she lost a little of her nerve – suddenly the adventure, the excitement she had so craved was now a little too real.

'We can't turn back now,' Marlena whispered, and Ilse wondered whether it was a statement or a question.

'Ilse? Ilse Klein?' A red, sweating face appeared from the entrance to the offices which sat at the side of the factory, a brass plate on the door announcing to all who came that Klein Engineering and Manufacturing lay just behind the black lacquered door.

Ilse looked to the man, who seemed familiar – a short, portly man whose shirt buttons stretched against his girth; his tie so tight around his neck that it looked like it was cutting off his circulation. 'Oh, my word! I have not seen you since you were a little girl! You had pigtails back then and were always trying to pull your hair free, do you remember?'

She tried, but she couldn't place him.

'It's me! Bruno! Well, Herr Schindler. Please don't say you don't remember me? I work with your father – have done for years.'

It was then that the memory resurfaced. Yes. She remembered him now. He would come to the house with his wife for dinner sometimes and always bring her sweets and chocolate.

'Herr Schindler, how lovely to see you.' She held out her hand for him to take, but he abruptly took her into a bear hug, his dampened body pressing firmly against hers.

'My, my,' he said, letting her go and looking at her from head to toe. 'You've grown up, haven't you?'

Ilse took an extra step back away from him, not so much to cause offence but enough to put a little more distance between herself and him.

'I'm here to see my father,' she said. 'Would you be able to take us to him, please?'

His piggy eyes were still roaming her body. Realising that she had said something, he replied, 'Yes, yes, of course,' holding the door open for them, making sure that he moved ever so slightly into them both as they passed.

Her father's office sat on the third floor with a huge glass window that looked out onto the factory below.

As soon as Ilse and Marlena entered, Ilse's eyes went to the window, looking at the bobbed heads of workers on enormous machines that spouted out steam, hissing and gasping. The air in her father's office was close, with a scent of oil and grease that she didn't much mind. Her father sat proudly behind a polished mahogany desk, piles of papers obscuring most of him, but his face that peered out was delighted to see her and for that she felt reassured that all would go to plan.

'Ilse, is everything all right?' His pleasure was quickly replaced by worry, and he scrunched up his brow as he looked to the door, perhaps expecting her mother to enter too.

'Everything's fine, Father. You remember my friend Marlena, don't you?'

'Oh, of course, of course.' He stood and held out his hand to shake Marlena's, a gesture that seemed so strange for him to make to a friend of his daughter's that he had known for years.

'What can I do for you? Do you need money for shopping, is that it?'

'Father.' Ilse sat in the chair that faced his desk, offering the other to Marlena. Surprised by her formality, her father sat down too, his fingers steepled together as she spoke.

'You know how Mother wants me to marry, but she says that I am stubborn and lazy and that no man will want me. Well, I think I have found a solution to the problem.'

'Oh, my dear Ilse. You know what your mother is like,' he replied, but she couldn't help noticing how his eyes flicked to the door again – just in case her mother should appear.

'You know what she's like,' he continued. 'Pay no heed. You'll find a match when you are ready. I am sure of it.'

'But, Father, I was thinking that perhaps I should work, perhaps if I work, I will learn how to be less stubborn and lazy and then perhaps Mother would be proud of me,' she said sweetly.

He leaned back in his chair and let his hands drop to his lap. 'You don't have to work, Ilse. There's no need for anything like that. We have enough money. So many girls, they have to work, but you don't.'

Ilse could feel her explanation and her need to be there slipping away. 'I know I don't need to, Papa,' she said, emphasising the childish Papa, as opposed to the formal Father, just to see him smile at her. 'But I would at least like to understand your business, our family business. Even if I don't technically work – I'd like to at least understand what it is that you do. I've been trying to explain to Marlena what you do, but I know I am not doing it justice. Please, Papa – won't you show us around – show me where you come to work each day and then maybe just consider letting me work here a little?'

'I'll tell you what.' He sat forward and rested his arms on the desk. 'I'll show you around and I'm sure that once you have seen what I do, you will be readily put off at the thought of working here! But no matter. Because you have shown willing and shown you are not lazy as you mother says. And we can tell her that, can't we? It may improve her mood.'

'We can, Father.' Ilse grinned at the skinny face of the man that was her Papa – a man so scared of his wife that he could not be the one to tell her that Ilse came to the factory – they had to do it together.

Buoyed by her achievement, she linked arms with Marlena as her father took them to the factory floor, introducing them to people whose faces were as red and sweaty as the horrid Herr Schindler. They seemed uninterested in the boss's daughter. And Ilse did not blame them. They were tired, hot, working in a factory that heaved with noise – so loud, so confusing it was, that Ilse soon asked her father if they could step outside a moment to catch a breath of air.

He led them to the rear of the factory, to a loading dock that was swollen with wooden crates, all marked with the Reichsadler, the eagle burned into the wood, blackened and ominous.

'Father, did you not say you were building another factory?' Ilse asked. 'I told Marlena you were – I am sure you said you were building another one.'

'Indeed' – he smiled at her – 'over there.' He pointed in the direction of the field that lay behind the loading dock, although there was not much of a field left. In its place was a cavernous hole where the tips of heads could be seen bobbing from inside it.

'The foundations are done. Just need the concrete to go down in the next few days, then the rest of it will be up before you can blink!' He laughed.

Marlena, who had stayed quiet the whole time, suddenly turned to Ilse. 'I think the heat and the noise have made me unwell, Ilse!' she cried. 'Please, I don't feel so well.'

'Sit down, catch your breath,' Ilse told her, helping her to sit on the concrete slab and lean her back against a crate.

'Father, could you get Marlena a glass of water and maybe something to eat? I don't think she ate before she came here.'

'Shouldn't we get her inside? I can fetch Schindler to help —' her father began, already reaching out to try and help Marlena to her feet.

'No! I mean, she needs to sit outside – she needs the fresh air, don't you, Marlena?'

Marlena played her part well and nodded slowly. 'Please, Herr Klein. If you don't mind.'

Her father agreed and disappeared inside the factory.

'We need to be quick.' Marlena jumped to her feet. 'But how are we going to get the money to him – there are what, four or five guards there.' She pointed in the direction of the hole in the field where two guards had appeared above the men inside, holding guns in their hands but seemingly uninterested in watching their charges as they spoke to one another. Another two stood lazily against a fence, both smoking, leaving a whisper of grey in the air.

'We'll talk to them,' Ilse said. 'To those two at the fence. Then the other two might come. I'll flirt with them a little, ask for a cigarette and then when no one's looking, you go and find him. He's in there. In that hole somewhere – you just need to find him.'

'I don't know, Ilse.' Marlena licked her lips. 'I don't think we can do it.'

Ilse looked to the guards, to the men in the hole and then to her friend whose hands were now shaking.

Before Marlena could stop her, she jumped off the loading dock, glad that she landed well and quickly walked up to the smoking guards. She had said that she would do this and she would. She would prove to Tadeusz, to Marlena and to herself that she was brave, she was serious, and she was no longer the selfish child they still thought she was.

The guards noticed her, and immediately turned to face her.

'Good afternoon!' she called out to them. 'I was just wondering whether you had a cigarette I could have?'

The men brushed their hands against the guns in the holsters, then quizzically looked at this woman who was clearly not a worker – she was dressed in a navy-blue skirt, her pale blue shirt tucked neatly into the waist, a long brown coat completing her look. She saw their expressions quickly go from suspicion to wonder and then, to interest.

'Who are you?' one of the guards asked, a man whose pock-marked cheeks were still slightly pink with youth.

'Frauline Klein,' she answered authoritatively. 'My father is Herr Klein, the owner of this factory.'

Immediately the two men fumbled about in their pockets for a cigarette, both of them retrieving silver cigarette cases at the same time.

She laughed. 'Oh how generous – whose will I choose?'

'Please. Take as many as you like,' the one with pockmarks said.

She slid one from the case and waited for the other man to light it for her. Trying not to gag, she dragged and then blew out a thin plume of smoke.

'Tell me, what is happening over there – Father said something about foundations?' She laughed again. 'But I don't want to admit to him that I don't quite know what that means. Would you be good enough to show me?'

'It's rather muddy – you'll ruin your shoes,' the young guard warned. 'We shouldn't really. I don't think we should.'

'Oh, come now.' Ilse dusted an imaginary speck of dust from the guard's lapel. 'Just a little peek and then we'll say nothing more about it. I'm wonderful at keeping secrets, you know.'

The pockmarked man returned her smile, and she knew then she had won.

'Follow me,' he said, crooking his arm for her to take as if they were out on a stroll in the countryside.

A few feet away lay the hole that had been dug. She allowed the guard to help her up the mound of dirt so that she could peer inside.

There she saw the faces of the workers – drawn, pale, their eyes trying to flit to her to look, but then in fear darting back down to their work – shovelling soil out of the pit, onto the banks, then again, and again.

She quickly scanned the faces in front of her. She could not identify any of them as Szymon. Behind her, Marlena's voice called out, followed by her father's.

'We should go.' The guard was nervous now, betraying his youth. 'Your father is calling for you.'

Quickly, she turned and with a flick of her ankle, her right shoe came loose. Pretending to walk away, she flicked the shoe backwards into the hole.

'Oh, silly me! My *shoe!*' she cried, and before the guard could jump in and retrieve it, she knelt down and looked at the nearest worker.

'You! You there,' she hissed. The man looked at her, his face stubbled with whitened hairs. 'Give this to Szymon Adamczyk,' she hissed again, reaching into her coat pocket and drawing out the envelope. 'Do it. Make sure you do it.'

The man was no fool and pocketed the envelope quickly and then bent down to retrieve her shoe just as the boy-guard was about to lower himself in.

'No need!' she giggled. 'This lovely man has helped me. Thank you, sir,' she said, turning to the stubble-faced man. 'Really. Thank you.'

Ilse wasn't sure whether she imagined it or not, but to her it seemed that he gave a slight nod of the head in agreement.

It was only as she was escorted away that she wondered if the man would pocket it for himself – whether the money would ever reach the hands of Szymon at all. But what else could she have done? Tadeusz would just have to be happy that she had tried.

Now they could only wait.

THIRTY-ONE
SZYMON

**Stalag VIII-A, Görlitz-Moys
June 1942**

'I still can't believe it,' Stanislaw exclaimed. 'I just can't believe it...'

Szymon, too, was still in a state of disbelief of what had happened that afternoon. He had seen the woman atop the mound of dirt that the foundations for the new factory had produced. He had seen her there with the young guard who looked little more than a large child, looking down and then she had seemingly disappeared. There had been whispers about who she was – perhaps. The boy's girlfriend? Surely not. Surely he could not have got a woman like that?

It was only when they reached the barracks that evening that Czeslaw, a fellow prisoner, a man nearing sixty who had volunteered to save his homeland, came to him in his bunkhouse and drew out from his trousers a thick white envelope.

'I didn't look inside it,' he assured Szymon. 'It's none of my business. But she was a pretty thing, whoever your girl is. And

that risk she took, well, I'd take my hat off to her if I had one!'
He rubbed at the thinning grey hair on his head.

Szymon waited until he had left to go outside and smoke
with the others to open the envelope and find it full of money.

The relief was indescribable. All at once he wanted to jump
up and scream and shout at the ingenuity of Ilse, at the plan-
ning by Tadeusz and Mr Gliński, but all he could do was
quickly hide the money out of sight and now find a way to get
some of it into Groening's hands.

'What are you grinning about?' Stanislaw grumbled, as he
walked into the barracks, his clothes soaked through from the
recent rain shower.

'Today at the factory. My cousin sent someone who gave me
the money. We have it!'

Stanislaw stopped in his tracks and turned his full attention
to Szymon.

'We can see if Groening is keen to earn something extra,'
Szymon explained. 'We can do it now!'

'All right, all right, keep your voice down!' Stanislaw
warned him. Moving closer to Szymon, he asked in a hoarse
whisper, 'How much?'

'Enough. Probably his month's wages.'

Stanislaw's eyes widened. 'Just think, if we weren't here and
we had that money what we could do with it! Me...' Stanislaw
went to his bunk and began removing his damp clothes. 'Me, I'd
find the best restaurant in town and order everything on the
menu and then a bottle of red wine to finish it off.'

'So, what do I do now?' Szymon interrupted his friend's
daydreaming. 'I'm at work again. How can I speak to him freely
like before?'

Stanislaw looked at him, brow furrowed. 'You're looking
very ill again, Szymon.'

'I feel a bit better—' he started to reply.

'No. No. I think you *are* ill. Not too ill to go to the infirmary, but maybe too sick to go with the work detail. Give me some of the money, and do it quick.'

Szymon handed over a few notes. 'This should do the trick,' Stanislaw said, then re-dressed himself in his wet clothes and left Szymon sitting alone in the bunkhouse.

It wasn't until that evening, when the beds were full with tired bodies, all of them curled up like babies under thin blankets that Stanislaw returned, a triumphant glow on his face. Before Szymon could ask where he had been these past two hours, the doctor he'd seen in the infirmary entered behind Stanislaw, followed by a guard called Schiller who was as wide as he was tall.

As they approached him, Szymon could hear the huff and puff of Schiller as he walked, his face growing red with the exertion.

'Here he is. Had a fever before, but I think it is gone now,' Stanislaw said.

The doctor made a feeble attempt to look in Szymon's eyes, throat and ears, then announced in fractured German that he needed to stay in the barracks for a few days.

'He can talk. He can walk. I don't see why he can't work,' Schiller announced in response to this news. 'I think he's fine.'

A look passed between the doctor and Stanislaw that Szymon interpreted as meaning unless he, Szymon was signed off the work detail, the doctor would not be getting any money.

'It is very difficult,' the doctor said, measuring out each word. 'You see, if he work, and if he die at work, then all the illness come out of him. And everyone will get it. *Everyone,*' he emphasised and stared at Schiller.

'Why? What has he got? Take him to the infirmary.'

'No. No need. Just here. Rest a few days and then he is well and it will go.'

Schiller looked to Szymon, then the doctor, trying to decide. 'You say if he *dies*, that's when others get sick?'

'Yes. Anyone near him.'

Schiller grimaced. Szymon knew that Schiller enjoyed doing very little, and his favourite job was taking the men to work, where he would then sit and eat all day, chatting as if he hadn't a care in the world. He would not risk this.

'Fine. Just for one week,' he finally said. 'Then he's back at it, you understand?'

The doctor nodded and smiled for the first time and Szymon imagined that his palm was itching for those few notes that Stanislaw had promised him.

As soon as they were gone, Stanislaw began to laugh and soon it became infectious – each of the prisoners joining in at getting one over on Schiller.

'The bastard is as stupid as he is fat!' one man remarked. 'Stanislaw, think of other things we can do to him!'

They spent the rest of the evening coming up with more and more ridiculous things they could do to Schiller to embarrass him and fool him and for once, in the cold, damp barracks that Szymon found himself in, he felt a sprinkle of happiness.

The following day he was glad to see that the rain had eased, and that he could sit on the steps of the bunkhouse, simply waiting for Groening to appear.

At midday, bored and sure by then that Groening was not going to show, he heard a light whistling, getting louder and louder, and finally Groening appeared.

'Herr Groening!' Szymon stood. 'You carry such a melody.'

Groening grinned and stopped walking, keeping a few feet between them. 'Why, thank you. I do feel on a summer's day that a whistle, a tune, lightens one's spirits.'

'Indeed, it does. I am honoured to have heard it.'

Groening looked left to right, then took a step forward. 'You know, I'm not supposed to talk to you. And you are certainly not supposed to talk to me.'

For a split second, Szymon's heart stopped. Groening had turned into one of the other guards.

'Not that anyone knows I'm talking to you,' he continued. 'They give me this job to stroll around empty barracks all day, with no one to talk to, so I am not sure what they expect.'

Szymon let out a breath of relief. 'A man must have someone to talk to. He cannot be silent all the time.'

'Yes! Quite! I mean, I am not like a woman who wants to gossip all day long, but back home, I had friends, family and we would talk about our day, discuss books we had read...' He looked wistfully off into the world beyond the fences.

'Books are a passion of mine too,' Szymon replied, seizing the opportunity and for a few minutes, they discussed their favourite authors, stories they had read as children and how it was such a simple pleasure in life that they could not under-stand people who said that they did not read.

'You must miss home,' Szymon said.

'I do. I miss a lot of things...'

'It must be hard to enjoy oneself here. Especially if one's wages are slim.' Szymon shot the suggestion out – he had to.

Groening cocked his head to the side. 'I suppose. I mean I'm not saying that our Führer in all his wisdom is not giving us enough money, but there are times when I wish for a little more. I could perhaps dine in a nice restaurant with a pretty lady should she so wish, or I could send my mother a gift...' He shrugged.

'That is what I would do too,' Szymon agreed. 'I would buy books though as well, I think!'

'Ah-ha! Yes. Books. I'd buy them also.'

There was a lull in the conversation as Szymon tried to think of how to word what he needed from Groening. How could he say that he had money? Stanislaw seemed to be able to do it with other guards and the doctor of course – he should have asked him how to word it!

'Well. I'd better be going.' Groening made to turn away, then thought better of it. 'By the way, if I don't see you again before you leave, I'll say goodbye now.'

'Leave?' Szymon asked.

'Um...' Groening looked like a child that had just let out a secret. His eyes once more scanned left and right before he came close to Szymon. 'Look. I probably shouldn't have said anything. Really, I shouldn't,' he whispered urgently. 'Don't tell anyone else – any of the others. We don't want a riot on our hands, and it would get back that I had said something, you know?'

'I promise. I won't say a word.' Szymon placed his hand on his chest. 'But tell me, where are we going?'

'I shouldn't say, I really shouldn't,' he muttered again.

It was then that Szymon seized upon the moment. He felt for a note in his pocket and handed it to him. 'I think you dropped this,' he said calmly, keeping his eyes level with Groening's.

Groening looked unsure, then with a slight nod of the head, took the proffered note.

'A place called Bergen – another prison camp. In the north. You leave in four days on the first train out.'

Groening quickly walked away from him, his hand already ferrying the money to his pocket.

They were leaving and heading north, to Bergen, a place Szymon had never heard of. They had to move fast, that much was clear.

Four days. That was all they had.

THIRTY-TWO

MIA

Görlitz

'Now you tell me your story,' Marlena demanded, abruptly stopping her account. 'You know everything now. Now is your turn.' She folded her arms authoritatively.

'But you haven't told me about what happened next. What happened, Marlena?'

'That part is not my story to tell.'

'Then whose is it?'

She shrugged. 'Maybe Tadeusz. Maybe your grandmother. Szymon too, but he is dead now.' She looked at the window, where outside I knew the graveyard sat. I shivered.

Tired and lacking in any sort of energy to argue with her, I pushed myself away from the table in order to get to my feet. 'We should see Grandma,' I told her and made to stand.

'Sit!' she commanded.

Oddly scared at her tone, I did as she commanded.

'Now. You *tell me* your story so that when we go to the hospital today, I can tell my friend – my closest friend, that you are OK. That you have spoken so all the ghosts inside you are gone and now you are strong again. You promised me. We made deal!'

'I don't want to.' I stared into my empty coffee cup. I had hoped that by buying myself some time with Marlena going first, then one of two things would have happened – either I would have found the courage to put into words what I was dreading to say, or Marlena would have forgotten that I had to tell her a story next. It seemed that neither one had transpired.

'Come, Mia. You promise me. Please, I promise you it will be good for you.'

She reached out and her fingers traced one of the bruises on my arm. It was still blue, even after a month. I didn't want to tell her what it had looked like at first. How it was so red that I had thought my blood was going to push through the skin, of how it had quickly turned black with violent purple edges and that I had worried that it would forever mark me.

Her fingertip gently circled it over and over again.

'I – I don't know where to begin,' I murmured anxiously.

'You start where you like. It doesn't matter to me,' she said kindly. 'Mia, look at me.'

I raised my eyes to meet hers. 'This thing. This thing on your arm – I don't know the English word for it. But I know that it has come from someone else. Yes?'

I nodded and swallowed a lump in my throat.

'I just want you to say, in words what happened to you. What this man did. You need to, Mia. You need to not be afraid to say the words. You cannot be afraid to speak.'

I chewed on the inside of my lip as I thought back to that relationship and swallowed deeply again, still not managing to get rid of that ball in my throat that was making it hard to think straight.

'Go on. Be brave,' Marlena urged.

'It's hard to say. I don't know. I mean, Will, my boyfriend, he was fine at first. Everything was fine,' I began.

'But then it wasn't fine?' she prompted.

'No,' I said, feeling the tears streaking down my face. 'No. Then it wasn't fine at all.'

Bit by bit, through tears, through a snotty nose, I managed to tell Marlena my tale of woe. A tale that I still could not believe had happened to me.

I was doing well at work and then I met him in a bar. It wasn't anything big; I don't think I even liked him to begin with – he was too slick, too confident. He was a banker, in the City and I don't know, there was just something about him that I was attracted to and was repelled by at the same time.

He was nice at first. Too nice. He saw that I was not as interested in him as perhaps other girls had been, so he bombarded me with romance. Flowers, chocolates, notes at work – anything and everything he could think of to make me his.

I held out for a few weeks until a friend at work said that he was dreamy, that I wouldn't find anyone else like him and I decided then to give him a chance.

It was the worst decision I ever made.

After about six months of romance, trips away and spending all our free time together, I finally fell for him – head over heels like a lovesick puppy. But it was then that the real Will made an appearance.

Slowly at first – almost imperceptibly. He would comment on my clothes, my weight, but in such a way that it didn't seem like a criticism – he was clever.

'Darling,' he'd say, 'you'd look so good in this dress, but I'm not sure it will fit you right.'

I know it sounds stupid that I didn't pick up on it. I should have – would have – but in my addled, lovesick mind he was saying things for my own good.

He bought me a gym membership – 'We can go together,' he had said. But he never came with me, and instead would ask me each day how long I'd been there for, how well I was doing and he was so proud of me.

I had basked beneath his praise – I sought it out as the months went on. I wanted to be perfect for him, all the time.

The problem was that he began to take up so much of my life that my work started to suffer.

'Don't go to Spain,' he'd say when I had a two-week work trip with the company partners. 'I'll miss you too much.'

He went on and on, so that in the end I called in sick, and we spent two weeks together at my flat, cosied up in bed, watching movies, and I thought it was the most romantic, perfect thing ever. I loved how I could snuggle into his neck, inhaling that scent that was just him – a mixture of tobacco, of aftershave and his sweat – a scent that now makes me nauseous.

We had been together for about a year, maybe a bit more, when one evening everything changed. I was getting ready to go out with him, a new red dress that he had bought me hanging up as I did my make-up.

He had stormed into the flat, his face almost grey with anger. 'What the fuck are you doing?' he screamed at me.

I had turned to look at him, sure that this was some sort of joke that I didn't understand. Then, before I knew it, he raced towards me and hit me so hard in the face that I fell against the sink and slumped down onto the floor.

I sat on the floor, stunned. I raised my hand to my face and then saw my palm crimson red. My nose was busted.

'You bring this on yourself,' he spat. 'Do you know how hard my day at work has been? You didn't even ask! You just stand in front of the mirror, putting make-up on that face of yours, with no thought about what I am going through!'

'I – I didn't know you'd come home,' I spluttered. 'I was just getting ready for the dinner.'

'There's no dinner, stupid! If you'd given yourself two seconds to answer a call – yes! I called you an hour ago and you didn't answer – then you'd know it was cancelled. You'd know that I lost a shitload of money today and you'd be at the fucking door, ready to ask me how I was. But no – you're too stupid for that.'

I didn't know what to say. There was a voice inside me that told me he was wrong – that I should be angry with him, but I just couldn't believe what had happened, so I nodded along with him – appeasing him, accepting eventually that it was all my fault.

As suddenly as the rage had come, it disappeared, and he became remorseful. He cried and promised he would never do it again. That he was just so stressed it had all come out.

That evening he cleaned my face, dressed me in my pyjamas like a small child and put me to bed, all the while lamenting how sorry he was.

I'm ashamed to say that I forgave him. I believed that he hadn't meant it and would never do it again. I wanted the old Will to come back – the romantic one: the one that love-bombed me in the first few weeks of meeting me because he couldn't possibly see a life without me.

Of course, it didn't get any better. It got worse. The beatings became more frequent. The apologies less and less, until I was sure that I was the one to blame for the situation. That I had to be perfect for him at all times, wait on him hand and foot. But it was never enough.

At work, I couldn't concentrate. I spent so much time thinking about him – wondering what mood he would be in when I got home, what I should cook, what I should wear – that soon my boss noticed and I knew, deep down, that my career was coming to an end.

The day he broke up with me was strange. I'd come back to my flat which he had basically lived in for the past two years, to find him sat on the couch, an unusual smile on his face. There was a moment of pure fear at seeing him there – a moment when I wanted to run out of the apartment and never come back. But conversely there was still love there – still this desperate feeling I had of wanting him to love me like he had used to. I pulled the sleeves of my hoodie over my arms, covering up the damage he had inflicted the night before: hitting me over and over again as I raised my hands and arms up to protect my face, he had sent my skin into a kaleidoscope of bruises.

He stood, took my face in his hands, and didn't yell at me because I had flinched at his touch.

'Sweetheart, you look exhausted.' He led me to the couch.

'I'm OK,' I said brightly, not wanting him to start a fight about who worked harder and how pathetic I was for being tired.

'Look. I know things have been a little – *tricky* lately.' He smiled at me. 'But I think it's just all come to a head, hasn't it?'

I nodded, not sure what else I was supposed to do.

'You see... The thing is, we're not right for each other. You've tried, I see that and I appreciate it. But at the end of the day, there's nothing left – no love left.'

I opened my mouth, wanting to protest that I loved him. That I couldn't be parted from him, but he shushed me.

'I've met someone else. Now, before you get all hysterical, I think we both knew it was going to happen. And really, what did you expect? The girl I met two years ago is gone and I'm not sure who you are any more. You used to be focused on your career, have friends – but now... I mean look at you.'

Again, I nodded. Stupidly agreeing. He was right. The old Mia was gone. The old Mia had friends, went out, worked twelve-hour days and loved it. Now, I was a mess.

'So you see why I had to look elsewhere, don't you, darling? I had no choice.'

He stood once more, then bent down and kissed me on the cheek. 'I've done what I can for you, Mia. I'm sorry that this might hurt you. But I think it's for the best.'

That's when I thanked him. I thanked him for trying to help me. I thanked him for being with me. Then I wished him luck in his new relationship.

And now here I was in a kitchen in Germany with my grandmother's best friend, weeping into her shoulder, shuddering with everything that had happened to me.

She rocked me like a baby and whispered that everything was going to be all right. That I had to let it out – I had to cry, scream and feel it all so I could finally put it all to rest.

I let Marlena hold me while I cried. He had abused me, had made me think everything was my fault, had eroded my confidence so that I was a shadow of myself – a ghost – just like the ghosts outside in the graveyard.

Soon, the tears stopped, and I became a hiccupping snotty mess. Marlena let me go and found some tissues in her handbag. She gently wiped my face, as if I was a small child in her care. 'Come,' she said. 'Let's go and see your grandmother, yes?' We are family. You are safe now. You will be you again. I promise. And we go and see her, and we tell her you are fine now. You will be you again, I promise you that.'

I let Marlena coddle me. She chose my clothes for the day and lamented that I seemed to have brought only baggy jumpers in greys and blacks, finally finding one that she decided would cheer me up. A pale blue sweater, tight-fitting, and a pair of jeans.

'There, *darlink*,' she said, observing me proudly. 'More like you, yes? No more hiding in big clothes.'

I hadn't even realised that my wardrobe had drastically changed in the final few months with Will. Gone was the colour, the figure-hugging clothes, short sleeves and dresses. I had to hide my arms lest people comment on the bruises that peppered my skin – some yellowing with age, some red, purple and blue with freshness.

Had everyone noticed? Grandma had known just from my tone on the phone to her, and perhaps my changed demeanour on our visits. But had everyone known? When I had gone to the shop, or at work, had everyone been commenting and feeling sorry for me?

'Come, be quick,' Marlena chided, as I dressed.

I did as I was told and let her slick some of her lipstick on my lips, mirroring her as she puckered her own together in a fake kiss.

'There. *Perfeck*!' she exclaimed.

The two of us left the apartment and were a few steps from the bottom of the staircase when Tadeusz's door swung open.

He seemed surprised to see Marlena with me and opened and closed his mouth as he reworded what he was going to say.

'Mia,' he greeted me. 'Marlena.'

'Tadeusz. *Darlink*,' Marlena purred and bustled past me. 'We are going to the hospital. Will you come with us?'

He shook his head. 'Mia, I need to talk with you. I could not sleep last night, and I need to tell you some things so that I can finally get some rest. Please. Will you come inside?'

I looked to Marlena to see what she thought and with a gentle nod of the head, she gave me her blessing.

'I come inside too!' she declared and pushed past Tadeusz. 'You never let me come here. I want to see!'

I followed Marlena inside with less enthusiasm than she displayed, oddly worried about what it was that he wanted to tell me.

I sat in the same armchair as I had the previous night and let Marlena and Tadeusz chatter for a moment in Polish. Then they both sat and stared at me for a moment, making me wonder what Marlena had just told Tadeusz.

'Marlena has said that she told you about Szymon bribing a guard? Yes?'

I nodded.

'OK. Then I will tell you how he escaped and then what happened after that. And then maybe you can make your decision.'

'What decision?'

Tadeusz softly shook his head. 'Not yet. First of all, I need to tell you about it. You need to see it now through *my* eyes. Let me tell you about the day Szymon escaped and then you can ask your questions, yes?'

The pair of them waited for my answer. Of course I was going to agree, but at the same time, I couldn't help but take some measure of pleasure in making them wait, just as they were doing to me.

'Fine. I agree.'

Tadeusz clasped his hands together and leaned back in his chair. 'So, the day Szymon escaped,' he began, 'that day changed everything for everyone...'

THIRTY-THREE

TADEUSZ

Görlitz
July 1942

The night before was humid – an Indian summer, they called it. The kind of heat that stuck nightshirts to backs and bedsheets to legs. The kind of heat that felt like a thick soup seeping through cracked windows and half-open shutters. When dogs were stupefied and could not bark if an intruder leaped upon them; when even the wail of the homeless cat was silenced, as was the sedentary hum of crickets in the long grass.

Crackles of thunder echoed in the night, as if someone upstairs were moving furniture, whilst flashes of lightning lit up the river, yet would not yield themselves to the comfort of rain.

Tadeusz felt an unease with the weather. It was as though the storm had come as a warning of something sinister. He held the final postcard from Szymon in his hand – reading the words over and over again. Szymon had bribed a guard called Groening. That morning, when they would be led over the bridge and past the graveyard to the train station, Groening would stop the line of men, seemingly worried about something up ahead. At that moment, Stanislaw, Pawel and Szymon would break free, head for the river and Groening would shoot at them, purposely missing them, and announce that they were dead to the other guards. It would be dark enough still for no one to know for sure, but Szymon had said that Groening could be trusted and that he would let them go free. All he wanted was more money.

Tadeusz was to wait for Szymon in the graveyard and somehow get them to safety. There were no instructions as to how he was to do this – no clue as to what would happen, and he wasn't sure that they should trust this Groening completely. Although the money that he wanted did indicate that he was willing to do it – for a price.

Tadeusz's uncle had secured the money. From where and from whom, Tadeusz did not know. He had prodded and probed at his uncle to tell him more, but he had refused.

That night, Tadeusz lay on his narrow bed, the window open letting in a hint of a breeze whilst his mind churned over the thoughts of what was going to happen in a few hours' time. Would it go wrong? Would Groening do what he was supposed to?

'Tadeusz!' A half shout, half whisper came from outside.

He turned on his side and propped himself up. Had he imagined it?

'Tadeusz!' The voice came again, more insistent now.

He stood and went to the window, seeing the shadowy outline of Ilse below, who waved her arm in the air in greeting.

'Let me in!'

Despite the seriousness of the evening, and the fact that in just a few hours he would be helping his cousin in a daring and dangerous escape, he felt a flutter of excitement at seeing Ilse, at letting her in and having her to himself for a while.

He reached the bookshop door, opened it and grasped the bell before it could announce a visitor and wake his uncle, who was sleeping in his office.

'What are you doing here?' he asked, as she pushed past him into the shop.

'I couldn't sleep.' She looked at him, her eyes bright even in the gloom. 'Can you? Could you sleep?'

He closed the door behind her and locked it.

'You shouldn't be here,' he said. 'What if your parents see that you are gone?'

'Who cares!' she responded.

He raised his finger to his lips and gestured at the office.

She nodded, then held her own finger over her lips, then she pointed upstairs.

'No,' he hissed. But she wasn't listening to him and had already made her way to the small staircase and was sneaking up each step.

He hurried after her, but she was quicker, and he found her sat on his bed.

'So, this is where you've been hiding then!'

'It is.' He closed the door and sat across from her in an armchair.

She switched on a small lamp and got up and closed the curtains. 'Much better,' she announced.

'Why are you here, Ilse?'

She sat once more on his bed and gave a slight shrug and began to finger at the corner of his pillowcase. 'Yesterday when your uncle told me that Szymon had the money and the escape was planned, I couldn't believe it. I mean, it's all happening so quickly, isn't it. Just three days ago, I got him the money and now he's going to be free.'

'He is. And thank you. I haven't seen you to say this, but from what my uncle told me, you were brave – and daring. I mean, throwing a shoe into the hole was ingenious!'

She grinned at him. 'You think so – you really think I was brave?'

'I do.' He sat beside her. 'Really, Ilse, we couldn't have done it without you.'

'So can I come tonight, with you to help?' she asked, her shoulder leaning against his.

He shook his head gently. 'It's not safe, Ilse. It wouldn't be safe.'

'Please,' she whined. 'I've been a part of it from the start and you can't cut me out now – not when there's a daring escape about to happen!'

He realised then that she had not much changed since she had been a girl. She was a woman, yes, but she had romanticised something that was life and death – she saw only characters in books, heroes and heroines and all the made-up nonsense that simply did not exist in real life.

'You should go home.' He leaned forward and placed his forearms on his knees, clasping his hands together.

'Why? Why can't I come and help you?'

'Because you can't, Ilse. I wouldn't want to put you in danger like that.'

'It's because I'm a woman, isn't it? If I were a man, you'd let me help you.' She stood up abruptly, stroppily folding her arms and looking at him like one of his teachers used to at school when he was making too much noise.

'No, I wouldn't. I wouldn't let anyone else help. I wouldn't risk anyone's life for this.'

'Fine,' she said. 'I'll go. But you know. You do need me. You'll see.' She laughed at him and left as suddenly as she had arrived, leaving Tadeusz wondering what she meant and whether she felt that little jump in her belly like he did when he saw her.

THIRTY-FOUR

MIA

Görlitz
Thursday, 11 February 1999

Suddenly, Tadeusz stopped. A silent look passed between him and Marlena.

'What, what is it?' I asked.

'There is nothing more there,' Marlena said, prompting Tadeusz to nod his head in agreement. 'Tell her about the morning – the morning you went to the graveyard.'

He opened his mouth, but I interrupted, 'What else happened that evening? Why did you stop? Is there something else that she said or did?'

Tadeusz dragged a hand over his face as if trying to wipe away the tiredness and perhaps something more. 'There is nothing else there, as Marlena said. Not all of my story is just mine,' he added cryptically.

Before I could insist that he tell me more, Marlena began to talk in rapid Polish, Tadeusz's head bobbing along in agreement.

'Now listen, Mia. You listen to this bit that Tadeusz can tell you. And then we go and see your grandmother, yes? It is a very big day today – you know, all the things we talk about before, and now Tadeusz, he is trying to do the same as you. You before are telling me something very hard for you to say out loud. Tadeusz the same. So listen and be patient.'

I couldn't not agree to her argument. If this was hard for Tadeusz to say, then I had to be less demanding. I knew, all too well and too recently, how finding the right words to say could be difficult, and once they were out, there was no putting them back.

'Please. Do go ahead if you want to, Tadeusz,' I said kindly. 'Really. It's up to you what you say. It's not for me to make you say something you're not ready to.'

'Thank you,' he said, wiping his face once more, then he gave a cough and began to speak once more.

THIRTY-FIVE

TADEUSZ

Görlitz
July 1942

Tadeusz left the bookshop at 3 a.m., closing the door softly behind him, noting the tinkling of the bell as he did so. Outside, the witching hour was upon the town; sleeping bodies twisted in their sheets as they dreamt, and Tadeusz remembered a tale Ilse had once told him, of how during the witching hour, the sick would die, and evil would be abroad.

Despite himself, he felt a shiver of fear as he passed the deep shadows in alleyways, wondering if the evil Ilse had spoken of might be lurking there, waiting for him.

From the deep blue of the night sky the screech of an owl came, and he tried to find it, hoping to see a good omen for what he was about to do. Would it work? Would Szymon be able to get free, and would this Herr Groening let it happen?

There was so much that could go wrong, and Tadeusz told himself that, no matter what, this time he would not leave Szymon behind.

He turned right, nearing the river, sneaking down the

embankment under the shroud of shadows until he smelled the familiar lemony scent of conifers and knew he had reached the graveyard.

He felt his way through the small gap between the trees, the rubbery-like stems leaving their scent on his fingers.

As soon as he was through, a chill washed over him that he suspected most people would find uncomfortable, but he knew this graveyard and found the cold it provided somewhat soothing.

He was unsure whether to stand or to sit – there was still an hour or so to wait, but he was afraid that if he settled himself down onto the damp ground, there was a chance his eyes would betray him and he would fall asleep.

Before he could make a decision, a rustle came from the undergrowth. Thinking that a river rat had made its home there, he began to stamp his feet on the ground to shoo it away.

'Calm down!' a voice came from behind a thickly ivy-covered headstone. A voice he knew.

'Ilse, what the *hell* are you doing here?'

Her face appeared from behind the tombstone, smiling and mischievous as if she did not realise the danger that she had put herself in.

'You know me,' she said, as she dusted the back of her black skirt that made her seem as if she had no legs in the thick darkness. 'I don't do anything that someone tells me to do. You should know that by now.'

He took a step closer to her and stubbed his toe on the stone, making him wince with pain and hop about as it spread through his foot.

Ilse laughed and then came to his aid, taking his arm and making him sit on the ground. 'It's fine,' she told him. 'Just a toe. Men make such a fuss about pain, you know.'

'Ilse,' he said through gritted teeth, 'I really don't think you realise the danger you are putting yourself in. Like I told you before, this isn't a game.'

'I know it isn't. Do you think I'm that stupid? I was just trying to lighten the mood – just like you used to. Don't you remember – when we were young, you were all smiley and happy, joking all the time and Szymon was the serious one. Now you've turned into him.'

'I lost my humour a while ago,' he said, taking off his shoe to inspect his big toe.

'When was that?'

'Ilse,' he sighed, 'just stop talking for a minute, would you?' He looked to her and saw that instead of being offended, she merely grinned at him, then closed her mouth with deliberate force, making it crease into a thin line.

He needed her to leave. She could not stay, but he wasn't sure how to make her go without literally picking her up and carrying her home and he knew that she would not go easily.

Before he could argue, a shout came from the bridge. It couldn't be – it was too early, surely? Tadeusz shoved his foot into his shoe and told Ilse to stay hidden behind the gravestone. For once, she listened and hid herself well.

He popped his head out through the gap and saw a clump of men stood under a bright street lamp, whilst shouts came from somewhere around them. He squinted, trying to see if he could make out Szymon amongst the group, but he could not distinguish one from the other.

Within seconds, two shadowy figures appeared, running in the direction of the river. More cries from the bridge followed, accompanied by the *ping ping* of neat gunfire.

It was time. He felt his heart racing as the two men ran through the shallows, water spraying up and catching the street lights. Was one of them Szymon? Which one? He ached to race out and find him but knew he had to stay and wait and Szymon would come to him.

Suddenly, the gunfire seemed much closer, and one man fell into the water, his arms outstretched as if he would be able to save himself.

Panic infused Tadeusz – this wasn't right. No one was meant to be shot! They were meant to be set *free*. His thoughts began to tumble, wondering if the man face down in the shallows was Szymon; then, relief hit him when as if from nowhere, Szymon appeared, half running, holding his own waist, his head bowed. He fell into Tadeusz's arms, breathing heavily, his chest sounding a sinister rattle.

'He's – he's...' Szymon tried to say, but his breathing would not allow him to get the words out.

Tadeusz dragged him into the graveyard and sat him down, leaning his back against the ivy-strewn gravestone.

'What's happened? What's wrong?' Ilse stood up and looked to Tadeusz with wide eyes. 'I – I don't understand.'

'Someone was shot,' Tadeusz said, and just as he spoke another round rang out, followed this time by a cry and a splash as the other man hit the water.

Tadeusz crouched down and held his cousin's face in his hands, feeling his cheekbones jutting out from his skin. 'Szymon, I'm here. Just breathe,' Tadeusz told him, but Szymon could not catch his breath and his eyes roamed wildly as though he could no longer control them.

'He's sick.' He felt Ilse next to him and watched as she reached out and placed her palm flat on his forehead. 'He's really hot. He's really sick, Tadeusz,' she said with a quiver in her voice.

Tadeusz stood. 'We need to get him out of here, now!' He grabbed one of Szymon's arms and Ilse took the other, both of them pulling him to his feet for a brief second before Tadeusz smelled it. Cigarette smoke. They were not alone.

'You must be Tadeusz.'

Tadeusz turned and Szymon slipped from his grasp and

tumbled back down, wheezing heavily.

'You see, I have a problem,' the voice said, stepping slowly into a patch of moonlight, revealing a young soldier, a cigarette clamped between his teeth.

It was then that Tadeusz looked down and saw in the other man's hand a gun, pointed at him. 'Herr Groening?' he stupidly asked.

'Obviously. Where's the money?'

Tadeusz dipped his hand into his pocket and drew out the wad of notes that his uncle had given him.

'Many thanks.' Groening took the money and pocketed it but did not move away. 'Now. Here's the problem I have.' Groening flicked hot ash at Tadeusz, where it smouldered for a second before disappearing into the darkness. 'Three men ran away, and, at the moment, I only have two. So there's a choice to be made, I suppose, and because I am a generous man, I'm giving Szymon here the option to get back in line with the others, or I can simply shoot him. Either way it matters little, but we must be pedantic about our number of prisoners, mustn't we?'

It was then that Szymon tried to speak once more. 'But you said... You promised...' he tried breathlessly.

'I say lots of things. And you don't honestly think I was friends with you, do you? That I would risk my *career* because of you and for a few notes?'

'But—' Szymon tried again, but he could not speak, so Tadeusz took a step nearer to Groening. 'You have the money, what more do you need? Just say he ran away, and that you couldn't find him.'

'And become a laughing stock? I hardly think so!'

'We'll give you more money!' Ilse's voice piped up and Tadeusz saw that Groening had not yet registered her, half-hidden in her dark clothing and the shadows.

'And who is this here?' Groening asked, a little amusement

lacing his tone.

'We'll give you more. Just let him go.'

Groening shook his head. 'Like I said, I don't want to be a laughing stock, now do I?'

'But he's *sick!*' Ilse cried. 'You can't take him back. Please.'

Tadeusz eyed the gun in his hands. Could he launch himself on top of it, perhaps, and give Ilse and Szymon time to get away? But then Ilse could barely support Szymon alone and how far would they get?

He could feel sweat collecting on the nape of his neck and tracking its way down his back. Then, he knew what to do.

'Take me instead,' he said. 'Take me. I look like him, I'm Polish, no one will know any difference. He cannot go – he's too sick. Take me instead.'

There was a ripple of silence before it was filled with a gruff laugh from Groening. 'You are joking, surely?'

'No. No, I'm not. Take me. We'll give you more money too. That way you win. Your comrades know you shot two men and brought back the third and each month we will ensure you are paid for this kindness.'

'How much?' Groening asked, wavering.

'As much as we can.' Tadeusz looked to Ilse, pleading with his eyes, hoping that she would agree to help, but she said nothing.

He turned back to Groening. 'You can have my parents' house. Szymon will give you the deed. It is yours.'

'It belongs to the Reich anyway,' Groening countered.

'Yes, but it will be in your name – yours not the Reich's. It is big – four bedrooms, acres of land. You can have it.'

'No...' Szymon quietly wheezed, but Tadeusz ignored him. 'Do it. You can give me a good beating if that makes you look even better. I don't care. Shoot me once I'm in line – just leave Szymon be.'

Groening flicked his cigarette and ground it into the dirt.

'The house, money every month, and any other favour I need,' he offered.

'Done,' Tadeusz held out his hand for Groening to take and shake, but he simply laughed at the gesture.

Quickly, Tadeusz undressed, stripping away his clothing and then began to undress Szymon, taking from him the thin light blue shirt he wore and brown trousers.

'Don't – don't do this, Tadeusz,' Szymon pleaded. 'You don't have to do this.'

'I do and I will.' He leaned in close to Szymon and kissed his cousin on the cheek.

'Come on, let's go!' Groening leaned in to Tadeusz and grabbed him roughly by the arm.

As he was dragged away, he saw Ilse, her face half-lit by the moonlight. 'Take care of him, Ilse! Please, for me. Take care of him and wait for me. I promise I will be home... please.'

As Tadeusz was pushed into line on the bridge, a few of the men who dared to raise their eyes from their boots gave him a funny look. Even one of the guards looked curiously at him.

'There's two dead in the river,' Groening spoke to the other guards. 'Just leave them there. The current will take them.'

'That was good shooting,' one of the guards congratulated him, and Tadeusz saw him clap him on the back. 'Two good shots. You'll drink with us tonight. Raise a glass. Just a shame you didn't get the other one.'

All at once, the guards' eyes were on him. He wished he could melt into the shadows and hoped that the light was not bright enough to show them that suddenly, Szymon was taller, broader and his shirt and trousers no longer fitted him.

Groening blew a whistle, the noise so shrill that the man next to him held his hands over his ears for a second before the men all started to walk forward.

'Better get moving,' Groening said, as Tadeusz walked past him. 'Better get rid of them all.'

THIRTY-SIX

MIA

Görlitz
Thursday, 11 February 1999

Tadeusz stopped speaking. His head hung low to his chest, and I was sure that he was crying.

'You took his place?' I gasped, repeating what he had just said.

'I had no choice. That Groening, he was going to kill us to show how he was a big, strong man like the other guards. What choice did I have? He was an evil man, Mia, you could see it, sly and delighting in the game that he had devised. Why Szymon had ever trusted him, I don't know. But then, Szymon did not see the bad in people – he never could.'

I shook my head in disbelief. Tadeusz took his place and went to Belsen. A place I knew about. A place where bodies were heaped in piles when the British arrived, starved down to the bone.

'Wait.' I suddenly realised something. 'You said that after this, I had a decision to make – what is it?'

A silent look between Tadeusz and Marlena made me

realise that there was something he had still not said. Marlena fired something off in rapid Polish and Tadeusz waved his hands about as he replied before they both fell silent once more.

'It is not for him to say,' Marlena finally said to me. 'It is not his story to tell. Like I said before, he cannot tell you this – it is only for one person to say.'

'Grandma,' I finished for her.

'Yes.'

I pushed myself up and looked to Marlena. 'We should go and see her. We need to go now.'

There was a fervour within me – whether it was the fact that I had unburdened myself to Marlena, or because Tadeusz and Marlena had trusted me enough to tell me what they knew, I just had to know what this decision was.

I had to let my grandmother tell her story.

THIRTY-SEVEN

ILSE

Görlitz City Hospital
Thursday, 11 February 1999

Where is everyone? It is almost the afternoon, and yet neither Marlena nor Mia have come to visit me. I have found that I do not like to be alone at the moment. I used to enjoy my own company, but now, my thoughts and emotions are so twisted and churned up that it makes me scared, as I am not sure what is real and what is not any more. And so, I write. I write whilst I can, because then at least I feel a little less alone and confused.

I wish they would hurry up and arrive. I have refused my pain medication this morning just so that I could stay awake and lucid enough to see them – to talk to them about some things that haven't been said yet and desperately need to be.

I have found myself crying this morning – off and on – not about anything in particular, but the tears just come abruptly and as soon as they appear, they disappear again, and I can't seem to understand what is happening to me or why I am upset.

I am not a crier; never have been. Maybe it is all the tears that I never cried trying now to escape me whilst they still can.

I feel nauseous again so have refused my breakfast and the nurse has chastised me and told me she will tell the doctor about it. I laughed at her – I'm dying; who cares if I eat the slop of porridge or a dry piece of toast?

Another nurse came in to remove the tray and asked me how I was feeling and whether she could call anyone for me. I stupidly told her to call my son, forgetting for a moment that he was dead, and then realising I had said the wrong thing, I began to cry.

She was kind, this nurse and held me whilst I sobbed, and once the tears had dried up, she sat and asked me about my son, about my family, and I told her what I could. I think I even told her things that were untrue – but that is just the cancer changing my memories.

'You must have been young, when you had him,' she said.

'Yes, I was. Very young.'

'Your husband must have loved you very much.'

I nodded but said nothing more.

As soon as she left, I wiped my face with a corner of the sheet. How stupid to cry about that and in front of a stranger! Why is my brain doing this to me?

My husband, the nurse had said. A *husband*. I suddenly find myself laughing. The word husband is so odd to me, I have never had one of those – I never had a wedding, nor someone to look after me.

Suddenly, Mia is here, beside the bed, and she is asking what I am writing. And I tell her I am writing that it is funny to think that I had a husband. She doesn't understand and I promise to stop now and explain myself.

A husband, I am thinking still – *how funny*.

THIRTY-EIGHT

MIA

Görlitz City Hospital
Thursday, 11 February 1999

'Grandma, what are you talking about?' I took the pen out of her hand and closed the notebook she was scrawling in, the handwriting so messy I wasn't sure it was even legible.

'A husband, Mia. I never had one of those, did I?'

I thought she was delusional, that the cancer had spread further, but she seemed bright-eyed and alert. 'You did. Remember Grandpa?' I asked her carefully, watching to see if she understood what I was saying.

'Marlena!' Grandma noticed her friend who stood in the doorway, chatting to a nurse. 'Come in. I expect she knows nearly everything now, does she?'

I looked to Marlena who grinned at her and then gave me a nod. 'She know, *darlink*, nearly everything.'

'You told her then. Spilled the beans. You said you would if I didn't.' Grandma let Marlena hold her close for a minute, then Marlena plonked herself down in a chair, leaving me stood at the edge of the bed, wondering what the hell was going on.

'You look confused, Mia,' Grandma said, then patted the bed. 'Come here. Come sit next to me.'

I sat carefully on the bed, scared to disturb the central line that snaked under the covers.

'You planned this?' I asked her, finally cottoning on.

She shook her head wearily. 'Not at first. No. But then, that day I mentioned Szymon, I knew my mind was doing strange things and that soon I might be saying all sorts of things. You see, I kept getting confused too – about Szymon – about who he was. Because he wasn't one person, was he – he was two. He was Tadeusz also. He became him that day he took his place. So sometimes when I think of them, it is as though they both become one and the same in my mind.

'Marlena told me that she had told you about my childhood and she told me that I should tell you about my life – about who I *really* am. She reminded me of a day when we had been at the graveyard and how I had been obsessed with a grave.'

'Otto's?' I asked her.

'Indeed. Otto's grave. I had said to Marlena that day that I hoped when I was dead, someone would remember me, and she reminded me of the fact that my closest relative didn't even know who I really was. So, I agreed. I said she could tell you what she could. But then there was a part that only I could say.'

'And Tadeusz, he was in on it too?'

It was then her turn to look confused. She switched her glance from me to Marlena and then back again.

'He came to see you. You not remember?' Marlena tentatively asked her. 'He say he read something to you?'

'No. Wait. Yes' – her eyes were scrunched up as she thought – 'He came, but he said some awful things, but I don't really remember them. The drugs do it – if I don't take them, I can think a little clearer, but that day I had taken them and I can't remember what he said. Did he say that he forgives me?' she asked Marlena.

'Why would Tadeusz need to forgive *you*?' I reached out and took her hand in mine. 'He told me how you had helped get the money to Szymon, how you were at the graveyard that night and how he had asked you to take care of Szymon.'

She nodded. 'He did ask me to. But that's the problem – one of them anyway. I didn't, did I? I ran away.'

'Where to? To England?'

'Yes. To England. But you have to know why I did – how I didn't have much choice in the matter.'

'I get tea, yes? From the machine.' Marlena stood. 'I get tea and you say the things you need to and I come back.'

'Bring coffee if you can. They won't give me coffee so try and sneak some in, will you?' my grandmother asked. There was a childish way in which she had just spoken with Marlena and all at once I could see that the old Ilse – the adventurous, happy, loving girl had not gone completely.

Marlena left us alone and I took the vacated chair, the warmth of Marlena's bottom still on the beige faux-leather seat.

'It's hard for me to tell you this, Mia, because I am not proud of myself at all, and I need you to understand that. I need you to understand that I was young and foolish and at times, stupid. No – don't try and interrupt. I was and that's a fact that cannot be disputed. Tell me you understand this before I start?'

'I understand,' I said, then saw her grimace with a sudden pain, holding her hand to her head and closing her eyes.

'No. No, I'm fine,' she told me. 'Do not under any circumstances get that nurse. I don't want medication. I need to stay awake. I need to tell you this.'

I sat waiting in the chair as she rubbed at her forehead, every ounce of me wanting to take the pain away for her, to feel it myself so that she wouldn't have to.

'Okay,' she said, letting her hand drop to the covers. 'Did Tadeusz tell you about the night before the escape – how I had come to see him?'

I told her that he had, but that he said there was a brief conversation and disagreement about her helping and she had left.

'Ah, he's still a gentleman then. Good. I'm glad.'

'What do you mean?'

'I'm glad he didn't tell you why I really went there that night. What had happened with me and Marlena and how perhaps, I sought something in Tadeusz that night to prove something to myself...'

Sitting back, I let her talk, let her get all the words out that she had never said. I wanted her to tell her story before it was too late.

THIRTY-NINE

ILSE

Görlitz City Hospital
Thursday, 11 February 1999

Again, Mia, I just want to tell you that I know how foolish I was
back then. I was always a little foolish – whether it was because
I was shielded from a lot of hardships because my parents were
wealthy, I don't know. But I often wondered if I had had
different parents, a different upbringing, whether that would
have made me a different person too – perhaps a wiser one.

It's too late to say now what would have been, or could have
been and, quite frankly, it wouldn't change anything at all.

Where was I? Oh yes. The night before the escape. It
sounds romantic, doesn't it? *The night before the escape.* Like a
book or a film that would give you this big action-packed adventure and you could feel it, see it, almost taste the danger.

I'm afraid I don't have the right words to evoke that for you,
Mia. I only have the words that are left in this mind of mine,
and every day, one by one they are disappearing.

That night, it was hot. I remember that. The air was so thick
you could almost feel that you could bite into it.

Marlena was at my house for dinner, and afterwards we had sat outside in the garden, going over and over again what had happened at the factory, how daring it all was and how my father was still mad at me for going over to the foundations that day. Thankfully, he had not told Mother about this escapade of mine, so for that I was grateful, and I was thus free from a serious scolding from her.

We talked that evening about a lot of things, I suppose. About what our lives would be like when Szymon was free, how we would all be together again, just like we had been that summer.

'Do you think you will fall in love with him again?' Marlena asked me.

The question had come out of nowhere it seemed, and I remember it so clearly – *do you think you will fall in love with him again?*

I assured her that I wouldn't – couldn't – that I wasn't sure if I had ever really loved him in the first place.

'And Tadeusz? You don't love him either?' she then asked me.

I had once more assured her that I did not.

'Good,' she had said. Then, she took my hand in hers.

She had often done this – we were friends, so it was entirely normal for us to be close in this way, but there was something different that evening. Something in the way she held my hand gently, the way she stroked the back of it with her thumb that made me suddenly pull my hand away.

She said nothing and neither did I, perhaps both of us afraid to put into words what Marlena really felt for me.

She stood after a minute or two, ready to leave, and I stood too. Before I knew what was happening, she had kissed me on my lips. A full kiss and I had responded.

Slowly, she pulled away and we stared at each other for a moment.

'I – I don't feel that way about you,' I spluttered.

'Are you sure?' she asked.

I wasn't sure, if I am completely honest with myself. I wasn't sure at all. I knew I loved her, but was that the same as being in love? What did I know – I had thought I was in love with Szymon, and it turned out I was wrong about that.

She didn't press me for an answer, but left me in the garden that night feeling confused and a little scared.

Was I like Marlena, I wondered? *Did I like women?*

I had always known that Marlena liked girls and not boys – neither of us had spoken of it because it wasn't something then that you spoke about. And I had often wondered if she could ever really be happy as her options were to live her life as a spinster, and have a companion, or marry a man and try to pretend she was someone that she wasn't.

I didn't want to be a spinster. I didn't want to be one of those women that were quietly gossiped about in parlour rooms by the likes of my mother and her friends. There was a teacher at my school who had never married, but she lived with another unmarried woman. To me, I couldn't see the problem, but I had once heard my mother and her friends talking about how unseemly it was, how she would quite rightly go to hell and that none of them thought she should be allowed to teach their daughters.

That humid evening, I sat with these thoughts in the garden, trying to unpick my feelings and I found that I could not.

I told you before that I was impulsive – that I never thought things through. It was to be my downfall – and yet I cannot regret it in its entirety because, my darling Mia, it brought me you.

If you haven't already guessed what I did, I'll tell you but without the details, if you'll spare me that.

I went to Tadeusz. It was that simple. In my mind I had to

see a man, right there and then. I had to see for myself who I liked and maybe prove to myself that I wasn't like Marlena at all. This will all sound so daft to you, dear Mia. But it is the truth.

Tadeusz had always liked me. I knew that – how he had always tried to make me laugh, or spend time alone together and I hoped that evening it would still be the case for him.

It's true what he said, that I asked to help with the escape – and indeed, I did want to help as I stupidly felt left out of the most exciting part. Once again, you can note my foolishness here.

But before that, before the disagreement, before I left to return home, change and go to the graveyard anyway, Tadeusz and I made love. At least, I think that's what it was – I would like to think that love was there somewhere, if not for both of us, then at least for one of us. For him.

Afterwards, I didn't feel ashamed for what I had done, nor did I feel any different, or that I'd proved anything to myself about where my true feelings lay. If anything, I felt powerful. I felt like an actual woman – that I had experienced something that only women do, not girls – women.

The two of us lay side by side, my head on his chest, listening to his heartbeat.

'Ilse,' he said quietly. 'I'm sorry.'

I propped myself up on my elbow and looked at him, resting my head in my hand. He seemed a little different to me all of a sudden. His face, a face I always thought I had known, was almost like a stranger's and I wondered if he were looking at me in the same way.

'What for?' I asked.

'For this,' he said, but he couldn't help but smile. 'We shouldn't have done this – it's wrong.'

I didn't *feel* as though what we had done was wrong, although I knew it was.

'Ilse, we should be together – properly,' he began. 'I always hoped that we would be together – you knew I always had feelings for you when we were younger, didn't you? Well...'

As soon as he said those words, I wanted to leave. I did not want to have this conversation and all at once I saw what we had done *was* wrong – not for me, perhaps, but for him. The words that Mr Gliński had said to me all those years ago, about being careful with other people's feelings, about handling their love for you with care, came rushing back at me.

It had been wrong. For me to do this to Tadeusz. To make him think that I felt something for him that I was sure I did not.

To stop him from saying anything more, I clambered over him and began to get dressed.

'Where are you going?' he asked, sitting up.

'Home, and then I will meet you at three in the graveyard,' I told him, as I pulled on my shoes.

'You're not coming.' He swung his legs out of bed so that he was sitting beside me.

'Of course I am.' I stood, not looking at him, scared that he would see my feelings, or lack thereof for him, right there on my face.

'Ilse, please.' He reached out and took my hand in his and then kissed my knuckles. 'I wouldn't put you in that type of danger. Not now. Not ever.'

I whipped my hand away with perhaps too much force and then caught sight of his reaction – hurt suddenly flashed across his face, but he said nothing.

'I'll be there at three,' I repeated and turned away from him.

'No, you won't,' he told my retreating back. 'You won't, Ilse. Because I need you to be safe. I need you to be here and waiting for me when I return.'

I think I looked back at him in that moment, but I'm not sure if I am imagining that. But in my mind's eye, he was sitting, the sheet covering his legs, his face a mixture of love, of concern and I think, of fear.

And that's when he said it. 'I love you, Ilse.'

I didn't answer. Instead, I left.

You see, Mia, why Tadeusz was angry with me. I was careless with his heart, just as I was with Szymon's. I was foolish and selfish, and I didn't think things through at all. I was too impetuous, too quick to act on any feeling or thought that came my way. In doing so, I broke the people around me, and I never apologised for it either. Not until it was too late.

But is it too late? Maybe if I tell you it all, you can speak to Tadeusz for me. You can tell him my regrets because he won't listen to me – he has never once since I came back allowed me to properly explain. But you, Mia. You can do this for me.

Let me finish.

Let me finish with what else happened. Let me tell you about how Szymon got free, but I became ensnared in a web of my own making.

That night, when we finally found him, Szymon was sicker than I ever thought it was possible for a human to be. He coughed and spluttered until he had no breath left, then would lie down, his chest rattling painfully as he gasped for air. His skin had taken on a strange yellow hue and his hands and feet were constantly cold whilst a fever raged on his forehead.

I tried to move him on my own, but I couldn't even lift his weight; his body slithered time after time from my grasp like a dead fish. I knew I had to get help, and waited in the darkness with Szymon's breathing dangerously shallow until I was sure that by then, that guard, Groening, and his men would be at the train station.

I raced to the bookshop where I knew Mr Gliński would be dozing in his office, too excited and perhaps too nervous to go home.

His face fell when he saw me. His untamed shock of white hair stuck up as if he had been electrified and the smile he greeted me with was soon replaced by a look of utter fear.

'What's happened?' he asked me.

'It's Tadeusz – and Szymon. I can't carry him,' I breathlessly told him.

He didn't stop to grab his coat but followed me out into the night and as we raced back to the graveyard, I told him what Tadeusz had done for Szymon – how he was now on his way to Bergen and that we would have to continue to pay Groening to keep us all safe.

'He saw you too?' Mr Gliński asked, his eyes wide.

'He did.'

'Then what must be done, must be done,' he muttered.

At the time I had no idea what he meant by those words, and it was only when I came back to Görlitz six years ago, that I finally found out.

I don't remember how we managed to get Szymon to Mr Gliński's apartment – not the bookshop which was further away. I don't know where he nor I found the strength to half carry him through the streets, and I don't know whether an angel or God was looking out for us on that morning as the streets stayed quiet – not a rumble of a car, not another footstep on those echoing pavements.

Mr Gliński tended to Szymon and told me I should go home before I was missed. I didn't want to stay, if I'm honest – I couldn't bear to look at the man who once, as a boy, I had loved. He looked nothing like the old Szymon. His hair was thinner and turning grey, his face so sallow and limbs so thin that I felt sure he was half-dead. But, at the same time, I didn't want to return home either.

I was scared. Truly scared. All my bravado, my naivety had been stripped away, leaving me fragile and in need of a reassuring shoulder to lean on, a hand to hold, or a quiet word telling me that everything was going to be all right.

'Go now,' Mr Gliński told me again as I hovered in the living-room doorway. 'Go, Ilse. Please. You must!'

I did as I was asked and walked home just as the birds began their wake-up call to one another, as the inhabitants of streets began to unfurl themselves from sleep and greet another day – a new day with fresh hopes and dreams.

I had neither of those things any more – hope and dreams were both forever banished from my mind.

I saw Szymon perhaps once more before I left, but I don't remember exactly when.

'Ilse,' he had said from his bed on the sofa, pillows brought from the bedroom and stuffed behind him so he half sat up, a thick duvet covering his frail body.

I went to his side and held his hand as he told me that two days prior to the escape, he had become ill once more, but he had pushed himself to still work, still act normally so that he would not be sent to the infirmary and miss his chance at freedom.

'You'll stay a while with me, won't you?' He grinned, and I saw a snippet of the boy that I had used to know.

I kissed his hand, then stood and kissed the crown of his head.

'I'll see you again,' I told him, leaving him there, with Tadeusz's old uncle, not realising that it would be the last time I saw him or Mr Gliński.

. . .

You may be wondering why I left – why I did not see them again. This is the hard thing for me to say, and indeed, I don't want to think about it too much. All I can, or will say is that I found out I was pregnant.

The baby was Tadeusz's, of course it was. That one night of foolishness, of wanting to see what it was like to be with a man, of being young and silly, and childish, had left me pregnant.

Of course, I had no idea what to do, or even who to talk to. Marlena and I had barely seen one another after what had happened, and I was almost afraid to tell her – to admit how utterly careless I had been.

Oddly, the person who came to my rescue was my father. A man who I had always earmarked as weak and under the rule of my mother noticed that something was wrong with me and saw that he had to help his little girl.

When I told him about the baby, when I began to cry and lean into him, feeling the warmth of his body on mine, I expected him to jump up and shout for my mother, I expected him to reprimand me, to call me a whore perhaps. I was – I deserved it.

Yet he was calm and measured. I did not tell him who the father was, only that it was someone I met in town, a soldier who was now gone, sent away to the front.

He listened to me berate myself, he listened as I told him I would have to kill myself – such was the shame I felt and the utter regret.

But he would not let that happen and told me I was to go to his brother, my uncle, in Belgium. A man who I had met only a handful of times, but who my father said would be able to take care of me in my situation. What he had meant by that I do not know, and only now, thinking about it, I wonder what he wrote in the letter to my uncle. Did he tell him to marry me off to someone? Did he tell him to help me get rid of the child? All I know is that I was so grateful for the lifeline, so grateful to feel that my father was in charge of this whole mess that I did not question a thing and I let myself be sent away, again, not realising that I was not to return to my home, to my friends, for the next fifty-five years.

Thinking back now, I see how I didn't take Tadeusz's affections into account. I can see that as clear as day. I thought of no one but myself in that moment – of the kiss I had shared with Marlena, the questioning I had to do after, and of wanting to always prove something to myself and anyone around me.

The problem with what I did, though, Mia, was that it didn't make me strong, or powerful. Instead, it broke me and took pieces away from the people I cared about.

In one fell swoop, I broke us all.

FORTY

MIA

Görlitz City Hospital
Thursday, 11 February 1999

When my grandmother finished talking, I noticed that Marlena had crept silently into the room. Her hands were still holding a cardboard carrier in which three Styrofoam cups sat.

'But you still loved me,' Marlena said with a sad smile. 'You forgot to say that.'

My grandmother smiled weakly, then raised a hand to her head. This time the pain made her clutch and grasp at her hair, causing her to fall forward in the bed. She wailed so loudly, and in such a high pitch that I expected to see nurses and doctors coming to her aid. But when no one did, I raced out into the corridor, calling for a nurse who followed me in, took one look at Grandma and hurried back out, only to return in less than a minute with a large syringe that she placed into the tube that ran into my grandmother's hand.

I went to her and held her small head in my own hands, rubbing at her hair, hoping that the drugs would take effect quickly, as Marlena rubbed her back, telling her to breathe, that it would soon be all right.

Soon, she started to relax in my arms, and I laid her back in her bed, sitting close to her and holding her hand.

'So, Tadeusz?' I asked quietly.

'Yes. Tadeusz,' she repeated, her voice falling away, as the medication coursed through her veins.

'You said before, it was funny that you didn't have a husband. Is that because Tadeusz was really my dad's father?'

It was then, suddenly, that the obvious hit me. *Otto.* Otto had been my 'grandfather's' name, or so I was told. Otto, whose name was on the gravestone.

'What was Otto's surname?' I quickly asked, scared that she would soon be asleep. 'Schaeffer,' she whispered. 'Schaeffer.'

Schaeffer. *My* surname. She had taken a dead man's name as her husband's to cover up the fact that she had got pregnant out of wedlock.

I thought she had fallen asleep, so stood and ran my hands through my hair, exhaling loudly. There was so much to unpack – so much I had learned about her in a day, that I needed a minute to get my head straight.

'You want another coffee?' Marlena queried.

I nodded. I grabbed my bag to leave when Grandma opened her eyes and pointed at her notebook. 'Take this,' she told me. 'Take it. Look at last year. There's more in there. I want to tell you myself, but I'm so tired now, Mia.' Her eyes were closing again, her voice soft with the promise of sleep. 'I'm so tired. But I wanted you to know. I wrote it down for you. Look at last year...' she trailed off.

I checked the monitor before I left her. Her heart was beating a steady rhythm, her pulse normal. I hated that she had gone into such a deep sleep in that way. It made me nervous that she had, in fact, been slipping away from me for the last time.

'Not yet,' Marlena said, as we walked to the cafeteria together. 'She won't go yet. I know her. She's still waiting.'

'Waiting for what?'

'For Szymon – Tadeusz. She's waiting for him to finally forgive her.'

We reached the cafeteria and collected our drinks – two weak-looking coffees that left me yearning for a proper latte or cappuccino.

'So, what you think?' Marlena stirred sugar into her drink, the spoon tinkling on the sides of the cup.

'About Tadeusz? About my grandmother? About me?' I half laughed, exhausted.

'I know. Is a lot. But she agree that you should know before she goes everything that happens. That way you remember her properly.'

I sipped at the coffee and welcomed the fact that Marlena was not talking for a minute. Around me, voices hushed in conversations, the scrape of knives and forks on plates were filling in the complete silence that I so craved. Yet it still gave me a moment to think.

Tadeusz was my grandfather.

My grandmother had not waited for him.

She had not cared for Szymon as she had promised she would do.

Marlena was in love with her.

My grandmother may have returned that love – but she had not said: she had neither confirmed nor denied what feelings she had either way.

And then there was me. There was me telling Marlena about Will. About how I had been weak and afraid. How I had let a man do that to me and change me from a happy young woman into a shell of a human being.

There was so much there to think about, so much to question, to perhaps even cry about that I didn't know where to start.

It was then that I saw Marlena had delved into my handbag and had retrieved the notebook of Grandma's that she had urged I read.

'Where we start?' Marlena's eyes were scanning the pages, and suspiciously found an entry far too quickly for her not to have seen it before.

'We start with this, yes?' She waved the notebook at me.

'I'm not sure, Marlena. I'm so tired... My brain is in such a muddle – I don't know whether I can take any more today.'

'I get you another coffee,' she insisted. 'Is not much. Few pages. I read them to you. Is near the end now – the story nearly over and then we talk and then you think about decision Tadeusz say to you.'

'What does that even mean – what decision?'

'He want to know if you will be his granddaughter. He want to know whether he is family I think. He want to know whether you will forgive him.'

'Forgive him for what?'

'For not forgiving Ilse. For holding on to pain all this time and not letting her be free.'

Before Marlena began, she took out a scrap of paper that had been wedged inside the bound pages.

'There is a note, here for you.' She scooted it to me and I read:

Dearest Mia,

Please read this, after I am gone. Please try and understand who I once was and who I am now. I leave you with this chapter of my life to give you some comfort and any gaps I am sure that Marlena will fill in for you.

I love you,

Grandma.

'What did she write?' I asked, not looking up from the note, not wanting Marlena to see that more tears had appeared in my eyes.

FORTY-ONE

ILSE

Görlitz
Thursday, 17 September 1998

Today the doctor telephoned me and told me that my tests conclusively show I have cancer.

It is strange, but I did not cry; I did not feel much if I am honest. He spoke of treatments, but advised that the probability of them working was slim to none, so I told him no – I would simply wait. He told me, of course, to tell family and friends, to give them a chance to see me and perhaps help me. But again, I have ignored his advice.

As I sit in my sitting room, Leonie the celloist has begun to play a mournful tune. I find it fitting this evening, and I add to my melancholy by looking out into the graveyard where that daring escape happened – where Tadeusz was taken away and Szymon was given to me to care for.

Do I remember how I felt that day? Yes, I do. I was afraid – probably for the first time in my life. A proper fear of knowing that something so terrible had just happened – those men, shot dead, the water carrying them away, and Tadeusz taken away to

God knows where. I had wanted to run home and hide under my sheets like a small child and try and pretend that it had never happened, but I did not – of course I didn't.

Fear followed me after that day – I could never quite escape it. All those years that I had yearned for adventure were upon me, but what I hadn't considered was that adventure, at least for me, was not exciting, as I had thought it would be. Rather it was wrapped up in a cloak of panic and a stomach-churning anxiety that forever stayed with me, up until now – up until this day when I have been told I am going to die.

There is one particular memory of mine that is mingling with the music of the cello. Leonie had begun to play Bach's Cello Suite No. 1 in G major, Prelude. I know this piece so well and as I think back to leaving my home, to what happened to me, I always, for some reason, have this music in my mind – as if it is a soundtrack to this moment in my life. I once told Marlena this, that if I were to pick a piece of music to be a backdrop to my life over those months, this is what I would pick.

It's not a sad piece of music; it isn't joyous either. I suppose each person would find something in it just for themselves. For me though, it matched my feelings – one minute happy, a girl dancing and laughing by the river with her friends, the next a frightened young woman – sent away to Belgium, to an uncle I barely knew, leaving behind everything I had known, traumatised and depressed, to meet my fate.

FORTY-TWO

ILSE

Bruges
September 1942

I arrived in Bruges in the dead of night – the witching hour, when all the world sleeps yet some are tormented by nightmares and worries. As I walked the cobbled street, the moon the only light guiding my path, I remembered what my grandmother had once said, that it was during the witching hour when the sick died, when babies due to be born found their way out of their mother's bodies and when, if there was any evil abroad, it would creep out of the shadows and find its prey.

None of those memories comforted me on that walk; death, babies, evil – yes, babies: that thought scared me as much as death. I knew that what was in my belly was mine, but I am ashamed to say now that at the time, on that cold, lonely street, with just a suitcase in my hand, I wanted to reach through my skin and rip it from my body. I was scared of it. Scared of what was going to happen because of it – what had already happened because of it.

Bruges resembled something out of medieval times, which did nothing for my humour and anxiety. The buildings seemed to dip towards me, their shadows lengthening as my footsteps echoed in the tiny alleyways where water dripped from leaking gutters and the wailing and screaming of cats as they fought knocked over a plant pot, sending the animals scuttling into the darkness, leaving a spatter of terracotta fragments on the cobbles.

I kept moving, my hand in my pocket fingering the address Father had written down for me. I had memorised it, and yet, I was still so afraid to lose that scrap of paper.

I repeated it over and over in my mind, so that even today I cannot forget it: 25 Verversdijk, Bruges–Ostend Canal.

I had no idea where I was going, other than the rough directions given to me by the conductor at the train station who spoke to me only in French – *a droit, a gauche* – I knew right and left but still, it felt a flimsy map for me to follow and soon I found myself in a narrow alleyway bordered on either side by high walls and was sure that I had taken a wrong turn and would soon forever be lost amongst these streets. Just then I smelled the hint of something familiar – of fresh water – a canal!

I raced to it, desperate to get out of my narrow confinement. As soon as I reached the end of the alleyway, there it was – a strip of glorious water, silver in the moonlight. I leaned against the railing and dropped my case at my feet that I now realised were burning with blisters on my heels and on my big toes. There was a brief moment when I felt that the water called to me. It sounds ridiculous, I know. But in that moment of tiredness and fear, I felt that the water wanted me to leap into it – to let it consume me and drag me to its depths, always to be a part of it.

I even set one foot on a bottom railing, so strange was the instant urge to obey this command and I only stopped when a man, perhaps travelling to work early in the morning, squeaked past me on a bicycle.

'*Ho!*' he shouted at me, his crackly voice echoing, bouncing off the buildings that edged each side of the river so that I was sure it had woken all who dwelled in them.

'*Ho!*' He shouted again.

I turned to look at him and saw he had stopped his cycling, resting one leg on the pavement to give him balance.

I did not bother to say anything and ferreted about in my pocket for my uncle's address. He took it and held it close to his face, then said something that I did not understand.

'*Sprechen sie Deutsch?*' I asked him.

I saw him wrinkle up his nose as I spoke, then he shook his head and simply pointed at a three-storey house only a few yards away.

I nodded my thanks and took the address back, placing it once more in my pocket.

Picking up my case, I followed where he had pointed and saw the number 25, shiny in copper on the red front door, reminding me all at once of Mr Gliński's bookshop.

I knocked lightly and found that the door gave way underneath my pressure, creaking open to reveal a darkened, dirty hallway, stale air wafting out into the night.

'Uncle?' I asked the darkness, hoping that he would appear.

But there was no answer, so I took a tentative step inside and closed the door behind me.

'Uncle?' I asked each room, turning on lights as I went. Each room gave no reply, so I moved upstairs, finding bedrooms neatly made, then the master bedroom with the covers heaped into a pile on the floor.

Making my way downstairs again, I found the kitchen. Perhaps he had gone out on some important business, I told myself as I searched the cupboards for food. Finding only a mouldy loaf of bread on the sideboard and a half-drunk cup of tea that sprouted a layer of green growth, I sat at the kitchen table, placed my head in my hands and wept.

The next thing I remember, it was morning, and I woke with my head on the kitchen table, my arms underneath, fizzy with pins and needles.

My mouth was dry, and I moved my tongue about a few times, trying to moisten it. I stood and found a glass, ran it under the tap and gulped back water.

'Uncle?' I cried out again into the nothingness and once more received no reply.

He would be back soon, I told myself. Wherever he had gone, he would be back soon. Father would have telephoned or sent a telegram. He wouldn't have left. And yet, my eyes could not tear themselves away from the mouldy bread and tea, the lack of food and the open front door. If he had only popped out, why had he left rotting food about?

I knew, deep down, that he had obviously left days earlier, never receiving whatever message my father had sent, and that I was here, alone, pregnant, in a strange country where I couldn't understand anyone and they couldn't understand me.

I suppose at that moment I should have broken down, I should have cried more or screamed or something – but I did not. Instead, I went in search of my uncle's telephone, and finding that he did not have one, began to inspect what I decided would be my new home.

I did not get far. I had scarcely managed to reach the living room with its plush red sofas and heavy bookcases when the front door swung open to reveal a man, wearing a long beige coat and dark hat.

Stupidly, I asked, 'Uncle?' knowing full well that the man before me with his slim, young face was not my craggy uncle with his pot belly and ruddy cheeks.

The man seemed not to hear me and began to shout at me in that same language I had heard at the station, and then in French. Finally, he spoke in English, so perfectly that I knew that he was from England. I had learned a little in school and could follow what he was saying.

'Who are you?' he demanded angrily, his hand suddenly reaching inside his coat.

To this day, I can't tell you why I did it. Maybe I knew somewhere in the recesses of my mind that I was in a very dangerous situation, or maybe my tiredness and confusion of the past few days overcame me, but my answer was simple – 'Ilse Schaeffer.' Schaeffer – like Otto Schaeffer, the man who was buried in the graveyard that I spent so much time in, the same name that I had traced over and over again with my finger, wondering who he was and what kind of life he had led.

The man removed his hand from his coat and beckoned me to come to him. It was then that I realised I still had my *Kennkarte* in my pocket, my passport too and I had just given a false identity.

So, I did as I knew how to do – gleaned from my mother – I started to cry. Big, fat ugly tears that streaked my face and I am sure alarmed the strange man. It worked, and he came to me and made me sit on the sofa, then scurried off to the kitchen. In that moment, I reached into my pocket and shoved my documents down the side of the couch, resuming my crying when he came back in, a glass of water in his hand.

'Calm down,' he told me, now in German, kneeling in front of me as I took the glass from him and sipped at the water.

'German, yes?' he asked.

I nodded.

'Why are you here? Do you know Herr Klein?'

I shook my head as I drank, scared to say anything lest I say the wrong thing, even though I wasn't sure what the wrong thing was at that point.

'Why are you here?' he asked me again, his narrow dark eyes flitting to the door and back again.

I did not answer him, and was glad that he finally answered for me. 'A refugee?' he asked, nodding at the one suitcase that sat forlornly in the hallway.

'Yes,' I said confidently. 'I was tired. I'm pregnant and I saw the door open, and I just needed to rest.'

I was hopeful that this would be enough for him to leave me alone – I was a refugee – a German fleeing danger, but again, I was not sure *which* danger he need me to be fearing – was I someone persecuted or was I fleeing from the British and their Allies? Which side was I on? I waited for him to tell me.

He removed his hat and ran a hand over his head, slicking back his black hair. 'Ilse Schaeffer,' he repeated to me. 'A refugee.'

'Yes,' I said.

He stood and held out his hand for me to take. 'You need to come with me. You need to come now.'

I stared at his hand for a few seconds before taking it. You may read this and wonder why on earth I did so. He was a stranger – but what else could I do?

He picked up my suitcase and led me out into the street, the canal flowing lazily, people scurrying about to and from work, children in prams, dogs yapping from gardens – it was all so normal and yet I was with a man who I did not know in a country I did not know, being taken to goodness knows where.

He made me walk quickly alongside him and soon we reached a car that he told me to get into. He sat behind the wheel and roared the engine into life, racing away from my uncle's house with so much speed that it made me turn and look out of the rear window to see if we were being followed.

There was no one there.

'It's all right,' he glanced at me as we drove, 'you're safe now.'

'Who are you?' I managed to ask, trying not to let my voice betray my nerves.

'I can't say,' he said and grinned at me. 'But I can say that the man's house you chose to rest in was not a good choice.'

'Why not?' I felt bolder now as we left the city behind, green fields opening up on both sides.

'I can't say,' he said again.

'Are you English?"

'Is it that obvious?' He gave a nervous laugh. 'I thought my accent was rather good to be honest.'

I assured him that his accent was fine, and logged away in my brain that he was English and therefore, I was a refugee fleeing my homeland after my husband was killed for opposing Hitler. The story came to my mind so quickly and with so much detail that I often thought since that I would have either made a wonderful spy, or a great author.

'You remind me of my sister, you know,' he said, and then quickly shook his head as if he wished he had never said anything.

'I do?' I prompted.

He did not answer.

'Where are we going?'

'I shouldn't be doing this,' he said through gritted teeth, as he took a tight bend at too much speed, and in such a way that I wondered if he were speaking to himself. 'I shouldn't. It's not the done thing, you know. But there you were, sat there, crying and pregnant and looking just like my sister...'

He trailed off and we spent the rest of the drive in an uncomfortable silence. I wasn't sure what to say to him, and thought it best that for once, I took my mother's advice and shut up. Within an hour, we arrived at a small cottage tucked away amongst a thicket of fir trees.

He got out of the car and opened the door for me, once more offering me his hand. I decided there and then that I trusted this man. And once more, if you are reading this, you would think I were mad. But there was a way about him – the door opening, the offering of a hand, the softness of the way he spoke to me when I cried – that told me that he wasn't going to hurt me.

As soon as I was out of the car, I realised that we were near the sea. I could not see it, but I could smell its salty freshness in the air, tickling at my nostrils with its promises of adventure.

Despite the situation I found myself in, and despite the past few days, I still felt that flutter of excitement that I had always felt at the sniff of an adventure – whether it be falling in love, clandestine meetings, or helping Szymon escape. I could not help it; it was hardwired into me – and it was something that I knew that from now on I had to suppress. My childish, romantic notions of adventure had to be tucked away now – they had not only got me into this situation in the first place, but they had put others in danger. And, there was the matter that I was going to be a mother and that meant the old Ilse had to depart.

The man led me inside the cottage where I was greeted with two more strangers – both men, one sporting a thin moustache and a craggy face, the other slim, blond and with a sort of vacant look about him.

They all spoke in English at once, in such a flurry that I could not understand them, but I knew that they were talking about me, as every second or so their eyes landed on me, questioning who I was and why I was here.

The man who had brought me here soon got exasperated with them and raised his voice, silencing the pair of them.

'We'll help her,' he said. 'Now. Ilse. Tell us your story.'

This I understood and took a chair at a rickety table that sported half-drunk glasses of whisky and a deck of playing cards.

I cannot remember what I told them in its entirety – but I told them what I had already imagined: that I had been married, and indeed the wedding band that my father had given me and told me to wear on my finger confirmed this for them. That my husband was Otto Schaeffer; that he was an opponent of the Nazi regime and that he had been killed, but I had escaped, coming to Belgium to try and find a friend whom we had once known.

The men asked for dates, more names, street names even, and whenever I did not know what to say or became overwhelmed, I cried and rubbed at my stomach and soon their questions ceased.

They let me rest in a bedroom upstairs, and within two days, I was ferried to England, where once more I was questioned and then placed in a boarding house in Cheltenham with a couple called Mr and Mrs Jacobs, who treated me with kindness – too much kindness that I certainly did not deserve.

It was some years later that the man who had saved me in Belgium found me and visited me. My son was five years old and playing in the garden on a tiny bicycle that the Jacobs had gifted him for his birthday.

I knew him before he said a word – the same shifty eyes, the same kind demeanour – the strange man of Belgium.

'Mrs Schaeffer?' he asked, tipping his hat that had not changed one bit.

'Yes,' I answered in English now, noting the smile on his lips as I did so.

Over tea and biscuits, he told me that he had been working for the British intelligence when he found me, and that Otto Klein had absconded after realising that the British were seeking him out for playing a part in sabotaging their communications.

'When I found you, I didn't know what to think! There you were, crying and pale and my sister, you see, had just become pregnant and I saw so much of her in you that day that I did something I most certainly should not have done.'

'You showed me kindness,' I told him. 'It was simply kindness.'

'I shouldn't have, though. You could have been anyone – you could have been a spy, but I let my emotions take over me. I believed you.'

As I offered him another biscuit, he reached out and placed his hand on my wrist, stopping me from moving the plate any further. 'Ilse Klein,' he said.

I didn't breathe. I didn't move. He had found out who I was, perhaps who my father was and now he was here to take me away.

He removed his hand, then stood and looked out through the front window at the scrap of a lawn that my son was playing on. 'That's a strapping lad you have there. Strapping. My sister, she lost her baby during birth. It was a boy too.'

Then he turned and left the house without a word of goodbye.

What can I say to defend myself? I don't suppose there are any words.

When I think back now to those days, I see how foolish I was. How I was a young woman who delighted in excitement and perhaps the danger and romance of it all. I didn't see then how naive and careless I had been, how each decision I made changed the course of so many lives. My only defence is that I was young. Young and stupid.

When my son and his wife died, I assumed that was my punishment for what I had done. I had disappeared from Tadeusz's life, pregnant with his child and never told him until years later – when too much had happened, when too much bitterness had seeped beneath his skin. He wouldn't talk to me, wouldn't let me explain how scared I had been, how confused I had been by everything and how, as much as I hated to admit it, I did not love Tadeusz – not in the way that he wanted me to, and how he deserved to be loved.

And then there was Szymon. Szymon who was so ill, wasting away in front of my eyes, who still held a flame for me, even after all those years, and who had begged me to stay with him because he was so afraid.

But I had thought of only myself. Of how scared *I* was. Of how I could not imagine my life with either of them, and could not bear the repercussions that would come when I told my mother I was with child and of course unmarried.

I know the pain I caused. I know it was unfair of me to keep Tadeusz's child from him. But then I also know the pain of losing my child, of losing my family, and being left with a small child, with you, Mia, to take care of, who was so vulnerable, so utterly at sea with what had happened that my pain seemed more important to me than anything I had caused to others.

It was only when you had left home for university that my thoughts, memories and guilt found a way back to me. I was absorbed in them from the moment I woke to the moment I fell asleep at night, and most of the time I would dream about the past and wake up feeling more tired than I did when I had gone to bed.

That was when I knew I had to return to Görlitz. I had to face the past and face what I had done, and maybe find some way to unburden myself. But, as is the way with things, it didn't work out as I had hoped and I ended up staying here, hoping each day that maybe, just maybe, Tadeusz would allow me to apologise, and would finally give me some relief.

FORTY-THREE

TADEUSZ

Görlitz
Thursday, 11 February 1999

Tadeusz could not settle. He had tried to go to the bookshop after Mia and Marlena left, but had reached the corner of the road and then he had turned back, this time heading east to the river.

It was as though he had no control over where his feet would take him, and he barely thought about the direction he was walking, knowing full well where he would end up.

Reaching the graveyard, he had to push through thick brambles that scratched at his hands and managed to rip a small hole through his left trouser leg. Normally, this would have bothered him, but not today.

He found what he was looking for, a sunken piece of earth underneath the weeping willow, just at the edge of the graveyard. He remembered how he had come here and buried Szymon himself, in the dead of night, not caring if he was caught. He had thought then that the worst had already happened, so what did it matter to him if he was arrested for burying a body?

He lowered himself onto the damp soil and with his fingers began to pick up loose cigarette butts, a crumpled beer can and a few stray packets that some youths had no doubt left behind on one of their midnight forays.

He didn't blame the youngsters for coming here to hide away from prying eyes. Why would he? He had done the same. He just wished that they would take whatever they had brought with them home, and not leave it here to rot along with the dead.

'I have to forgive her,' he told Szymon. 'I have to let it all go now, don't I?'

He imagined his cousin's reply – that he had told Mia to try and understand the past – to understand the whole to be able to make any sense of it. But had Tadeusz taken his own advice? Had he really examined his past?

He reached into his pocket and took out a neatly folded pile of letters. He had thought he would give them to Mia to read – these same letters that he had read to Ilse whilst she lay in hospital, trying to finally tell her all his feelings in one go so that she might understand why he had resisted talking to her.

He remembered the day that she had come back to Görlitz, arriving on his doorstep with a smile – that smile – that had never left her.

'I need to talk to you,' she had said. 'I need to apologise.' She was older, certainly, as they both were. But to him she was the same Ilse, and for a split second he felt a rush of warmth at finally seeing her again, which quickly disappeared.

He thought he knew what she was going to say – that she was sorry for leaving. Sorry for not caring for Szymon.

Instead, she handed him a photograph of a happy couple, the man wearing a blue checked shirt, a child on his lap, pigtails in her hair. 'That's your son,' she had said.

He had known that she had got married – that she was a Frau Schaeffer now – and he knew, too, that she had had a child. But was it really his?

'I'm sorry I didn't tell you. I'm sorry that you never got to know him,' her words rushed forth, one on top of the other with such speed that he wasn't sure he had heard her correctly. 'He died. A while ago now. But her,' she pointed at the child, 'That's Mia. Your granddaughter. She's at university now. You could meet her if you like?'

It was then that he stopped staring at the photograph and handed it back to her.

'Keep it,' she urged.

He still held it out for her to take.

'Are you not going to say anything? Are you not going to let me in so we can talk about this?' she pleaded, her eyes moist.

Tadeusz shook his head and closed the door. He would not, could not speak to her.

She did not give up and daily would knock on his door, visit the bookshop and then, when an apartment became free in his building, she moved in so that her visits, her pleas for him to talk to her only increased.

But he did not waver. Not once. He would not speak to that woman. He did not want to think that he had a son – why, because he had never had a chance to know him, and now he never would. He found it almost cruel that she had told him about this – what was he supposed to say, supposed to think now? Had she expected him to envelop her in an embrace, tell her he loved her and that he could not wait to meet his grand-daughter?

Well, if that's what she had been waiting for, Tadeusz decided that she would be waiting the rest of her life.

'I was so bitter,' he said to Szymon's grave. 'So bitter. I let it consume me. I thought about sending her the letters, these letters over and over again, but oddly, I liked to keep them with

me so I could read them, so I could revel in my anger and everything else that came with it.'

'*But it wasn't just about Ilse not telling you that you had a
son, was it? It was something much more, much deeper than
that,*' Szymon's imaginary voice asked him.

'I suppose you're right,' Tadeusz sighed. 'I became this way
after the war ended. I became this way before I ever knew I had
a son. It was easier, though, wasn't it, for me to blame her for
everything?' he asked the dirt that he had been absentmindedly
tracing a finger through, leaving the name Szymon in large
letters that he knew would soon be smoothed away by the wind
and rain.

There was no answer this time from the imaginary Szymon.
All Tadeusz heard was the singing of birds, the rustle of leaves
and the slow *lap, lap* of the water at the river's edge.

He unfurled the letters and began reading them to himself.
This would be the last time he would read them, he decided.
He would give them to Mia and ask her to forgive him for being
a grumpy, bitter old fool.

FORTY-FOUR

TADEUSZ

Bergen Belsen
October 1942

Dear Ilse,

It is I. 'Szymon'. It is strange to me to have this name, as we both know why. I cannot be explicit in what I write you lest someone find these ramblings, but I hope that one day, they find their way into your hands.

I hope that you and my cousin are safe. Has he recovered some? Is he well? I wonder constantly what is happening – how he has taken my place now above the bookshop, how you visit him each day, talking to him and perhaps even reading to him. I imagine that your presence gives much comfort to my uncle, who delights in seeing you each day and sees how much you care for Szymon.

It is hard for me to tell you where I now find myself. Each time I have thought of the words to describe it, they fall flat and utterly useless. Perhaps there are no words and perhaps one day, someone will come up with new ones that accurately describe the horror of this place.

We were transported here by train, in cattle cars that still held the scent of long-gone animals, musty and mixed with a hint of sulphur from their excrement. Piled into these boxes, we found ourselves arm to arm, stood upright, with no way to sit down to relieve the aching in our legs. It lasted a day, perhaps a little less. I can't be sure as time did that strange thing it tends to do, distorting itself and everything around it. All I know is that we arrived at a train station, the ground a quagmire after recent rains and the sky hidden by tumultuous clouds.

We were not to stay long at this station and were soon ordered to march, two by two, guards on horseback and motor-cycles on either side of us. I found the sight humorous. So many guards for so few men, many of whom were coughing from the TB they had contracted in the Görlitz camp, others limping from sores on their feet from their forced labour, and others who looked almost translucent, so thin they were – their faces gaunt, eyes hollow sockets. Why did the guards think that we could escape them? There was no way we could have done so.

Our friend Groening did not accompany us on this journey, so other than the few men I find myself among, no one has said a thing. Why would they? They have their numbers, their pris-oners and to tell you the truth, I do not think they even see us as human. We are all one face, one body. Has he been paid? Has he done anything to Szymon? I worry still that he will not leave you all alone, even when you have paid him. I hope that he does. I hope and pray that you are all safe.

The march lasted three or so hours and I itched to talk to the man I walked beside, to ask his name, to try and pass the time. But we were not permitted to talk and found that out the hard way when someone at the rear of our column dared to speak to his fellow prisoner and was punished with a thwack of a baton on the back of his legs that saw him crumple to the ground in an undignified heap.

When we finally stopped, we were met with the sight of barbed wire fences, tall towers that were manned by men with guns, and soldiers that held in their hands leashes attached to barking dogs, who seemed to salivate when they saw us.

I immediately felt an unease at this place. This was not a barracks for POWs, this was not a place where we would stay, work and maybe be set free. It felt to me, even before I stepped inside, that this was a place of death and many of us, if not all, would end our days here.

Perhaps it was the smell of the place – rancid, like rotting meat, or perhaps it was the vigour with which the guards eyed us like vermin, ready to be extinguished.

I soon found out, after walking through the gates, why it smelled the way it did, why they looked at us the way that they did, and of course why I felt the unease I did.

Dead bodies greeted us. This I am certain of. And yet, they walked and talked, wearing striped uniforms, stars stitched onto them, some with the letter P, some with F. They were so thin that to them, I am sure, we all looked hugely and grotesquely fat. They were walking skeletons, their skin taut, thin as paper pulled over bones, their eye sockets seemingly bulging, their eyes almost falling out of their moorings.

We walked past them as they huddled in groups. All men, all eyeing us with worry. But was it worry for us, I wondered, or for them?

Our induction into this place did not take long. We were stripped of our clothing and given rough, used uniforms, that had holes in the material, and smelled of something that I cannot place – but it was a scent that I wished never to smell again.

Our heads were shaved, and we were made to have our photographs taken. I stood in front of that camera, realising that this was only the second time in my life that I had had my likeness shown on a shiny photograph. The first time had been when I was with my parents, and I was perhaps fourteen years old. We had had a family portrait taken in Görlitz by a man who made us pose in certain ways and in front of a red velvet curtain.

We had smiled for that photograph – the three of us. And now, here I was, standing once more in front of a camera, but this time without my parents who were still gone – their whereabouts unknown, without my hair, without my clothes. I did not smile.

My new lodgings is a large barracks, the *Häftlingslager*, three bunks, with two men apiece in each. Already cramped and stinking of sweat and bodily fluids, I was to sleep here, I was told, eat here, and stay here. There was no work detail. There was nothing to do and nowhere to go.

Holding a dirty blanket that I had been issued, I made my way through the narrow aisles of that bunkhouse, the ghostly faces of my fellow inmates watching me as I walked.

'This one is free,' a voice came from a top bunk, at the rear of the building. Polish – a welcome sign. 'Just come on up.'

Careful not to stand on the inhabitants below me who were curled up like kittens in their beds, I stepped up and felt a strong hand pull me into what was my new home.

'Janek,' the man said. He smiled at me, showing a black toothy gap where his two front teeth should have been. 'Ah this!' He pointed at the gap. 'Kicked out if you can believe it. I saw you arrive. Polish – I knew it as soon as I saw you and I thought to myself, Janek, get that man in your bunk and you can at least talk each day and pass some time!'

Despite our surroundings, Janek spoke as if we were simply friends, perhaps comrades in the army at a training camp. Noticing my reticence and perhaps the worry and fear that had no doubt drawn itself across my face, he stopped smiling. 'Just tell me your name,' he said. 'They can't take that from you. Tell me your name.'

It was a simple request, wasn't it, to tell someone your name. I had been doing it since I was a child. But this was the first time that I had to pause – I had to think. I was no longer who I used to be – here I am *Szymon*.

FORTY-FIVE

TADEUSZ

Belsen Bergen
February 1943

Dear Ilse,

When I wrote you last that was a while ago, and for this I am sorry. Although, I am not sure why exactly I am apologising as I have not managed to find a way to send the last letter to you –there is no way to get a letter out of here even if I wanted to.

The added problem I have found is that writing paper, pencils and pens are in high demand here, yet there are very few to be found. Everything works on a bartering system, and unfortunately, when I arrived, I had little to barter.

But it is funny how inventive you can become when you need to be. I have found that whilst I do not have anything physical to barter, my skills at storytelling are in demand. This may sound strange to you, but you must understand that time here is one of our enemies. Time means that you are able to think about how hungry you are, how cold you are, how you wish to be home. With no work detail, we have little to occupy us, and we seek out ways to get through each day from sunrise to sunset and try and find tiny glimpses of joy in something – anything.

I never thought of myself as a storyteller before. But one night, my bunkmate and close friend, Janek, could not sleep. He had succumbed to a fever, and a cough which was making its rounds through each bunkhouse, taking a few lives along with it each time it made contact with a weary and skeletal body. Janek was quite robust, however. He had arrived here an overweight soldier from Kilice. He credits that he is still alive to the fact, that as he said, he had a lot of weight to lose.

Janek is not fat now. He is like the rest of us I suppose. Although there is no real way of knowing what we look like. I do not like to look at my body – I did that perhaps a month ago and saw my own ribs protruding in such a fashion that I was sure they were trying to escape my own torso. But I can still see how I have changed. My forearms, once strong and wiry with muscle are now devoid of much else but a little skin and bone. I try not to look at them either.

Anyway, Janek. Janek and the storytelling. I apologise once more for the diversion. It is hard to keep thoughts together, to know what I want to say and to put them in some order that will make sense to you. I do wonder if any of this will make sense to anyone who has not had to be here.

Janek. Storytelling.

Janek could not sleep. He asked me to talk to him whilst the others slept. He wanted to stop thinking about the rattle and wheeze in his chest and the heat that covered his body. So I told him a story. I felt in that moment like my uncle. How he would read us stories that summer in that cool bookshop to keep us out of the heat. How we learned so much from Mr Conan Doyle, from Shakespeare and Mr Dickens, of course. He introduced us to Polish writers, German writers, English writers and, in those days, I did feel as though we left Germany and travelled the globe.

My story was about two boys who found treasure on a river-bank and then travelled the world. Although it came from my imagination, there were some parts of it at least that were rooted in truth.

Do you remember when we first met? That day it was raining and cold and we had dragged ashore a muddied box that had fallen from a boat. At the time, I was sure it would contain treasure, or money, but it didn't contain much apart from old clothes.

How disappointed we were! The story I told Janek, though, had none of that disappointment. And soon I found that others who had been trying to sleep had now turned their attention to me and were listening intently. As soon as I finished the tale – the two boys had travelled to Egypt as a map they had found in their treasure chest had told them they must go there – the other men in the bunkhouse cried out! They wanted more. They wanted to find out what would happen next for these two boys and implored me to think of something that would extend the story.

And I did. The following days I thought of new adventures and would recite my stories each evening, and in return for my storytelling I have so far received a pen, which was stolen from one of the guards, three sheets of paper, also stolen, four ciga-rettes and a piece of bread.

You cannot understand how these small gifts bring so much joy! Upon receiving the bread, I almost wept. We are served nothing much more than weak coffee, stale bread, thin, watery soup and if we are lucky, porridge, and here was this man, this tiny man, with black spectacles that constantly fell from his face because there was no fat on it to keep them in place, with a lump of his bread just to hear a story. That's how much stories matter here. They give us an escape, perhaps a little hope, but most of all, they stop us from thinking how hungry we are all the time.

I have just realised that I have just one sheet left, and I must be careful now with what I write and what I say. I need to decide what is important.

The cold here is different. It is everywhere, especially now that we have had more snow. We are not given any more blankets or extra clothing to keep out the icy air that constantly nibbles out our skin, finding its way inside and settling on our bones. The guards here do not care if we die from it. In fact, I think they would prefer it – there would be less of us to look after.

They say we are POWs, and that we will get 'exchanged' at some point for our German counterparts, and yet, no one has saved us, no one has bartered for our release.

Instead, the guards have now found work detail for us. At first, I was happy to hear this news. I was tired of trying to pass the time in the bunkhouse each day, but as soon as I was taken to my 'work', I wished to be back.

We are to build more bunkhouses made from thin slats of wood for some new 'prisoners' and they do not tell us when they are coming, who they are for. I overheard one guard talking to another, who said that the camp would soon be overflowing, and trains were scheduled to arrive in the spring – from Poland and France.

'More Jewish pigs,' one guard spat.

'And their offspring,' the other said with no hint of emotion.

There are Jews here, but I have not met them as they are kept separate from us, yet I hear that their treatment is worse than ours – they are in overcrowded rooms, fed a little less, and if you believe Janek, which I do, he says there are pits of naked bodies – all of them skeletal, their faces twisted in torment.

As I worked, my hands turning blue with the cold, and then the fingertips to white, I tried not to think about the people who would be living in these huts and bunkhouses. I tried not to think that in some way I was helping the Germans to do this to so many. But then, what choice do I have? It is not as though I can escape – I have seen others try and they were promptly shot by hidden shadows in the tall towers, their bodies left on the ground for the crows to pick at.

I have to keep going. I have to work, and try and ignore how each day I feel weaker, how my chest feels tight and I find myself coughing more often than not. I have to try and not think about how my skin feels in pain from the cold, how no matter what I do to warm it, it will not, and how I dream at night of the summer we were all together, desperate to feel that heat on me once more.

I have to try not to think too much, not to wonder what will happen to me next, or if I will even survive this.

FORTY-SIX
TADEUSZ

Belsen Bergen
August 1943

Dear Ilse,

You may notice, as do I, that my handwriting has changed somewhat. I find that holding a pen these days is getting harder and, after a few minutes, my hand begins to shake. That is what hunger will do to you. It makes you so weakened that holding a pen is too much.

More prisoners arrived in April and then again in July. The camp is now teeming with what they call 'hostage prisoners'. To me, however, this is not a place where we are likely to be exchanged for other prisoners, this is not a prisoner of war camp. I don't know what name to give it exactly, but all I can feel is that it has been designed in such a way to either work us to death, starve us to death, or wait until a disease finds us and carries us away.

So many have already departed through a wave of typhus that hit us in spring, and those that died were not permitted a burial as we know it. Instead, we were to throw them into a pit that was already full with decaying corpses as the crematorium cannot keep up with the demand of the dead. Janek and I were given this task, and I will not go into the detail of it – all I will say is that the faces of those whom I had to 'bury' that day will forever remain etched in my mind. At night, they haunt me, and during the day, my eyes cannot help but look to the open, festering holes in the ground where they lay.

The amount of death here has brought many rats, and as the heat hammers down on us this summer, it has become even worse. Once more, the guards have no desire to rid us of this new problem, and we are left to our own devices regarding how to kill them.

Although this may sound strange to you, it has become something a sport for us and each of us in our bunkhouse are keeping tallies as to how many rats we kill in one day. I have been rather productive and have created traps made from discarded pieces of wood from work detail, nails and pieces of wire.

Janek on the other hand has killed none. He is a pacifist, he says, even though he was a soldier in the Polish army, and refuses to kill anything – even a fly. It's quite something to watch him as an insect lands on his face and he becomes still, quiet and patient, and waits for it to leave of its own accord. At first, I was sure he would give in and at least swat it away, but he has not. He sits as still as a statue and simply waits. I must say I envy this about him. He has a calmness in him. Even the way in which he walks around the camp would make you think he were out for a stroll on a warm summer's evening, going nowhere in particular but simply delighting in the activity.

I asked him how he did this – and perhaps why. We all feel frustrated, angry, with a thirst for escape and minds that constantly think about life outside of here, but he does not.

'You have only one option,' he told me one evening, as we sat outside, our backs against the bunkhouse, staring at the fence and the trees beyond – freedom was always so close yet at the same time, so far away. 'You have only one option,' he repeated. 'You cannot control what is happening to you here, but what you can control is your mind. You have to train it to think a different way, and, in that way, you are not letting them win. They cannot break you if they cannot break your mind.'

'But *how* do you do it?' I demanded of him. 'It is easy to say – control your mind – but how do you do it?'

'With practice,' he said. 'Every day, whenever you get a thought that you know will make things worse – for example thinking about your past, or what is going on around you – you then have to decide to tell yourself that you won't think about it. Instead, what you will do is turn it around. Take work detail, for example. Yes, we are hungry and tired. Now, I could concentrate on those thoughts, or I could think, *I am going to work, and when I do, I am going to try and find a small piece of joy in it.* So I think about the fact that I am going to spend time with you, and with my other friends. I know we will talk; perhaps someone will tell a joke. And when I move, when I walk, I won't drag myself, letting the guards see that they have defeated me. No! I will walk as a free man, feeling the warmth of the sun on my back, the crunch of the ground under my feet. These are small joys – very small, but if I concentrate on them long enough, they begin to fill my mind and stop me from thinking about the worst of this place.'

'Everything is the worst,' I complained. 'There is no joy here.'

'You must try.' He nudged me as we sat together. 'You must try or you will not survive. Even if you finally get free, your mind will still be locked away in here, so you will never survive.'

I will tell you that I have tried to do as he says. I have tried to change how I view things, but as soon as I see something joyful – perhaps a flutter of leaves in the breeze – I am suddenly taken home once more, and I think of the trees in my parents' garden and wish, no, *long*, to be there.

For me, there is no joy here.

FORTY-SEVEN

TADEUSZ

Belsen Bergen
December 1944

Dear Ilse,

There is a change in the camp. Not only have we almost doubled in size – people are literally everywhere, but work detail has ceased, and the mood has shifted with the guards. Janek says it is because the Allies are getting closer and soon the war will be over. We are desperate for more information and have tried to bribe guards to find out information – any information that may give us hope that we will soon be free.

The guards, however, give us nothing. They remain impassive, but you can see that they have changed slightly – a worry-worm of fear creases their brow, they talk together in small groups in low voices, they smoke more and their eyes, which once remained still and focused, roam about as if at any moment the British will arrive.

We talk at length in the evenings now, about what will happen when the Allies get here. We come up with strange and unusual punishments for our captors, and have decided that the best idea yet is to make them stay here and live the rest of their lives as we have. I like this idea very much, and the thought of revenge is keeping me warm at night.

Janek tells me that I have let bitterness into my heart and that it cannot be good. He says that I need to forgive. But I think he is mad. How can one forgive these brutes? These people that call themselves human? I would not do to an animal what they have done to us. And they continue to do it.

Food has been reduced further. Some days we do not eat at all. As more people have arrived, no extra water or food has accompanied them, and day by day we are all wasting away in front of each other's eyes.

But, it could have been worse for us. I could not imagine that things could have been worse than this, but one of the new arrivals, Bartosz, has told us of the horrors from the other camps. One such place is called Auschwitz – a name I have heard before, as I think it is where my parents were sent, and to hear about what has happened there only makes the bitterness in my heart grow and get stronger.

He and others arrived on a train, much emaciated like the rest of us, limping with sores on their feet, coughing, sneezing and some barely breathing, they were added to our bunkhouse late one night and have not been given their own space – because of course there is no place left to house them.

Bartosz spent two years in Auschwitz, he says, and he was brought here because the guards there were trying to hide their crimes as the Russians were getting closer. He was amazed when he arrived here to find that there were no 'gas chambers', as he called them; no routine shootings nor cruel torture. He was also amazed that there was no work detail and that the days were our own. We tried to explain to him that this was not a holiday camp, and the food, if we had any, was simply soup, watery and with little sustenance, but he seemed not to care. As soon as we confirmed that we had heard of no 'gas chambers', he visibly relaxed.

The gas chambers he speaks of are shower blocks where prisoners were marched, straight on arrival from the train – women, children, young, old – it didn't matter who was picked to go to their deaths, he said, there was no thought put into it other than killing.

'I worked in one of them,' he told us all one evening, smoking a cigarette that Janek had given him, having assured him that he need not barter for it – it was a simple gift.

'You cannot imagine what it was like to go into the shower block when they had finished doing what they did. Piles of bodies, naked, slumped on the floor. We had to carry them out and take them to the crematorium ovens and burn them. You cannot imagine.'

When he told me this, I thought of my parents. I imagined them in the ovens. I imagined them gasping for breath in a shower room as a gas was poured in, robbing them of all air.

I tried to do what Janek did, and not think about it, and I tried to find some hope that maybe like Bartosz they were still alive, and maybe they, too, would be sent here. But there is something in me that knows that that will never happen. I know somehow that they are dead.

FORTY-EIGHT

TADEUSZ

Celle, Germany
August 1945

Dear Ilse,

I write this to you from a small hospital in Celle. There are many of us here, all thankful to be out of that place – to be fed, warm and have a bed to sleep in that did not contain lice, in a room that did not have the constant scratching of rats.

A man beside me is from another camp. He is thinner than me – if you can imagine it – for I can see every rib, every bone in my body that juts from under the skin as if trying to force its way out. He is so thin, however, so malnourished that even the feeding tube they have placed in his nose makes him vomit and soil himself – his body is so unused to food that it is now rejecting it. I pray for him. How can I not?

This hospital is not as calming as I had hoped it would be. Although, after what we have all been through, how could it be?

At night, there are so many sounds. It is a cacophony of nightmares. Each man is still chained to his experiences and even the sweet release of sleep will not let them have rest. They cry for their mothers, their fathers, their wives, their children. They cry out names and swat at the air with their arms as if trying to rescue them.

I do not sleep at night. I cannot. I am afraid that during those dark hours I will find myself back in Belsen, back with no food, no warmth and no hope of survival. Instead, I sleep during the day – a twilight sort of sleep where I can still hear what is happening around me, but I fall and dip in and out of dreams that make little sense to me. And for that I am glad.

The man in the bed on the other side to me told me this morning that his name is Jedrick. He was in Belsen too, although I do not recognise him and am sure we have never met. He is an amiable sort, and reminds me much of Janek with his outlook on life.

'Did you see their faces?' he asked me. 'The guards, when the British walked in. At first, they were smiling – you remember – offering them cigarettes and then, when they realised what was going to happen – I mean. Their faces fell! Having to dig graves! They didn't see that coming, did they?'

I agreed that they did not.

Jedrick would not stop talking, all about the things he had seen, and how his friends in the camp had died before his eyes. He talked so much about it that it made me think, really think about the day that Janek died.

I did not tell you about this. It was as though I was afraid to put what happened into words, on paper, as if by not doing so, it wouldn't be real – could not really be true.

I realise, too, that I have shielded you from the terror and the daily life that I have had these past few years. It is as though there are not the right words, the right descriptions to adequately explain my feelings, nor the place itself. Each time I try and think of a word, it feels useless, and I wonder if new words will soon be invented in order to convey the horrors of the place.

I will try to tell you about Janek. I will try as Jedrick next to me talks and talks, and I realise that he is afraid of the silence – he is afraid not to talk – he needs to keep talking to feel alive.

Janek died on a Thursday, in February of this year. He died lying amongst the already dead, his head on the chest of a man who had died two days before – a man we did not know.

The diseases that plagued the camp seemed to get worse, and by the time Janek died, bodies were piled high. When I say piled, I mean it. And they were left, strewn out on the ground whilst rats and flies found their next meals on the measly bits of flesh that still clung on to their bodies.

Janek had been sick with dysentery. Every time he ate, it would go straight through him, and even if he had not eaten, his stomach would cramp and convulse until he screamed with pain.

We knew of three other men who had been taken away with the same thing, and we had heard that they had been given an injection to kill them. When Janek found out about it, he begged me to promise him that I would not let him be taken away.

He lay in his bunk for four days, writhing and twisting about, a delirium making him see his family and he would talk to them and plead with them to get a doctor.

The utter uselessness I felt in those days consumed me. I could not help him, I could not make him well. All I could do, and all I did, was give him water to drink – even giving him mine, knowing that he was so dehydrated that I could manage a day without water, but he certainly could not.

By the fifth day, his body was so wasted away that I was sure his skull had shrunk and his eyes grown bigger.

'Don't let them take me,' he said, drawing me close, his ragged voice so weak and so quiet.

'I won't,' I promised again.

'You'll promise me something else too?'

'What? Anything.'

He had smiled at that response. 'Good. Promise me you will find joy again. Promise me you won't let this place ruin you. I worry for you. I worry that you have let bitterness into your soul and that you will keep it there.'

Before I could answer him, a guard marched into the bunkhouse, screwing up his face with the distasteful smell and sight of us all.

'Get out! Now!' he yelled at Janek who quite obviously could not, and did not move.

'Now!' he yelled again and came to Janek's bunk, pushing me aside, grabbing his arm and yanking him from the bed with such force that his body bounced as it hit the floor.

Janek was so weak that he did not cry out, and stared unblinking at the guard who stood over him.

There was a second, perhaps less, but it seems longer to me now, that there was utter silence in that bunkhouse. Not one man breathed. No one moved.

The second ended.

The guard dragged Janek by his arm out of the bunkhouse, leaving us all watching with horror. He was going to the infirmary which meant only one thing.

We followed the guard and Janek outside and saw the guard drag Janek to a pile of bodies, some of which had already started to decay – their skin falling away to reveal the whiteness of their bones.

The guard walked up to us and stood, a smile on his lips.

'He's dead,' he told us. 'He's dead, or almost is. Leave him there. If I find out that any of you have fed him or given him water, I will make sure that you are next, is that clear?'

There was a collective murmuring amongst us all and nodding of the heads. We knew we had to leave Janek outside in the cold, his only companions the dead bodies which he lay amongst.

The guard found this whole thing amusing – a game I think and ensured that there was always a guard outside of our bunkhouse, watching us all to see if we would go against his command.

To say that I wanted to go to Janek is an understatement. I could not concentrate on anything else but him and my eyes sought him out amongst the dead for the next two days. Watching and hoping that by some miracle he would be able to stand up himself and walk back to us.

Of course he did not. And by the third day, the guards who had been watching us fell away, which meant only one thing. The game was over. Janek was dead.

The feelings of guilt have plagued me ever since. I should have done something, but even now I don't know what I could have done. I was so weakened by the lack of food and water, so broken down by the constant fear of death that the guards promised, that I became a statue and did not, could not move.

Do you think he forgave me, Ilse? Do you?

Can I forgive myself?

I hope that when I am home, I can find some comfort, some joy to be with you again. I think of you all the time – of that night we spent together and how I told you I loved you, but you did not reply. A lesser man would take that as meaning that you do not love me. But I refuse to believe that. I think you do, and I think you were simply scared to say it.

I hope so.

I hope that you love me, and I hope we will be together soon.

FORTY-NINE

TADEUSZ

Görlitz

March 1946

Dear Ilse,

I write this for me. Not for you.

I need to get these feelings out, put them on paper and never look at them again. I need to let out everything that is consuming me – and part of that is the anger I feel for you. The hatred I have for life.

I returned home to Görlitz, to my uncle and the bookshop, wanting to go across the river to my own home, but the pedestrian bridge is now gone, destroyed in the war and the only way across is the vehicle bridge further away. Of course I can use it. Of course I can find my way home again, and yet, when I saw the bridge gone, it felt to me like a sign – that I was never meant to get home so easily. And anyway. What is home any more? My parents' house? They are dead. They died in Auschwitz. I have no home.

Marlena would not give me your new address. Do you remember her? I ask this with utter scorn in my voice because she was your best friend – and more, and yet she tells me that you barely write her, barely tell her anything. You have cut her from your life so easily, without so much as an explanation, that I wonder what kind of woman you have become.

You *promised* that you would wait for me. You *promised* that you would be there for me when I returned. It was the only thing that kept me going – that hope that one day we would be together. You promised you would care for Szymon too. And yet, when I returned, he was being taken care of by my uncle, whose own health had deteriorated so that when I came back to the bookshop, it was as though I had returned to the camp – two men, trying to help each other, half-ghosts, with one foot in the grave.

Szymon was alive only one month more when I returned. On those final few days of nursing him, he told me about his time in the camp, about that French composer who found some way of creating something beautiful amidst such ugliness. He told me that he had asked you to stay with him, and that you had said that you would, but that you simply... disappeared.

Where are you?

Marlena says that you are fine. That you are well, but that she will not tell me any more – she tells me that you want to start a new life, with no thought of the past. I laughed when she said that to me. I laughed so hard that I began to cry. We all want to forget, Ilse. We all want to start afresh, but for me, at least, it seems that this is not possible.

But *you*. You get a fresh start. You get to be *free*. You have been able to disappear into nothingness, without so much as a goodbye or an explanation, leaving me with a dead cousin, a dying uncle, and my own shadow for company.

My uncle – how he has changed. His spirit for life seems dimmed, his eagerness to read, to learn and to teach others has all but gone. I assumed that it was because of Szymon, of the hardships we had all felt during those years, but it is something much deeper than that.

Groening.

Do you remember that name? That guard who shot those men as they waded out into the river, that man who was the devil himself – a man I made a deal with to save my cousin and yet Szymon is now gone.

I asked my uncle how he had managed to pay Groening all through the war, how he managed to keep him at bay. He told me that once he knew Groening had seen you, that he could not let the brute live – he knew, you see, the danger it would bring to your front door, not just to you, but your family too. How ironic is that? That he wished to save a German family – a family who by all accounts were a part of the death and destruction of his own people. But he knew you – or at least he thought he did – just as we all thought we did. He wanted to protect the young woman, the girl he had known, and he could not let Groening live.

How he killed him, I do not know. He wouldn't say. All he would say was that 'Ilse is safe now. What had to be done was done,' and mumble into his chest about all those that we have lost before crying for hours at a time.

You see. That night, that decision by you to come to the graveyard even when I told you not to, resulted in the living death of my uncle. He saved you, but I am not sure that you deserved to be saved.

Do you know that I buried Szymon myself? Does that image of me, digging a hole, under the night sky, whilst cold rain fell, turning the earth to mud move something in you? Does it make you feel a glimmer of my *pain*?

I had to bury him myself. I owed him that at least, to give him a final resting place that had meant so much to him – so much to all of us that summer when we were young – in the private graveyard by the river.

There is no headstone, no marker that he is there. But I know he is, and at least there is that. At least he has me to remember him.

Will you remember me, I wonder? Will you remember that one night we spent together that, for me, meant so much, but maybe to you, meant very little?. I sit here now and think I have been a foolish, lovestruck boy. You did not love me. You felt nothing for me, and when I look back, I can see now that you were lying to me, and more importantly to yourself.

There is an anger that fuels me now, Ilse. An anger not only directed at you, but at everyone. I see them all, walking about, rebuilding lives, finding happiness with the few people that they have left in their lives, and I cannot find any joy, no snippet of respite in the long days that keep me here, working, caring for my uncle and seeing that I have no one, nothing left.

At night, I lie in bed and think about Belsen. I think that it would have been better that I died there and that the likes of Janek lived. He would have been able to find some happiness, I am sure of it. He would have sought out the simple pleasures of the turning of a season from winter to spring, delighting in the tulips and daffodils that bloomed and bobbed their heads merrily. He would have seen that as a reason to keep living. But when I see the flowers, I want to rip them from the ground and shred their petals. I want the world to match my insides – grey – I want the world to stop mocking me with the promise of new life. I want to not be in this world any more.

There is a guilt too – one which frustrates me. A guilt that asks me every day why I was allowed to survive. Why me, and why not someone like Janek who would be able to cope in the world outside, who would be able to find some joy. This guilt mingles with the bitterness, with the anger like a toxic poison, and at times, I no longer know where one feeling starts and the other ends.

I do not wish you ill, Ilse. I do not wish for anything any

more. Every day is like it was in Belsen – a day of survival. And that is what I must do. Wake up each day now and try and survive. Janek was wrong. There is no joy in life. There can never be joy again.

I will not write again. I will not see you again.

But like I said. These words are mostly for me. They are words you will never read. They are just that. Words. And they will eventually disappear. Just like me.

FIFTY

MIA

Görlitz
Thursday, 11 February 1999

Marlena and I sat in Room 31, across from a nurse's station whose phone endlessly rang.

We sat together in that room, one of us on either side of the bed, holding my grandmother's hands as she slept.

A nurse had come to fetch us from the cafeteria – Grandma's breathing had become shallow, she had said. And then she spoke the words which I had been dreading to hear – *It's time.*

I could not think about what Marlena and I had read in her diary – of her escape to Belgium, of how it could have gone so terribly wrong for her once more. I did not have time, nor the energy or the wherewithal to put it all together – this immense story of so many people's lives that I had come to learn in just a few days. This immense story that included my own.

As we sat, Marlena murmured prayers in Polish, reaching out now and then to place her palm on my grandmother's cheek – just to feel her one last time.

Her breathing became worse as the minutes ticked by, and I

could not grasp how just a few hours before she had been sat in bed, telling me about who my grandfather really was, how she had felt guilt all these years for keeping it all a secret and how she had tried to make amends by coming back home for her final few years.

'It happens this way sometimes,' the doctor told us. 'It's better this way than it dragging on.'

I wanted to tell the young doctor with his small, damp hands that he was mistaken – that there was no way that this could be better. But then, Marlena agreed with him.

'It is better, Mia, that she goes before it gets worse, before the pain and her thoughts are so bad that she is not herself any more.'

Since crying earlier in the day with Marlena, it was as though I had turned on a tap that could now not be turned off. They leaked down my face without my even knowing about it, causing me to constantly rub at my eyes, making them redder than they already were.

'Did she love you, Marlena?' I asked, as the day morphed into night, the bright hospital lights causing too much glare in that quiet room.

'She loved me as well as she could,' Marlena said. 'Maybe not as I loved her, but she loved me.' She nodded to herself, then began to cry and repeat over and over again, 'She loved me.'

I was sure my grandmother did love her. I was sure at one point she loved Szymon and even Tadeusz. I think she was full of love, full of life and vigour when she was young and some-times it took her over, making her make bad decisions, making her at times a little selfish.

But I was glad to know that she had loved and had been loved. All the years she had cared for me in that quiet, distant way of hers, with no real friends, no love other than from me, I felt comforted that at least once in her life she had experienced so much love, all for herself.

A cough at the doorway interrupted the silence. Tadeusz was standing there, turning his hat around and around in his hands.

'I saw you hadn't come home,' he whispered. 'I thought maybe something had happened.'

Marlena went to him and whispered in Polish, Tadeusz nodding along, his eyes not leaving my grandmother's prone body.

'May I?' he asked me, gesturing at the bed.

I nodded my consent and watched this man – my grandfather – go to my grandmother and sit gently beside her, taking her hand in his. Then he bent down, placed his mouth close to her ear and said, 'Please forgive me, Ilse. Forgive me before you go.'

Her eyelids fluttered as he spoke, and I was sure she was going to open them, but she didn't. Then he whispered, with a catch in his voice, 'I forgive you. But you never needed it. I was the one at fault. Forgive me, Ilse.'

Suddenly, she took a deep breath. Tadeusz sprang back from her and all three of us stared at her, thinking she was going to speak.

Then she exhaled. Heavily, slowly, until there was no more breath in her body.

I am not sure how much time passed before one of us spoke – and I am not sure who spoke first. But all at once, a nurse rushed in, Marlena wailed and Tadeusz stood dumbfounded at the end of the bed.

'Is she…?' I asked, knowing the answer but needing the nurse to say it anyway.

'She's dead, yes,' she said.

FIFTY-ONE

MIA

Görlitz
Thursday, 11 February 1999

That evening the three of us sat in Tadeusz's apartment, each
one of us holding thick tumblers of vodka, each one of us seemingly unwilling to break the grief-laden silence that hung in the
room like an impenetrable wall of fog – a silence so thick, you
could not see through it, could not find the right words that
would make it dissipate.

A clock ticked the seconds away on the mantelpiece – time
was still moving on its relentless march. My head was warm and
fuzzy from the alcohol, and as I concentrated on the ticking of
the clock – on the absurdity that time still dared to push on, that
the world outside was still living – I found it strangely funny
and began to laugh. First a titter, then the laughter and the grief
overcame me, and I began to howl with it – a howl that soon
turned into a mixture of tears and incomprehensible sentences
that resulted in Marlena taking me into her arms and holding
me tightly until my tired body relaxed.

'It just doesn't seem real,' I sniffed. 'It can't be – we were talking to her earlier, and now – she's just gone!' I raised my arms in disbelief and then my eyes immediately went to the window, searching for the crumbling gravestones.

Tadeusz saw me, and followed my gaze.

'Come,' he said, and stood up, placing his drink on the table. 'Come, let us go and tell Szymon, let us go and say our own goodbyes.'

I did not have the energy to have an opinion on the matter and allowed Marlena to take one arm, Tadeusz the other, and in the inky blackness we made our way outside and across to the river and to the graveyard.

Tadeusz held a torch, the beam picking out our route – when had he got that, I wondered? I shook my head and realised that the alcohol had had much more of an effect than I had thought – my brain seemed thick and slow as I shook my head, all my thoughts fumbling about but none making any sense.

Tadeusz pushed back spindly bare branches to reveal the graveyard, the torchlight bouncing off the headstones and finally resting on a patch of earth underneath a willow tree.

'He's here,' he whispered, and next to me, I felt Marlena shiver.

Tadeusz bent down and whispered something in Polish, then he turned to me and Marlena and beckoned us to come closer.

It all seemed too macabre, and all of a sudden, I wanted to return to the flat. But then the realisation hit me that it was my flat now – no longer my grandmother's, as she would never be coming home.

'Come. Come and speak to him,' Tadeusz was insistent.

Marlena stepped forward and my soggy alcohol brain could not refuse, and I went with her, both of us crouching down to look at soil, weeds and blades of grass.

'I want to get a headstone – I always thought that I would,

but I knew I would have to ask permission and admit that I had buried him here and I knew that it was probably not possible. So. Here he is. I know he is here and now you know too, Mia, so you can visit him when I am gone and talk to him.'

'Have you told him?' Marlena whispered. 'Have you told him about Ilse?'

'I did. I imagined that he spoke back to me. I imagined that he said that she was there with him, both of them looking down on us and hoping that we do not hurt any more. It is funny, though; I have imagined his voice for so many years that sometimes it feels so real to me that I think it is him talking to me.'

I wasn't sure what I was supposed to do – or say – so I simply stared at the ground, trying not to think that a body lay a few feet below.

'It may be too soon,' Tadeusz said quietly, 'but have you made a decision yet?'

'A decision, what decision?' I asked, thinking he was perhaps asking me about her funeral, about where she would finally come to rest.

'Marlena said she explained...' he trailed off.

'I did, Mia,' she said gently. 'Tadeusz he has been thinking about the past, he has been trying to maybe make it sleep forever. He wants to know whether he can be a part of your life – he wants to find happiness, I am thinking.'

'I do, Mia,' he agreed with Marlena. 'When you first came here, I was bitter and foolish. I was so consumed by the past that I could not understand that there was perhaps a better future awaiting me. With Marlena telling me what to do—'

'I no tell you what to do!' she interrupted. 'I am just saying to you that you must stop being so old and sad.'

Tadeusz let out a small laugh. 'All right. With gentle *prodding* from Marlena, I realised this was my last chance to have a family. But I needed to forgive myself first, and I am asking you now, if you can forgive a foolish old man for being so hateful towards your grandmother. And, whether you can accept me as part of your life. I realise we may never be close, we may never see each other again when you leave, but at least it would give me some peace to know I did something right in this life. It produced you, Mia – it produced a granddaughter that I sorely want to get to know if you will allow it.'

His words were so measured, so heartfelt that I could not deny him his request. So much had happened to them all over the years and in the past few days, so much had happened in my life, that anger, resentment and bitterness had no place within me now.

'I've made my decision,' I told him. 'I forgive you, even though there's nothing to forgive.'

'There is—' he started.

'No,' I cut him off. 'There isn't. We're family.'

FIFTY-TWO

MIA

Görlitz
March 1999

The day began as a bleak, sullen morning with heavy clouds that promised rain. By the time that we reached the crematorium, the sun peeked out from behind the clouds, and I stood for a moment, wondering if it were some sort of sign.

We were a paltry group of three. Me, Marlena and Tadeusz. In Grandma's will she had specified that she did not want a church service – no one was to speak about her, no one was to try and remember her. She simply wanted to be cremated and her ashes spread in the graveyard by the river, the graveyard that had strangely been a part of her childhood, where a name purloined from an old stone had dictated who she would be in her adult life.

I liked the symmetry of it – that she would be at rest where she fell in love, where she made friends, where she had been most happy. She would rest near Szymon, who had loved her dearly – properly, with such force that when he was young, he had felt so nervous in front of her, so bowled over by the light that shone out of her, that he had become meek and mild in her presence.

No matter that she no longer loved him, at last she would be *near* love – she would be close to it.

I did find it strange in a way that she didn't want to be buried with her son, my father, back in England. But as her will had said, she had wanted to be scattered on her home soil. England was not her home – it never had been, and I did wonder whether she ever really felt she'd found a home. Her parents' home was one of anxiety for her; her home in England fraught with loss; and her final home, a home she had chosen to try and make amends, had been the place where she had found out that she was dying. Had she ever been happy?

I thought back to the girl that she had once been, full of life and dreams of adventure. She didn't care what people thought of her and her impulsivity drew people to her, but at the same time pushed them away.

We three stood as the coffin disappeared behind a curtain and a man dressed in a black suit told us that was it and that the ashes would be given to me within a week.

It seemed wrong that this was her farewell – that no music had been played nor words of remembrance uttered.

'I know where we should go.' Tadeusz took my arm as we exited the crematorium. 'I know where we should go to remember her.'

I let them lead me away from the crematorium, as I tried not to think about my grandmother's body in that simple wooden box, slowly disappearing behind a red curtain approaching a heat that I couldn't even begin to comprehend.

The taxi that had brought us sat waiting idly, the man behind the wheel – a young man who still carried the remnants of pockmarks on his cheeks – listening to the Foo Fighters blaring out on the radio, with no thought as to what was happening only yards away from him.

Tadeusz gave him the address and then told him, quite firmly, to turn the volume down.

None of us spoke, making the driver feel that he had to fill the silence. He spoke in rapid German to Marlena who fired something back that I couldn't catch, but whatever she said to him quietened him immediately.

Within ten minutes, we were back in the town centre and the taxi slowed, pulling up in front of Mr Gliński's bookshop.

Tadeusz waved a note at the driver who snatched it away and the three of us got out, standing for a moment in front of the shop where my grandmother had spent quiet and happy times.

It was only when we entered that it hit me: this was where my grandmother and Tadeusz had conceived my father – this was my beginning and as much as it was a building that meant something to Marlena, Tadeusz and my grandmother, it also meant something to me too.

It was then that I cried.

I had not cried much when she died. I had even swallowed back those early tears I had cried about Will and the trauma of our relationship and had not allowed myself to indulge in it any more. But now I let it all out, in amongst the most famous writers in the world, weeping for everything I had lost and everything my grandmother had stopped herself from having – love, friendship, peace.

Marlena wrapped her arms around me, drawing me to her and I did not resist. I let her hold me as I wept, and she shushed me like a small child, finding comfort in the touch of another human for once – not feeling the need to flinch and pull away.

Tadeusz coughed, once, then twice, alerting us both to his presence. He held in his hand a bottle of champagne, grinned at us and ushered us into the rear of the shop, allowing me to sit on the regal purple chair, pouring us all glasses that overflowed with the vigour of the bubbles.

'To Ilse!' Tadeusz raised his glass.

Marlena and I followed suit, then I took a sip.

'And to Mia,' Tadeusz was not finished. I swallowed quickly and half raised my glass. 'Why me?"

'To Ilse's granddaughter who brought us all back together in the end, and to my granddaughter who I hope to get to know before it is my time to leave.'

I looked to Marlena who gave me a gentle nod, and then to Tadeusz – my grandfather, his wispy hair mussed like cotton candy from the heat in the shop – and realised that I wasn't alone. These people were my family now.

'And to me,' I raised my glass, 'And to my grandfather and to my aunt Marlena too. My family!'

We each clinked glasses, and I saw Tadeusz reach under his spectacles for a quick second to wipe a tear away.

'You'll go back to England now?' Marlena asked.

I drank back a gulp of champagne, almost draining the glass. 'Not yet,' I replied. 'I think I'll stay a while.'

FIFTY-THREE

MIA

Zgorzelec
Monday, 2 August 2004

If at all possible, the heat is worse, but the woman at the café, whose name I now know is Krystyna, has moved a fan from inside to put it next to me, blowing warm air on my face. It does little to help, but she has been so accommodating to me these past few weeks as each day I have descended on her café to try and make sense of the story I have just completed.

She has asked questions, and I have tried to answer them as best that I can, and within a few days she became quite engaged with the tale, and would happily re-translate the postcards and letters for me, adding in bits of history that she knew herself from that time.

My grandmother's diaries, though, I did not let her read. Instead, I used the German I had learned and translated them well into the night. Even I felt like I was snooping on my grand-mother's innermost thoughts, so I couldn't very well let Krystyna read them, no matter how well-intentioned she is.

I think I have read my grandmother's diary ten times over. It is not really a diary, I suppose. Really more of a confessional journal that she rarely wrote in until she found out that she had cancer. I suppose she knew then that she was running out of time and if she were ever to get her thoughts, regrets and sins on paper, that then was her only chance.

They were not an easy read. Especially when I realised that many of the entries were written when I was just a few streets away in her apartment. The thought of her sitting in the hospital at night, the cancer spreading rapidly, revisiting the guilt that had plagued her all those years made me cry. I wished she had spoken to me instead. I wished I could have offered her some words of comfort and told her that she had no reason to hate herself as she did – she was not a bad person, she was in a situation that she had no idea how to get out of.

It pains me even more that she cut herself off from life in order to punish herself and that she was filled up so tightly with guilt and regret that there was no room for joy, no room to forgive herself even.

I wish, too, that she had seen that Tadeusz, my grandfather, and I had formed a relationship. It was awkward to start with, neither of us quite sure how to be granddaughter and grandfather to each other. But bit by bit, and along with encouragement from Marlena, we somehow managed it.

Tadeusz is not well now either. He is cared for by me and still lives in his apartment, and Marlena lives with me with her *meny* dogs. Her mobility has declined, so she sits most days at the window, looking out onto the street then to the river beyond, and gives me a running commentary of the life that is happening just outside.

But now, I am a part of that life. Like that woman I saw on my second day here with her polka-dot umbrella. That day I had wondered about her life and what one day mine could be. And between Tadeusz and Marlena, I have found a place for myself.

'Are you free tonight?' Krystyna asks. 'I have a friend I want you to meet. I told him that you work at the bookshop, and he is a librarian – I think you will both like each other!'

I look up and grin at Krystyna, who I now consider my friend and agree to meet her at a local wine bar after I have seen to Tadeusz and Marlena.

'Your family comes first,' she says.

I nod. They do.

Soon, I will walk over the bridge again and will stop as I always do, right in the middle, Görlitz to my left and Zgorzelec to my right, a foot in each country, a foot in each moment of my past, my heritage, my family.

A LETTER FROM CARLY

I want to say a huge thank you for choosing to read *The Postcard*. If you did enjoy it, and want to keep up to date with all my latest releases, just sign up at the following link. Your email address will never be shared and you can unsubscribe at any time.

www.bookouture.com/carly-schabowski

What is history, and how do we consume it? These are the questions that I ask myself before writing any book, and indeed, for *The Postcard*, this was no different.

I believe that our histories are handed down to us in a myriad of ways – of course through fact, but also though that dubious lens of memory, of familial storytelling and of the blanks in history that we fill in ourselves.

The inspiration for this novel came about after a research trip to Poland, whereby at a local flea market, I bought a post-card that was written during WW2 (the very same image that is included in this book). It was a plea from the sender to their uncle to send more books, and upon more research I found out that the sender was indeed in a POW camp in Germany.

It was such an odd request that it intrigued me, and the possible stories of this person's life would not leave me alone. Who was he? What books had he read? What had happened in his life prior to and after the war?

As the questions piled up, I sought answers to them and

again, another piece of information came to me, a story about a priest, Maximilian Maria Kolbe, who offered to die in place of another at Auschwitz. This ultimate sacrifice led me to create a story of two cousins, one who would offer to take the other's place when they were being led to Belsen.

And what about Ilse? She, too, became an interesting character for me – a girl who had been brought up in Görlitz, a place prior to WW2 that had Poles and Germans living side by side. It made me question what a German woman might do, if her friends from before the war now found themselves in danger. Would she help them? What would become of their friendships?

Ilse's granddaughter became an important character here, as she, just like me, is trying to very carefully piece together a jigsaw of stories and fill in the blanks when the ghosts of the past remain silent. It is her own trauma, her own past that fuels her on this journey to try to find peace, not only for those who were left, but for herself too.

What I hope I have done with *The Postcard* is situate you in a time and place, taking multiple stories and multiple lenses to look back at the past so that it feels an authentic portrayal of what could have been and of what was. I hope, too, that I have given voices to those ghosts who wished to speak.

I hope you loved *The Postcard* and if you did, I would be very grateful if you could write a review. I'd love to hear what you think, and it makes such a difference helping new readers to discover one of my books for the first time.

I love hearing from my readers – you can get in touch through Twitter.

Thanks,

Carly Schabowski

KEEP IN TOUCH WITH CARLY

twitter.com/@carlyschab11

BIBLIOGRAPHY

Biniaz, Benjamin: Religious Resistance in Auschwitz: The Sacrifice of Saint Kolbe: https://sfi.usc.edu/news/2016/08/12019-religious-resistance-auschwitz-sacrifice-saint-kolbe

Blitz Konig, Nanette. *Holocaust Memoirs of a Bergen-Belsen Survivor: Classmate of Anne Frank* (Holocaust Survivor Memoirs World War II). Amsterdam Publishers. Kindle Edition.

Bourke, J. (2004). Introduction "Remembering" War. *Journal of Contemporary History*, 39(4), 473–485. http://www.jstor.org/stable/4141406

Carter, J. A. (2003). Telling Times: History, Employment, and Truth. *History and Theory*, 42(1), 1–27. http://www.jstor.org/stable/3590799

Hasian, M. (2001). Anne Frank, Bergen-Belsen, and the Polysemic Nature of Holocaust Memories. *Rhetoric and Public Affairs*, 4(3), 349–374. http://www.jstor.org/stable/41940587

Krammer, A. (1992). [Review of *Sitting It Out: A World War II POW Memoir*, by D. Westheimer]. *Air Power History*, 39(3), 55–56. http://www.jstor.org/stable/26272246

Marx, E. (2015). That's How It Was: A Report on Westerbork and Bergen Belsen (1945). *Irish Pages*, 9(2), 72–101. http://www.jstor.org/stable/44508352

McMullen, John William. *The Miracle of Stalag 8A (Stalag VIII-A) – Beauty Beyond the Horror: Olivier Messiaen and the Quartet for the End of Time* (p. 103). Bird Brain Publishing. Kindle Edition.

Night Will Fall, (2014), directed by Andre Singer.

ACKNOWLEDGEMENTS

As always, a big thank you goes to my agent Jo Bell, who has shown me that there is no way I would be able to do this without her! Not only does she manage to talk me down off many a self-doubt ledge, she is funny and kind and is always on my side.

A thank you to Jess Whitlum-Cooper, my editor, who has toiled away on this book with me and helped me to make it the best it can possibly be.

My sisters, mum and dad get a big thank you too for once again dealing with my whinging. How they haven't disowned me yet, I do not know!

There are so many people to thank that if I named them all, it would be another book in itself, but I have to say thank you to Michal Rodzynski for helping with translations once more, and a thanks to my neighbours, Sarah Lunde and Doug Parmenter for putting up with me sitting in the garden and asking them for synonyms and various bits of prose when my mind wasn't working.

Lastly, a HUGE thank you to you, dear reader. Because without you, I would not be where I am today, and that is a fact!